CW01090897

An Inspector Ruiz Mystery

THE
FIFTH
COLUMN

James García Woods

LUME BOOKS

LUME BOOKS

This edition published in 2021 by Lume Books
30 Great Guildford Street,
Borough, SE1 0HS

ISBN 978-1-83901-440-6

Typeset using Atomik ePublisher from Easypress Technologies

www.lumebooks.co.uk

This is for Eric, my dad.
and also for:
Collette, my sister, and Steve, her husband, who have given him
a wonderful home.

Prologue

As the hands of the ancient town hall clock creaked round towards midnight, the villagers of San Antonio de la Jara began to trickle into the main square, and soon almost the entire population was gathered together.

Most of the small towns on the plain held their *fiestas* during the warmer, gentler summer days, but San Antonio took a kind of perverse pride in the fact that the obscure saint who was honored in their *pueblo* had his day amidst the chill winds of February.

Strictly speaking, the saint in question – a minor martyr of the early church – was *not* being honored at all that year. His church had been burned down, the fat parish priest had fled. And even as the church still burned, the saint's statue – along with that of the Blessed Virgin – had been paraded through the smoke-filled streets to invite derision, instead of the customary veneration. The war which had torn the country apart had also all-but killed religion – as it had killed so many other traditions.

Yet the expulsion of God and all his angels did not prevent the people gathered in the Plaza Mayor from throwing themselves into the celebrations with a gusto which was uniquely and gloriously Spanish. If anything, the villagers displayed even more exuberance at these *fiestas* than ever before, because they were acutely aware that although life had never been anything but hard, it could be about to get much harder. They knew – even if many of them would not admit it – that not all the sons and brothers who were fighting on the front line would eventually return. They understood – without actually putting it into words – that the day might soon come when a hostile army would appear on the horizon, and a fresh wave of killings would begin. And so they ate and they drank, they danced and they sang – and they told themselves that if this were to be the last *fiesta* they ever attended, they would make sure it was a good one.

The tall American standing on the edge of the crowd shook his head in wonder. Spain was not just another country, he thought. It was another *world* – a world he could never even have begun to imagine back home, but one which he had now embraced and was more than willing to die for.

He let his mind drift back to New York City, where his epic journey had started.

"Tell no one where you're going," the secretary of the selection board had told him, as he'd stood there, bursting with pride that he'd been chosen as one of the vanguard. "No one! Do you understand? Not your friends! Not your family! Your departure must be kept secret at all cost."

It had been an impossible instruction to obey, of course. He had confided in his favorite cousin, who had passed the information on to his friends, and when he finally made his way down to the docks, it had been as part of a small procession.

But he had not been alone in his weakness – in his betrayal of Party discipline! Once he arrived at the pier, he came across at least another hundred young men like himself.

All of them carrying the identical cardboard suitcases that the Party had issued them with.

All of them surrounded by a knot of anxious relatives.

There had been government agents on the dock, too – hard faced officials who asked them where they were going and warned them that it was illegal to travel to Spain. And so all the earnest young men, many of whom had never told a real lie in their lives, made up stories – that they were writing a book, that they were going to search for their roots in France, that they were interested in learning how to produce wine. The government agents had not believed them, but since it was still permitted to go to France, all they actually could *do* was to issue dark warnings about what might happen to the travelers if they attempted to cross the border into a country split in two by a bloody civil war.

The American grinned as he remembered the mixture of farce and desperation that border crossing had actually involved. The volunteers had been taken by train to Perpignan, where, to avoid being conspicuous, they had been split into smaller groups of around a dozen men each.

His group had been summoned to a café in the center of the town.

"You go tonight," their contact had told them. "Now listen very carefully, and follow my instructions to the letter. Until you reach the taxis which are waiting for you at the edge of Perpignan, you must show no sign that you know one another. I will leave this café first, and you will follow me, one at a time. You must always maintain a distance of at least thirty meters between yourself and the man in front of you. Is that clear?"

Had he ever really imagined that a group of twelve young men – obviously foreign and carrying identical cheap cardboard suitcases – could walk through a small French town, in an awkward crocodile, without being noticed, the American wondered, looking back on it.

If he had thought it, he'd have soon seen the error of his ways. Hundreds of locals, out for their evening strolls, had spotted them and called, "Viva España." A gendarme on duty at one of the intersections had even gone so far as to stop the traffic for them, and given each one of them the clenched-fist Communist salute as he passed by.

But there had been nothing even mildly amusing about the next stage of the journey – scaling the Pyrenees. The French smuggler who guided them had taken the crossing in his stride, but after several hours of steady climbing – up from the mild foothills into the icy mountains – many of the young Americans would have been happy to simply lie down and die.

Despite the hardship, they made it.

They had *made* it!

They were not yet at the front, doing what they had come to do, but at least they were in Spain, preparing for their great adventure.

The young American frowned. He should not think of it as an adventure, he thought, rebuking himself in the absence of anyone else to do the job for him. He was not in Spain for the excitement and the personal glory. He was there as one tiny part of a larger movement which would bring fascism to its knees. And yet it was hard *not* to feel the thrill of anticipation – to see himself, in a minor way at least – as heroic.

He let his gaze sweep across the square.

At the local people, dressed in their Sunday-best clothes.

At his comrades, wearing a motley collection of uniforms, many of which had been bought at army surplus stores back in the States.

He examined the houses which ringed and bounded the square. They were three or four stories high – though they had surrendered a portion of their bottom floors to create a covered arcade which offered protection from both the sun and the rain. The beams of these houses were seasoned wood, the supporting pillars made of stone. There was not a steel girder in sight.

The whole place breathed history, he told himself. And when he said *history*, that was exactly what he meant. He was by no means an educated man – not in the formal sense of the word – but it did not require years of study to get a sense of the atmosphere of the place, to feel the impulses, the hopes and fears, of countless generations reverberating through the soles of his thick boots.

The town had existed when Columbus set off to discover the New World. Saint Teresa of Avila had established a convent here when his own country had not been a country at all, but merely a loose collection of isolated settlements. But, on one level at least, the past was not important – because it was only by ensuring the future that the past would be allowed to survive.

Earlier in the day, fireworks had arrived from Valencia – the town which had housed the government since it fled from Madrid. Now the rockets were in place, the giant Catherine wheels had been firmly fixed to wooden posts, and the display was about to begin.

It was a pity to have to miss the fireworks, the American told himself as he made his way round the edge of the square, but to a man who had pledged his whole life to the betterment of generations as yet unborn, it was only the smallest of sacrifices to make.

He turned onto one of the streets which led out of the plaza. The houses on both sides of him were in complete darkness now that the people had congregated in the main square.

Or rather, *nearly* all the people had congregated, he reminded himself.

Apart from him, there was one other person at least, who, because of the urgent matter which needed attending to, had turned his back on pleasure.

The blackened shape of the church loomed up in front of him. Located as it was, in the center of the village, setting it ablaze must have posed considerable threat to the houses surrounding it. Yet such was the hatred of the Church in this area that, the American was willing to wager, the inhabitants of these houses had been as enthusiastic as anyone else about setting the fire.

He reached the burned-out building, and stepped through the gap where had once been a solid, hardwood door. The walls had survived the conflagration, but the roof had collapsed, and looking up, he could see the stars glittering in the black Castilian sky.

As his eyes became accustomed to the darkness, he found he could distinguish the far wall of the church, in front of which the altar and its accompanying statutory had stood. But he could detect no movement – no sign there was another living soul inside the shell.

He shivered, though not because of the cold. He had long decided that Marx was right when he'd said that religion was the opiate of the people, yet he could not completely cast out the feeling of awe he had experienced as a child when, every Sunday, his mother would take him to their local church to praise a god who, it was promised, would one day deliver justice to his people.

Standing there, in what had once been the aisle, he remembered the feel of his mother's hand – damp yet reassuring – and the sight of the big man in the pulpit who had talked with absolute certainty about the days of glory to come.

The memory made him laugh. It was a soft laugh, yet, in the absolute stillness of the ruined church, it seemed almost like a scream.

From the square came the sound of the first explosion.

Soon, the night sky would be lit up with crimson and yellow sparks.

Soon, there would be the roar of battle without any of the horror which followed such conflicts.

He strained his ears, trying to isolate sounds of movement within the church from the cacophony which had begun outside.

"Is there anybody there?" he asked.

But only the silence answered him.

He was beginning to feel slightly nervous – though he had no idea why he should – and despite the fact that it was a cold night, he felt drops of sweat starting to form on his powerful neck.

"I ain't here to play no games," he said.

He realized he was speaking louder than was strictly necessary, as if to give himself courage.

But why should he *need* to do that?

Perhaps because, though he had no evidence to back it up, he was sure that he was being watched.

"You said somethin' about there bein' a traitor in the battalion," he called to the silent, unseen observer. "If you're right about that, then we gotta talk it through – while there's still time."

He heard the banshee wail of the rockets, and the bang-bang-bang of the ripraps. But they were all some distance away, and belonged to a world in which the joy of living was all that mattered – and in which treachery played no part.

"I'm gonna count to ten, an' then I'm headin' back for the square," he announced. "One… two… three…"

The frenzy of noise from the plaza swelled as he counted. The firework display was approaching its climax.

"… four… five… six…" he continued.

The flash and explosion from deeper inside the church came so close to one another that it was impossible for his mind to separate them. The pain – burning its way into his chest – arrived a split second later.

Breathing was suddenly an almost impossible task, and his sturdy legs no longer seemed capable of supporting his weight. So this was what it was like to be shot, he thought, as his knees buckled underneath him and he fell in a crumpled heap on the stone floor.

It hurt more than he had ever imagined it could. Yet at the same time he felt a sense of inevitability – as if it had always been intended that this pain should be his.

There was the sound of footsteps now, starting from behind one of the store pillars, beating out a heavy tattoo as they got closer. The American would have liked to raise his head – to look up at the man who was approaching him – but his body was working so hard at registering the pain that it had no strength left for any other activity.

The sound of the footsteps ceased, and he could see a pair of boots a few inches in front of his eyes.

From somewhere deep inside himself, he found the power to speak.

"Why?" he grunted, blowing a bubble of blood as the word emerged from his mouth. "What have I done wro…?"

The figure beside him bent his knees, and something hard and cold touched the fallen man's head.

A pistol barrel! It could only be a pistol barrel!

Let me live! the wounded man pleaded silently. I don't mind dying – but not like this! Spare me, so that I can at least do some good before I go.

The man with the gun breathed in deeply. Perhaps he could read his victim's thoughts and had some sympathy with them. Or perhaps he needed the extra air because killing another human being – even when it was necessary – was still a momentous act. Whatever his reasoning, it did not deter him from squeezing the trigger which propelled the bullet into the fallen man's brain.

There was one last wild burst of explosions from the square, and the *fiestas* were over for another year – or maybe forever.

The killer buried his gun deeply in his jacket pocket, and walked quickly away from the scene of his crime.

Chapter One

Paco Ruiz stood on one of the middle rungs of his ladder, surveying the hundred or so meters of ploughed-up no-man's-land which ran from the edge of his own trench to the line of sandbags marking the beginning of the fascists' trenches. Seen from the air, he imagined, the trenches would be gaping wounds, savagely slashed across the innocent landscape, but the men on the ground – like him – had a very different perspective. To them, the trenches were a series of uncovered tunnels which cramped and confined them – and all too often served as a gateway to death.

Earlier in the day – before the clouds had dispersed and the sun made one last half-hearted appearance before starting to set behind the hills – it had been raining down mercilessly on the Jarama Valley, and Paco found himself wondering if the enemy were feeling as wet and miserable as he was. He guessed they were, though he couldn't know for sure.

There were *so many* things he couldn't know for sure – starting with the composition of the enemy forces. It was possible that the men who fired the odd, half-hearted pot shot at him were regular Spanish troops – soldiers who were already serving in the army when the war started, and had followed their rebel generals because that was what soldiers did if they wished to avoid being shot. Or they could be conscripts – peasant boys pressed into the army once the rebels had overrun their villages. They might be Moors, the hardened troopers who General Franco had used with so much effect to crush their own countrymen in Morocco – and *his* own countrymen during the Asturian miners' strike of 1934. They could even be Irishmen – General O'Duffy, with his six hundred Irish volunteers, was rumored to be somewhere in the area.

Whatever their nationality, they weren't going anywhere else in the foreseeable future. The battle for the Jarama Valley had been hard fought – 25,000 casualties on his side, 20,000 on the other – but for the moment there was an almost perfect balance of forces, and wherever the breakthrough in the war came, it would not be on this front.

"Excuse me, captain," said a voice to his left.

Paco climbed back down into the trench, and turned to face the man who had addressed him. He was a young private – probably no more than seventeen or eighteen.

In the early days – Good God, had he really just thought about them as the *early days*, when the period he was talking about was less than *nine months* earlier? – well, back then, anyway, the militiamen Paco had fought with had all been around his own age, but the Republic's new regular army seemed to be populated entirely by men who were little more than babies.

The private was standing there awkwardly, aware that he was being inspected by one of his superiors and seemingly unable to find the courage to speak again until he was spoken to.

"Yes, what is it?" Paco asked.

"They want you back at field headquarters, sir."

Sir! There had been no ranks in those first few days of the Civil War. Everyone had been called 'comrade'. But it could not have gone on that way, Paco recognized. They had been facing a trained army, and if they were to succeed, they, too, needed to be trained. He was glad that things had changed, and yet there was a part of him which – obstinately and irrationally – missed the spirit which had existed during the fierce battles in the Guadarrama Mountains.

"So they want me back at headquarters, do they?" he asked. "And who are *they*, exactly?"

2

The private shrugged. "They didn't say. Only that you were to come immediately."

Paco nodded. "And who did they say they wanted to see? *Captain* Ruiz? Or *Inspector* Ruiz?"

The private looked confused.

"Are there two of you?"

The army captain – who had once been a policeman – shook his head.

"No, it's me they want, all right."

He took a packet of Celtas from the pocket of his combat jacket, and offered it to the private.

"Smoke, son?"

The private took one – but hesitantly.

"We'd ... we'd better go, sir," he said, as his superior struck a match and held it out to him.

"Yes," Paco agreed, lighting his own Celtas and then dousing the match. "I suppose we better had."

The temporary field headquarters had been established in what had once been the home of one of the valley's landowning *caciques* (as the pre-revolutionary political bosses had been known). There were three flags flying from the top of the building now – one to represent the Spanish Republic and its democratically elected government, another belonging to the Communist Party, and a third with the insignia of the Socialists.

Armed guards, looking very bored, stood on duty outside the house, and several military vehicles were parked in front of it.

Yet apart from that, the village looked much as it must have looked before the war broke out.

Peasant women, dressed entirely in black, still passed by carrying bundles on their heads.

Skinny donkeys, weighed down by their loads, still ambled reluctantly up the street.

Mongrel dogs snarled menacingly at each other.

And old men, wearing berets, and with cigarettes drooping from the corners of their mouths, sat in the village bar drinking glasses of wine.

In some villages in this devastated country, it was almost possible to believe the war had never happened, Paco thought enviously.

The nervous private handed him over to a sergeant who had obviously been waiting impatiently, and the sergeant led him down a corridor, stopping only when he reached a heavy oak door.

"They're in there," he said.

They again.

"Who are they?" Paco asked.

"They've come from Valencia," the sergeant answered, as if that were all the explanation that was needed.

And in a way, it was. Since early November, when the Prime Minister had come to the conclusion that Madrid was about to fall to the enemy any day, the government of Republican Spain had resided in Valencia.

"You'd better knock, sir," the sergeant said.

"Aren't you going to announce me?"

The sergeant shook his head.

"I've got other duties."

Then he turned on his heel, and was gone.

Paco stood staring at the oak door – and thinking about the past. He had once been a policeman – a good one – but even before that he had been a soldier, fighting in Spanish Morocco – and now it was in the hands of the soldiers that the future of Spain lay. If the unnamed "they" had called him from the front line in order to resurrect his policeman self, he wanted nothing to do with it.

He knocked on the door, and when a voice called out, "Come in!" he turned the handle and stepped inside.

There were two of them, sitting behind the *cacique's* long mahogany desk. One was a gray-haired man in his early sixties, the other a sharp-faced, much younger man with burning, ambitious eyes.

And they were both wearing lounge suits!

4

It was months since Paco had seen anyone in a suit. Before the Rebellion, he had worn suits himself – everyone who was not a manual worker had been expected to – but from August onwards, no one in Madrid had appeared in anything but overalls or a military uniform.

"You are Francisco Ruiz?" asked the sharp-faced younger man.

"I am," Paco agreed, noting his questioner had used neither of his titles – and wondering whether that had been deliberate.

"Take a seat, Señor Ruiz," the young man said, indicating a low chair which had been set up in front of the desk.

"I would prefer to stand," Paco told him.

For a second, it looked as if the sharp-faced man would insist.

Then he nodded his head and said. "Very well, if that's your choice. My name is Enrique Muñoz, and my colleague is Don Luis Ortega. We are here on official business, the direct representatives of President Azaña."

In other words, they were political time-servers, Paco thought.

Which was just another way of saying that they would be well versed in playing the games of manipulation and advantage, which would ensure that whatever else happened, *they'd* manage to retain their comfortable berth.

It was incredible that after all that had happened in the previous few months – after society had been turned upside down – he should still find himself talking to men of the same stock as the ones who had made his life so difficult in the old days.

What *had* happened to the revolutionary spirit?

Muñoz consulted the cardboard folder in front of him, though Paco suspected he already knew all the details it contained by heart.

"It seems that before the outbreak of hostilities you were a homicide inspector in the Madrid police," the official representative of the President said.

The outbreak of hostilities! Paco repeated in his mind. What a neat, clinical – governmental – way to describe a situation in which thousands on both sides had been massacred.

"Yes, I was a policeman," he replied flatly.

"A *homicide* policeman," Muñoz repeated, in case the man standing before him had missed the point.

"A homicide policeman," Paco agreed.

"There has been a murder," Muñoz told him, "a particularly unpleasant one, as a matter of fact."

It would always be a case of 'matter of fact' with people like these. Paco did not even try to feign surprise.

"There have always been murders – most of them particularly unpleasant," he said. "There was no reason to suppose that they would stop just because of *the outbreak of hostilities*."

"This isn't just *any* murder. It has very serious political and military implications."

Muñoz looked as if he expected the ex-policeman's tongue to hang out – as if he were a dog, suddenly aware of the possibility of being fed a juicy bone. Paco took some pleasure in disappointing him.

The sharp-faced young man and gray-haired older one exchanged questioning glances.

Then the gray-haired man – Don Luis – said. "If we lose Madrid, Señor Ruiz, we have lost the war. That wasn't always the case, but it is now. It was in Madrid that we first halted fascism and …"

"*We?*" Paco interrupted. "I don't recall seeing you up in the mountains, when my comrades were dying like flies all around me."

Don Luis frowned, as if considering delivering a stinging rebuke. Then he shrugged, just as his partner had done earlier, and said, "We all do what we can – or what our age allows us to do. But to get back to the point – it is Madrid which stands as an all-important symbol for the continuation of our struggle. If it falls, the heart will be gone from the cause. The Republic will be like a balloon without any air in it. Flat. Useless."

Don Luis sounded as smooth and glib as every other politician he'd ever met, Paco thought. But for all that, he was right – lose Madrid and the cause was also lost.

"Go on," he said.

"Do you recall what that traitor General Mola said about a fifth column?" Ortega asked.

"He said that there were four columns of his soldiers marching on Madrid, but that they had a fifth column to assist them – the men loyal to the rebel cause who were already in the city."

"Exactly," the gray-haired man agreed. "And it is not only in the capital that there are fifth columnists at work."

The man was dangling the bait like an eager fisherman waiting to lure a hungry fish, Paco thought – but he was not ready to throw himself on the hook quite yet.

"It's only to be expected that there are people who support the rebels behind our lines," he said. "Just as there must also be people loyal to our cause who have been trapped behind the fascist lines."

"Would you agree that Madrid would have already fallen to the enemy had it not been for the help of the International Brigade?" Ortega asked, suddenly changing tack.

"Yes," Paco said.

How could he deny it? When the first battalions of the brigade – Germans, French, Belgians, Englishmen and Poles – had marched into the capital in November, they had given new hope to a populace which believed the city lost. More than that – the foreign soldiers had taught the eager but untrained Spanish volunteers *how* to fight. And they had been willing to lay down their own lives alongside those of their Spanish comrades in defense of a republic which was not even their own. The same had been true of the Americans in the Abraham Lincoln Brigade, who had fought side by side with his men in the Battle of Jarama. Republican Spain owed them all a debt it could never hope to repay.

"Would you also agree that we need the continued support of the brigade if we are to win this war?" Ortega asked.

"I'm an infantryman," Paco said. "I know about hand-to-hand fighting on the ground. I know how to kill a man, and the best ways to avoid being killed myself. I have no knowledge of overall strategy."

The gray-haired man sighed.

"Very well," he agreed. "But would you believe me if I told you that is the case?"

Paco looked into the other man's eyes, and saw that beneath the veneer of the politician, there perhaps lay the soul of an honest man.

"Yes, I'd believe you," he said.

"The enemy obviously believe it, too," Muñoz interrupted. "More than believe it – they have done something to ensure that it doesn't happen."

"Even in a group of like-minded comrades, there will be differences," Ortega continued. "They are bound together by their common ideology, but they are divided by their own personal experiences of life. And these personal experiences create animosities which, while they remain suppressed for most of the time, can surface in times of difficulty."

"Is all this generalization leading anywhere?" Paco asked impatiently.

"Once these differences emerge, the cause of them must be dealt with as soon as possible, if splits and divisions are to be avoided," Ortega said, carrying on as if he had never spoken.

"One of the International Brigade has been murdered," Paco said, finally seeing where he was leading.

Ortega nodded. "A member of the Abraham Lincoln Battalion was assassinated in San Antonio de la Jara, the night before last. His murder has caused a great deal of dissension."

"You mean that other members of the brigade suspect that the murderer is one of his own comrades?" Paco asked.

"Yes," Ortega said. "Which is, of course, exactly what the treacherous fifth columnist who is behind the crime wants them to think. That is why the real murderer must be arrested as soon as possible. Which, in turn, is why you must leave for Albacete immediately."

"I can't do it," Paco said firmly.

"Why not?" Muñoz demanded sharply.

"Because I have a responsibility to the men I command. They've fought bravely, and it's my duty as their leader to see that as many of them as possible come out of this bloody mess in one piece. So, you see, you'll simply have to send someone else."

"There is no one else," Muñoz countered.

"No one else!" Paco repeated incredulously. "No other ex-detective in the whole of Republican Spain?"

"No one who is as a good as you were…"

"I can give you half a dozen names off the top of my head …"

"… and who is still alive!"

It was possible that Muñoz was speaking the truth, Paco thought. So many good men had died, and he would not be at all surprised if some of them had been his colleagues from the old days. But that didn't do anything to alter the situation he found himself in now.

"I'm still not interested," he said. "And as things stand, I'd be no good to you, anyway."

The gray-haired man frowned.

"No good to us? Why not?"

"Because of the kind of detective I was."

"And what kind of detective was that?"

Paco sighed. "When I investigated a case, I always started with a completely open mind."

"I imagine you did."

"It was the only way I knew how to work. But you've already told me the conclusion you'd want me to reach if you sent me down to Albacete."

"We've told you the conclusion that you're *bound* to reach anyway," Muñoz said.

Paco shook his head. "There's no such thing as 'bound to' in detective work. I know nothing about this particular case, but I do know there are a hundred reasons why one man might kill another." He began to count them out on his fingers. "Envy … jealousy … greed…" He stopped counting and spread his hand in a gesture of hopelessness. "The list is endless. And if I discovered that your American was killed for one of those reasons – and not by the enemy at all, but by one of his comrades – it would achieve exactly the opposite result to the one that you're hoping for."

Muñoz slammed his first hard on the desk.

"You *will* investigate it," he said hotly. "You will investigate it because it is what the President wishes. And you *will* reach the correct – and inevitable – conclusion."

"Even if I agreed to do what you want, I wouldn't even know where to begin," Paco protested. "How long have these *brigadistas* been in Spain? A month? Six weeks?"

Ortega gave a thin smile – the smile of a hunter who senses a false hope growing in the bosom of his quarry.

"Some of them have been here for even less time than that," he said.

"And do they speak Spanish?"

"A few of them might have picked up a little of the language."

"Well, there you are. They don't speak my language, and I don't speak theirs. How do you expect me to interrogate them when we can't even understand each other?"

"It's true that might present a difficulty in most circumstances," Muñoz agreed, "but fortunately that is not so in this case. You might not speak any English yourself, but," he glanced down at the cardboard folder, "you appear to have a friend who does."

Paco felt his stomach perform a somersault.

"I don't know what you're talking about," he said.

Muñoz looked down at the file again.

"It is widely known that you are involved in an adulterous relationship with an American woman who speaks excellent Spanish," he said. "To be specific – a Señorita Cindy Walker? Isn't that right?"

"You leave her out of this," Paco said menacingly.

"There is a war going on," the sharp-faced man replied. "It is impossible to leave *anyone* out of *anything*." He gave the folder another cursory glance. "Señorita Walker is working as an unqualified nurse. At the moment, she is based in Madrid, which, with the enemy bombardment, is a dangerous enough place to be. But it is always

10

possible she could be moved much closer to the front line – and, as we all know, there is even more danger there."

"If she's moved, and anything happens to her. I'll hunt you down, wherever you are," Paco growled.

"Perhaps that's true," the sharp-faced man agreed. "But killing me wouldn't bring Señorita Walker back to life, now would it?" He gave Paco another thin smile. "Look at it this way, Inspector Ruiz – if you were to agree to take the case, and she were to go with you to Albacete as your interpreter, you would both be a very long way from the front, and therefore quite safe. Whereas, as things stand, you could both easily be dead by tomorrow."

"You heard him," Paco said to Ortega. "He's threatening me."

The older man looked distinctly uncomfortable.

"He is ... er... only making plain the practical realities of war," he said. "We would not decide ourselves that Señorita Walker should be sent closer to the front – that is not within our remit. But the decision could be made from Madrid. All we are offering you is the opportunity to prevent it from happening."

"Bullshit!" Paco told him. "Politician's double-talk."

"Perhaps it is," Muñoz agreed. "But the fact remains, you still have two options. Either you go back to the trenches and abandon Cindy Walker to her fate, or you both go to San Antonio de la Jara. Which is it to be?"

"You know which it is, you bastard!" Paco told him.

"Yes, I do," the sharp-faced man agreed. "I knew long before you even entered the room. That is why I am the one giving the orders, and you are the one obeying them."

Chapter Two

If the train taking them to Albacete had been a racehorse, it would certainly have been put out to grass long ago.

Its engine wheezed asthmatically. Smoke rose reluctantly from its funnel as if from the lungs of an addicted heavy smoker. Even its wheels – clanking protestingly against the rails – seemed to be suffering from a touch of rheumatism.

From inside one of the rickety carriages, Paco Ruiz looked out at the vast, empty expanse of the La Mancha countryside which was slipping lethargically by. Once in a while, a small, sleepy village would appear through the window to break the monotony, but then it was gone again, and all that was left was rolling hills, scrub and clumps of sad-looking olive trees.

This was the heart of Spain, he thought – and it was a harsh, unyielding heart, which demanded much but gave precious little in return.

His own father had worked his modest plot of land not so far from here. The old man had slaved from dawn to dusk – and sometimes beyond that.

And for what?

No one had starved in the Ruiz family – that was true – yet when the old man had died, he had gone out of the world with no more than he'd had when he'd come into it. And it was the same with millions of other Spaniards. Yet despite that, the people loved the land, and would have withered away without it. Even he, a city boy for over a decade and a half now, didn't really feel at home until he was out in the *campo* of his childhood.

"What are you thinking about now, Ruiz?" asked a voice from the seat opposite his.

He turned his gaze from the window to the blonde woman, and experienced once again a feeling of wonder that this beautiful, intelligent, strong-willed *yanqui* should ever want to be a part of his life.

"I asked you what you're thinking about" Cindy repeated. "Is it the case?"

He shook his head. He'd been a real detective when she'd first met him, and there'd been very few moments – except when caught up in the heat of passion in the bedroom – when his mind *hadn't* been fixated on his investigation.

But now all that seemed like another life, and when he was called on to be a policeman again – as he had been in the case of the General's dog – it always took a while for him to stop merely *acting* like a detective and slip fully into his old role.

Besides, he was still assailed by the doubts he'd expressed to the sharp-faced man in the field headquarters, doubts which warned him that this wasn't a real investigation at all – that he wasn't actually expected to solve the murder, but merely come up with a solution which was politically expedient.

Paco looked around the carriage. There were not many other people traveling to Albacete that day, and of the few there were, most wore some kind of military uniform. It would be a very different matter on the train's return journey to Madrid. Then, it would be carrying rice and meat from Valencia to feed the capital, and perhaps a few weapons to help carry on the struggle with an enemy who had reached the very western edges of the city. That was why the Battle of Jarama had been so vital – *continued* to be so vital. Because if the Republic lost that battle, it would lose the railway line, and without its link to friendly territory, Madrid was finished.

In the old days, the train would have been crammed full of all sorts of people, Paco thought. There would have been weather-beaten peasants on their way to the market in Albacete, weighed down with fruit and live chickens. There would have been stiff clerks, dispatched by their masters in Madrid to check on how the provincial branches of their businesses were being run. And, of course, there would have been the priests and nuns.

There had always been priests and nuns on the train before the war – traveling from one of the many religious houses to another, visiting their relatives in the village where they had grown up, or answering a summons from their bishop. But now they had all either been banished from the territory the government controlled, or killed at the behest of an angry mob. The Republic – or at least, the workers and peasants who made up most of it – no longer had time for those they saw as the blood-sucking leeches who had lived for so long off the sweat and strain of others.

Paco lit up a cigarette. "Where's Felipe?" he asked.

Cindy smiled. "Where do you think he is? He's gone farther up the train – looking for something to eat."

Paco grinned. Constable Felipe Fernandez – who had been known to everyone in the Madrid police force before the war as *Fat* Felipe – had been involved in a perpetual search for food for as long as Paco had known him. And that had been quite some time. Felipe had been his partner for nearly a decade, and a few months earlier that association had almost cost the fat man his life. For a while, when he had been lying in hospital with half a dozen bullet holes in him, the fat constable had been losing weight, but ever since his discharge he had been working with the dedication of a zealot at returning his figure to its former podgy glory.

Paco was glad that he had Felipe working with him on this case. The constable was driven by stolid, unimaginative common sense, which Paco recognized as a necessary counter-balance to his own impulsive reactions (which were often completely off-target) and his occasional flashes of insight (which were usually stunningly right). But their relationship went beyond their work. Though he would have died rather than admit it openly, there was no one in the world – Cindy excepted – of whom the ex-inspector was fonder.

Felipe appeared, waddling between the rows of wooden benches, and plopped himself down heavily on the seat next to Cindy.

"Not a single thing to eat on this whole bloody train," he complained loudly. "The state things have been allowed to fall into, anybody would think there was a war going on." He scratched his ample belly. "Still, Albacete's quite close to the coast, so there should be plenty to eat there." A look of mild concern flashed across his face. "We *will* be in the area long enough to get a few decent meals down us, won't we, *jefe*?"

"*I* don't know," Paco admitted. "If the murderer takes one look at you and decides it's pointless to try and keep the truth from a man of your substantial girth for long, we should be out of there in a few hours. On the other hand …" He shrugged again.

"A man of my girth," Felipe muttered, pretending to sound offended. "That's really hurtful."

"I hope it takes a long, long time," Cindy said, then bit her lip as if she regretted having spoken.

Paco knew what she meant. They were very much in love, yet his duty – first as a policeman, then as a soldier – had conspired to keep them apart for most of the time they had known each other. This investigation would at least give them an opportunity to be together.

But wouldn't that just make it harder when they had to separate again?

The train, which could never have been said to be speeding, slowed down to almost a crawl.

Fat Felipe checked his pocket watch.

"We must be nearly there – and only three hours late," he said. He stuck his head out of the open window. "Yes, that's Albacete, all right." He turned his attention to Cindy. "Do you know anything about the town?"

"Very little," the American woman admitted.

"It's not much of a place to look at," Felipe told her, "but it's the offensive weapons capital of the whole of Spain. If you're ever robbed

15

at knife-point, you can be almost sure that the blade which the robber is threatening you with was made in Albacete."

Cindy grinned.

"Thanks," she said. "If I *am* ever robbed, I'll take real comfort from knowing that fact."

But it hadn't been a knife from Albacete which had put an end to the life of a *Yanqui* who went by the name of Samuel Johnson, Paco thought. He had been shot twice – once through the chest and once through the head. Before the war, it would have been a pretty safe bet that such a crime had been premeditated, but now there were so many guns around that the mere fact that a man was carrying one was no indication that he had murder on his mind.

Before finally being allowed to take a rest, the new recruits of the Abraham Lincoln Battalion of the International Brigade had spent an exhausting morning marching up and down the plain which surrounded San Antonio de la Jara. Now the men squatted on their haunches, eating their *bocadillos* and smoking their cigarettes as they had done during similar breaks on previous days. But today there was a difference. The easy camaraderie of their other marches had all-but disappeared. Instead of being the single unit that their commanders had been attempting to forge, the men had broken up into small clusters, drawn together either by the fact that they shared the same suspicions or because they belonged to that group on which those suspicions fell.

"Sam Johnson was killed because of who he was," muttered a Jew from Brooklyn, talking to three other Jews who had been brought up in the same orphanage as he had. "There can be no other explanation for it. And we, too, could be killed for who *we* are."

"'Spect this sort o' thing to happen in Alabama," one of the black volunteers told his companions. "Hell, they still got the Klan down there. Just didn't think it was gonna happen here."

"It was a cowardly killing," an ex-longshoreman called Ted Donaldson told the three other ex-longshoremen who had traveled out to Spain with him. "An' who should you be pointin' the finger at when somethin' cowardly happens? Why, the Yids!"

The sandy-haired sergeant, standing some distance away from his men, shook his head sadly. He could not hear what any of them were saying, but he could make a pretty accurate guess. It wasn't going to be easy to get these men to trust each other again, he thought. It wasn't going to be easy at all.

The train crawled into Albacete station, and came to a juddering, exhausted halt. The second it had stopped moving – even before the passengers had had the opportunity to disembark – the people who'd been standing on the platform were forming tight knots around the doors. They couldn't wait to get to Madrid – to be in the thick of the action.

Paco wondered how long their enthusiasm would last – how long they would have to be under constant bombardment before they decided that the tranquility of Albacete was not such a bad thing after all.

Fat Felipe took his battered suitcase down from the rack.

"We won't have to walk far, will we?" he asked, sounding a little concerned.

Paco grinned. "No. The commander of the Lincoln Battalion has been instructed to send someone to pick us up."

He had been expecting the 'someone' in question to be a man, but as they fought their way through the mob waiting to get on the train, he noticed a woman waving at them. She was around twenty-eight or twenty-nine, Paco estimated. She was wearing pants – which for practical reasons had become the fashion among women in the militias – and a combat jacket which did little to disguise her firm breasts. She had the long black hair and the dark eyes of a typical Spanish beauty, and most of the men on the platform who were not struggling to get on the train seemed incapable of tearing their gazes away from her.

The woman started to walk towards them, cutting her path through the crowd as if she were the only person on the platform. An ex-aristocrat, from her attitude, Paco decided. The sort of woman who, before the war, would have spent her days riding around her father's estate on a pure black stallion and her nights being waited on hand and foot by half a dozen servants. He wondered what had happened to make her decide to join the opposition.

The woman spoke, but to Cindy, not Paco – and in English.

"You the translator?" she asked.

"That's right. Cindy Walker."

"I'm Dolores McBride," the other woman said. "You can call me Doll – most *men* do, whether I want them to or not." She noticed Paco's raised eyebrow when she'd said her first name, and turned her attention onto him. "My father's Irish-American, but my mother's Mexican," she said, switching to Spanish. "I'm a journalist."

"I didn't know there was such a thing as women journalists," Paco replied.

"Maybe there aren't – here," the woman said.

"But in America …?"

"Not on any of the big newspapers back in the States, either. For all the talk of equality, a woman with *cojones* scares the hell out of most men. But see, I don't work for one of the *big* newspapers. I'm the Spanish correspondent of the *Moscow News*. That's Moscow, Russia, not Moscow Idaho. Also, as it happens, I'm the schmuck who's been given the job of driving the three of you out to the lovely town of San Antonio de la Jara – which is where the Abraham Lincoln Brigade is based, and where the murder took place."

Paco remembered how Cindy's American directness had almost shocked him when he'd first met her. But this woman was something else. She made his lover seem like a mere shrinking violet.

"So you're working for the International Brigade, are you, Miss McBride?" he asked.

Dolores McBride laughed.

"God, no! But the boys back at the base camp are expecting to be sent up to the front real soon now, and I figured it would have been a waste of time for one of them to come and pick you up, when he'd be much better employed learning how not to get himself killed."

It was a good point, Paco agreed, but he found himself wondering if that was the only reason this woman – this *journalist* who was no doubt in pursuit of a story – had volunteered to drive to the station and collect them.

Dolores McBride pulled a pack of American cigarettes out of her breast pocket, and offered them round.

"OK," she said, as she struck a match and held it under Paco's cigarette, "let's get this show on the road."

She led them to the barrier. Before the war, there would have been a railway official there to collect their tickets, but now that tickets – in common with so many other things – were distributed rather than bought, the only people standing there were two militiamen checking identification papers.

The four of them stepped out of the station into the watery winter sunshine.

"The car's over there." Dolores McBride said.

Paco's heart skipped a beat. The vehicle she was pointing to was a Fiat Balilla. He'd had one himself until the previous summer. It had been the only thing of any value he'd ever owned. And now it was gone – requisitioned by the Socialist Militia just as this one – as evidenced by the initials UGT crudely painted on its the side in white – had been requisitioned by the General Workers Union.

Paco didn't regret giving up his car – but he did miss it. He wondered where it was now. Probably blown to hell by a shell from a German tank on the front line.

Dolores McBride stopped in front of the car. "You're the Big Cheese, aren't you?" she asked Paco.

The *queso grande*?

"I'm sorry?" Paco said. "I don't understand."

"Are you the guy in charge of the investigation?" She glanced at Felipe. "Or should I be talking to your cuddly friend here?"

"I'm in charge of the investigation," Paco told her.

"OK, so one of the perks of the job is that you get to ride up front with me," Dolores McBride said, opening the door, pulling forward the passenger seat and indicating to Cindy and Felipe that they should clamber into the back.

Paco turned questioningly to Cindy, whose expression replied that since he *was* the Big Cheese, she supposed he had the place in the front of the car by right. But he could tell that she was not entirely happy with the idea.

Paco waited while Felipe eased his bulk into the back seat and Cindy had followed him, then slid in beside Dolores McBride.

The railway station, as was the case in most Spanish towns, was situated well away from the center of Albacete, and soon the Balilla had left all buildings behind and was crossing the Castilian Plain. Once again, as they passed gnarled peasants leading donkeys and gangs of burly workmen repairing holes in the road, Paco got the eerie feeling that the war he had just left behind him was really nothing more than a bad dream.

"Could you tell me what you know about the case?" he asked.

"Sure," Dolores agreed. "Sam Johnson was shot to death in a burnt-out church near the Plaza Mayor in San Antonio. So far, nobody's come up with any satisfactory reason for him being there. Death occurred shortly after midnight on Friday."

"How can you pin it down so accurately?"

"Easy. The town was *en fiestas*, and he was seen on the square just before the fireworks started. His body was discovered ten minutes later, by a local woman called Concha Prieto."

"What reason did she have for going to a burnt-out church at that time of night?"

Dolores McBride shrugged. "Who knows? Maybe she's one of the few God-botherers still left in town. Any more questions?"

"Yes. Could you please tell me all you can about Samuel Johnson's comrades?"

"That's a pretty tall order, Mister. What particularly do you want to know about them?"

"What are they like?"

The journalist snorted.

"That's the same as asking me what *dogs* are like. There's all sorts."

"Just try to give me some kind of overall impression, if you can," Paco persisted.

"OK," Dolores McBride agreed. "There are two things that most of them have in common. The first is that they're idealists. The second is that they were recruited by the Party in New York."

"The Party?"

The journalist turned her head slightly towards him, the expression on her face suggesting that she couldn't understand his obvious confusion, since there *was* only one party as far as she was concerned.

"The Communist Party," she said.

"So all the members of the International Brigade are also members of the Communist Party, are they?"

Dolores McBride sighed exasperatedly, as though she'd been through the same discussion so many times before – and with so many other people – that it was starting to bore her.

"As far as the Party is concerned, this war isn't about spreading communism but about stopping fascism," she said.

"You still haven't answered my question," Paco pointed out.

"No, the Lincolns are *not* all communists. Many of them are, but that certainly wasn't one of the requirements for recruitment. There are socialists in the brigade as well. And a fair number of other guys who don't have any particular political leaning at all – but just want to do what's right."

"So that's how they're the same," Paco said thoughtfully. "How are they different?"

"It's hard to know just where to start," Dolores McBride confessed. "One of the guys in the brigade is in line to inherit millions of dollars when his robber baron father finally kicks the bucket. Then again, there are others who haven't got a pot to piss in. There are men with a college education, and men who can hardly even sign their own names. There are kids still wet behind the ears, and there are guys who

21

it would be more than charitable to say are approaching middle age. A fair number of them have lied to their families about where they are – just like the Party asked them to – but there are others who don't even have a family to lie to. We've got ex-union organizers and civil engineers, shop assistants and carpenters, poets and sharecroppers. Some of the guys haven't had any kind of job since the Crash of '29. So like I said, all that binds them together is the fact that they want to do the right thing."

"But are they *really* bound together?" Paco asked, thinking of what the sharp-faced man had told him back at the front line headquarters.

"What the hell is that supposed to mean?" Dolores McBride demanded, bridling and suspicious.

"Tell me something about the dead man – Samuel Johnson," Paco said, changing the subject.

"He was a real great guy," the journalist told him. She was speaking seriously – and Paco thought he detected a catch in her voice, as if the subject was genuinely upsetting for her. "He was one of those who didn't have much of an education, but he was as smart as hell. And he had a heart as big as your head."

"So why is he dead?"

"Why do you think? He's dead because somebody pumped a couple of bullets in him."

"You're missing the point," Paco told her. "The main reason people get killed is because they're in the way."

"In the way of *what*?"

Paco shrugged. "It could be any number of things. Happening to be in the wrong place during an armed robbery. Having too much money and being unwilling to die so your heirs can spend it. Trying to take for yourself something that somebody else wants very badly. What I want to know is – whose way was Johnson getting in?"

"That's obvious," Dolores McBride retorted. "He was getting in the way of the fascists."

"He hadn't even finished his basic training, had he?"

"No, but …"

"And even if he had, why would the fascists single him out in particular for extermination?"

"Because he had great potential to be a leader. The brigade is much weaker as a result of his death."

"So you're saying that the fascists smuggled one of their men a hundred kilometers behind our lines just so he could eliminate someone who had the potential to be a leader?"

"What other explanation could there possibly be?"

Plenty, Paco thought – but obviously none that Dolores McBride really wanted to hear.

He thought back to the last case he'd been forced to investigate, when he'd been a prisoner of the rebel army up in the Sierra Guadarrama. The general in charge there had not wanted to believe that anyone from his own side had been involved in a crime, either. That was the trouble with wars – each person divided the rest of the world into black and white, and, unlike in real life, there was absolutely no room for shades of gray.

The car had been climbing a hill which would scarcely have been worth a mention had it been located at the base of the Sierra Nevada, but managed to achieve something like eminence in the middle of a plain. As the Balilla reached the crown of the hill, Dolores McBride said, "There's the town. That's where it all happened."

Paco looked down. The town – which was really no more than a large village – was situated on the bend of a small river. It had clearly once been completely surrounded by a wall, but over the years a part of its fortifications had either crumbled away or been pulled down. From its center rose a blackened church spire, and close to the church was the square of buildings which formed the Plaza Mayor. Paco guessed that to walk from the square to the edge of the town would take even the slowest moving man no more than ten minutes – and that one who was running could have covered the ground *much* quicker.

But he didn't think it likely that *anyone* had been running the night Samuel Johnson had been killed – at least, not if the murder had been premeditated. And it was more than probable that the killer had chosen his time deliberately – had waited until the town was crowded with people and filled with noise – before making his move.

Paco took out his pack of cigarettes, offered one to his driver, then passed the pack back to Cindy and Felipe.

If the killer were some outsider, as everyone seemed to want to believe, he thought, then the *fiestas* would have provided a perfect cover for his crime.

But if it had been someone from *inside* the town instead, that would have been equally true.

And Paco had a gut instinct that whoever had carried out the murder was not now behind enemy lines, toasting himself with good Rioja wine, but was somewhere in San Antonio de la Jara, waiting for the investigators from Madrid to arrive.

Chapter Three

The Fiat entered San Antonio de la Jara through an arched gateway which, unlike much of the rest of the town wall, had not fallen victim to either the harsh weather or the people's need for building material.

It was a narrow gate, just wide enough for a rattling farm cart, and most car drivers would have gone through it at a cautious crawl, in order to avoid scraping the vehicle against the stonework. But Dolores McBride was not most drivers – she hardly slowed at all, and the Balilla passed through the gap with just inches to spare on either side.

The street immediately inside the walls was narrow, too, and sloped upwards towards the center of town. It was made of rough cobbles worn smooth by generations of donkeys' hooves, and it had a drain running down its center. It was lined by two and three-story houses of various ages and in various states of repair, which huddled together as if they needed each other's support and assurance.

As the Fiat bumped and bucked over the cobbles, Paco glanced up at the small iron balconies which projected out from the houses. These balconies were where much of the life of the street went on. It was from here that neighbors, who could almost touch each other if they chose to stretch, would gossip. Lovers, as physically close to each other as they could ever be without a chaperone, would whisper terms of endearment across the divide. Young children would take their street-battles into the air, and hurl abuse – and sometimes objects – at each other from the safety of their own homes.

Washing hung from these balconies – shirts and sheets almost starched frozen by the cold Castilian winter air. On some balconies there were old olive oil tins, containing geraniums which shivered their way through this early month of the year and dreamed of the balmier times yet to come.

"Ah Spain!" the ex-policeman thought. It was easy to criticize it in so many ways, but he was sure there was nowhere else on earth quite like it.

Dolores McBride brought the car to a sudden halt a few doors down from the main square.

"This is where I've fixed you guys up with rooms," she announced. "It's conveniently located for the whole of the town, and the widow who lives here could sure use the money you'll pay her. OK?"

"Yes, it should serve our purpose perfectly," Paco said.

Dolores glanced from Paco to Cindy and Felipe and back again, as if she were counting heads. Then she looked Cindy squarely in the eye and said, "I'm assuming it's only two rooms that you'll be wanting."

"That's right," Cindy agreed tightly. "We'll just want the two."

Dolores McBride lit a fresh cigarette. "OK, dump your bags, and then we can get down to business."

"We can get down to business," Cindy repeated, in English. "I thought your job was finished as soon as you'd delivered us here."

Paco frowned. He didn't know quite what was going on between these two women – but he was almost certain he didn't like it.

Dolores McBride noticed Paco's puzzled expression – and grinned.

"Yeah – we," she told Cindy. "You'd be real surprised just how many of the pies around here I've got my finger in, Honey."

The widow who owned the house where Dolores McBride had booked the rooms was dressed in black from head to toe. She could have been as young as her early forties or as old as her late sixties – it was hard to tell a woman's age once she had gone into the mourning which would last her for the rest of her life.

Paco told her that he and his wife would like the bigger of the two rooms. The widow glanced down automatically at Cindy's finger, but made no comment when she saw there was no ring on it, though she would undoubtedly have done so a few months earlier.

The war had changed the way so many people saw life, Paco thought.

The room that he and Cindy were shown to was pretty much what he would have expected. Most of it was taken up by a cast-iron bed on which rested a lumpy feather mattress, but there was still just enough space for a cheap wardrobe, a chest of drawers and wash-stand. The small window, set into the roof, overlooked the street.

Cindy slammed her suitcase down on the bed, wrenched it open, and began to pull out her clothes as if she were in a hurry to find something which was buried beneath them.

"We can't have this, you know," Paco said quietly.

"Can't have what?" Cindy replied, manhandling one of her dresses as if it was an enemy who needed to be subdued.

"A detective needs co-operation to conduct his investigation properly."

"What's that supposed to mean?"

"It means that he can't afford to antagonize any of the people whose help he might need."

"Yeah, well, I'm not a detective," Cindy said, thrusting a coat hanger viciously under the collar of the dress.

"What's the matter with you?" Paco asked.

"Oh nothing! Everything's just peachy."

"Come on, Cindy!" Paco said.

"If you must know, I don't particularly like being treated like a piece of dirt just because I don't work for the *Moscow News*."

"Is that how Doll treats you?"

"Yes, that's how *McBride* treats me. Maybe you don't notice it so much in Spanish, but let me tell you, it's painfully obvious when she's speaking to me in English."

"I'll have a word with her," Paco promised.

"Sure! And a lot of good that will do."

"Would you care to explain that?"

"Yeah, I'll explain it! You've only just met the woman – and already she's starting to twist you round her little finger. You should see the way you look at her. Your tongue's hanging so far out it's a wonder you don't step on it."

She wasn't being fair, Paco thought. Yet, in a way, he could understand why she was getting so upset and talking about Dolores McBride as if she were a rival.

Dolores made her feel insecure. Not because she was undoubtedly very attractive. Not even because she was a very attractive *fellow* American. No, Cindy's real problem was that the woman she saw as competition for her Spanish lover looked Spanish herself!

"If I promise not to look at her again, will that make things any better?" he asked.

"Not if it takes an effort," Cindy retorted. "Not if you have to force yourself to tear your eyes away from her."

"I love you," Paco said. "I might occasionally look at another woman – what Spaniard could honestly say that he doesn't – but it will never go further than that. It's you I want – now and forever."

Cindy bundled her underwear into one of the drawers.

"Talk is cheap," she said. She slammed the drawer closed. "We're here to solve a murder, Ruiz. Let's do it quickly, so we can get the hell away."

The chill wind which blew down the narrow street leading up to the Plaza Mayor made the three visitors from Madrid shudder, but if it had any effect on Dolores McBride, she gave no sign of it.

The central square itself held no surprises. There was a fountain in the middle of it, and a moderately impressive building with a shield carved over the door at the far end.

"The town hall?" Paco asked.

"That's right," Dolores McBride agreed. "Or, at least, it used to be the town hall. But it's no longer the place where the bloated landlords get together to work out how to squeeze every last possible *centimo* out of the struggling masses. It belongs to the People now."

Paco coughed awkwardly. He'd never been happy with jargon, whichever side of the conflict it came from, and phrases like 'bloated landlords' and 'struggling masses' made him feel vaguely uncomfortable, even though – he had to admit – they were more or less accurate.

"It's not that we don't appreciate the guided tour you're giving us of this charming *pueblo*, Miss McBride," Cindy said tartly – and in English. "But, in case you've forgotten the fact, we're not here to take in the tourist attractions, but to solve a murder."

"Oh, so you're a detective as well as an interpreter, are you?" Dolores McBride asked with an innocence which was meant to fool no one.

"*Inspector Ruiz's* here to solve a murder," Cindy corrected herself.

"That's what I thought," Dolores replied. "And that's why I've brought you to the plaza. The town hall's serving as the Lincoln's base – at least until they're moved up the front."

Cindy studied the building as if she expected to learn something from it.

"It may be their base, but it seems really quiet to me right now," she said.

"Most of the battalion should be out on training exercises," Dolores replied, reverting to Spanish. "But the ones who Paco needs to talk to – the commander and the political commissar – will probably be in the office."

The ex-policeman found himself frowning again.

The ones who Paco needs to talk to, he repeated mentally – as if *she* knew who *he* needed to talk to.

Dolores' attitude was a perfect illustration of what was bothering him about this case. He was the acknowledged expert in murder investigation – but everybody else seemed to think they knew how he should conduct this particular one, and exactly what conclusion he should reach.

"You sure you want to do this?" Dolores asked Cindy, when they'd reached the town hall steps.

"Do what?"

"You've had a long journey from Madrid, and you must be feeling wrecked. Why don't you go back to your room for a little shut-eye, and leave the translating up to me?"

"I'm not tired," Cindy said, through clenched teeth. 'And since I'm the trained linguist here, I think I should be the one to do the translation."

Dolores gave her an unquestionably superior smile.

"You might be 'trained', as you put it, Honey, but I've been speaking both languages from the moment I was born," she said.

I really don't need this kind of complication, Paco thought – I don't need it *at all*.

He glanced across at Cindy, and understood from the expression on her face not only that she was waiting for him to say something, but exactly what that response was expected to be.

"Cindy's used to helping me in my investigations," he said aloud. "I think it's better if she does the translation."

Dolores shrugged.

"Whatever you say, *Queso Grande*. Mind if I show you where you can find the commander and the commissar – or will Señorita Walker take care of that, too?"

"By all means show us where they are," Paco said.

Dolores McBride stepped up to the door, and turned the big iron ring which was set in the center of it. The door swung open, and she signaled the others to follow her. She led them down a corridor, came to a halt at the third door on the right, and opened it without knocking.

A large wooden desk, which had probably once been used by the town clerk, took up at least half of the room they were entering. Sitting behind the desk were two men. They were both in their late twenties, but that was where the similarity ended. One was tall, and almost impossibly thin. His blue eyes bulged slightly, giving him the look of a highly excitable – and slightly nervous – hare. The other man was shorter, bulkier and darker. *His* eyes were almost hooded, suggesting that he always thought before he spoke – and that even when he did put his thoughts into words, they were not necessarily to be trusted.

"These are the guys from Madrid – the ones who've come to solve all your problems for you," Dolores said in English.

The thin American behind the desk stood up and extended his hand to Paco.

"I'm Matt Harris. It's an honor to meet you, sir."

"He says…" Dolores began.

"I understand," replied Paco. "Paco Ruiz." he told Harris. He gestured first towards Cindy, "Cindy Walker," and then Fat Felipe, "Constable Fernandez."

"And this is James Clay, our political commissar," Harris said.

The short dark man did not rise from his seat, but instead gave the three new arrivals a curt nod.

"Please be seated," Harris said. "I expect you've got some questions you want to ask."

"He says you've probably got some questions you want to ask," Cindy said quickly, giving Dolores McBride a pointed look.

The journalist hesitated for a second, then shrugged again and said, "I guess I'll catch up with you guys later."

"Tell Señor Harris that I wish to know what the murdered man was doing in the hours before he met his death," Paco said to Cindy, once Dolores McBride had gone.

Cindy translated.

"Immediately before his death, he was seen by several people standing in the town square," Harris said. "Earlier in the evening, he'd been visiting one of the families on the edge of town."

"Visiting them?"

"They'd invited him over for supper. He'd become quite a friend of theirs, considering the short time he'd been here."

"So he spoke Spanish?" Paco asked.

"No, but that didn't really seem to matter very much. The locals understand that we're here because we want to help them, and they've taken us to their hearts. Well-meaning people usually find a way to understand each other, even without a common language, you know."

"Who was aware of Samuel Johnson's plans for the evening?"

"I'm not entirely sure of that, but I imagine it would have been pretty common knowledge. Members of the battalion spend most of their time together, and nobody has any secrets."

Everybody has secrets, Paco thought. However open a man's life appears, there is always something which, for one reason or another, he wishes to keep hidden from others.

"Have you accounted for the movements of the other members of the battalion at the time of the murder?" Paco asked.

"Why the hell should we want to do that?" James Clay demanded, when the question had been translated into English. "Are you suggesting, even for a moment, that it might have been one of his comrades who murdered him?"

"Well, he certainly didn't kill himself," Paco pointed out.

"We don't *have to be* here in Spain," Clay said, with obvious growing fury. "We weren't drafted – we volunteered. Every man in the brigade is like a brother to every other man. We need each other. We trust each other. Losing a good man like Samuel Johnson is a loss to us all."

"Like brothers," Paco said, reflectively. "Possibly you are. But from what I remember from my religion classes, the first murder in the scriptures was when Cain killed *his* brother – and he wasn't the last sibling to do it."

"Do you really want me to translate that, Ruiz?" Cindy asked.

Paco grinned ruefully.

"Maybe it might be wiser not to," he agreed. "Ask Señor Harris when his men will be back."

But it was James Clay who responded to Cindy's translation.

"He wants to know why you should need to have that information," Cindy said.

"Because I have to question them," Paco answered. "And before Señor Clay goes off on his high horse again, tell him that even if none of the *brigadistas* had anything to do with the murder, one or two still might know something which will lead us to the killer."

In the exchange which followed, Paco could only guess at what was being said, though it seemed to him that Cindy was vigorously arguing his case, Clay was vehement on his opposition and Harris appeared to be attempting to steer some kind of compromise course between the two. Eventually Cindy asked a question, and Clay gave a reluctant nod.

"The Lincolns should be back in an hour or so," Cindy told Paco. "They will be instructed to go to the council chamber, where you will be permitted to talk to them."

"Talk to them? Or question them?"

"Mr. Clay agrees there can be no objection to you questioning them."

"But questioning them *how*? Can I talk to individuals? Or does he just expect me to throw out questions at the whole group?"

Cindy gave him an awkward little smile.

"I wanted to get *some kind* of agreement out of him, so I thought it was best not to be too specific about that," she said.

"You were probably right," Paco agreed.

"So you're happy with the arrangements?"

"Of course not. But at least it's a start."

"Is there anything else you'd like me to ask them about, while we're here?" Cindy said.

Despite the unusual circumstances, this was a murder case like any other, Paco reminded himself, and his best course of action would be to follow the normal procedures as far as possible.

"Has the body been buried yet?" he asked.

"No. They're planning to bury him with full military honors at dawn tomorrow."

"So where's the cadaver being kept until then?"

"In the house that used to belong to the priest."

"Ask them if I can see it."

Cindy conveyed the request. The commander nodded his head immediately, and even the political commissar did not seem to have any deep-rooted objections to the idea.

"When would you like to see it?" Cindy asked.

"Right now seems as good a time as any," Paco replied.

* * *

The priest's house was just one door down from the church, but had escaped the latter's fate when the townsfolk had gone on the rampage in the first few, heady days of the revolution.

Matt Harris slipped a bony hand into one of his pockets, and pulled out a large key.

"We considered posting an honor guard on the door," he said, almost apologetically. "Sam Johnson certainly deserved one. But then we thought about it, and decided that Sam would have preferred his comrades to use their time for their basic training."

He inserted the key in the lock, and opened the door. The atmosphere inside the house – a mixture of incense, piety and brandy – reminded Paco of the few visits he had made to his priest's house when he had been a child.

"He's been laid to rest in what was the priest's study," Cindy told him.

Paco turned the phrase over in his mind.

Laid to rest.

He had long ago ceased to believe in God, and with that loss had gone any belief that the human soul could survive beyond death. Yet, as always when faced with a murder, he could not quite bring himself to accept that the victim would ever be completely at peace until his killer had been found and brought to justice.

The coffin had been placed across the top of the priest's mahogany desk. A red flag, with a hammer and sickle clearly – and obviously deliberately – visible in one corner, had been draped over it.

"So, unlike some of the other Lincolns, Samuel Johnson was a member of the Party, was he?" Paco asked.

Clay nodded, and Harris said, "*Si, un buen comunista,*" his tongue curling awkwardly around the alien words.

"Could you open the coffin, please?" Paco asked.

Harris and Clay stepped forward, removed the flag, and reverently folded it up. The coffin, which the process revealed, was made of plain wood, in marked contrast to the expensive table on which it was lying.

34

Harris said something to Cindy.

"They want you to know in advance that he's naked except for the bed sheet he's draped in," she said.

"And why is that?"

"They didn't want to bury him in a uniform which was covered with blood. They've sent for a new uniform, but it hasn't arrived from Albacete yet."

Paco nodded.

"Good. That will make it easier for me to examine the nature of the wounds."

The two Americans lifted the lid of the cheap coffin, and moved to the side. Paco stepped forward. The wound in the dead man's chest was puckered, so it resembled an obscenely bloodied red mouth. The wound to the head was even messier. Though some attempt had been made to clean it up, nothing could disguise the fact that part of the skull had been blown away and some of his brain was missing.

It was obvious what had happened. The shot to the chest had been the first one, and had merely served to take Johnson down. It was the second shot – the one to the head – which had killed the poor bastard.

Yet even as he was examining the wounds and drawing his conclusions, only a small part of Paco's mind was focusing on the *cause* of death. The rest of it was trying to accommodate the shock he had received the moment he saw the body.

He had been told that Samuel Johnson was a brave man with a big heart. He had been told that though not educated, Johnson had been intelligent. But no one – not the sharp-faced man at the field headquarters, not the commissar nor the commander – not even the female journalist from the *Moscow* News – had thought to mention the fact that Johnson was as black as well-aged teak.

Chapter Four

"Do you smell something interesting, *jefe*?" Fat Felipe asked, as the two ex-policemen and their blonde *yanqui* interpreter left the town hall and made their way across the Plaza Mayor.

Paco sniffed, and felt the chill air rush up his nostrils. "I can smell donkey dung," he said. "And wood smoke. But in a place like this, I wouldn't call either of them particularly interesting."

Fat Felipe shook his head slowly – almost pityingly.

"You might have a good nose for crime, but you've none at all when it comes to food," he said. "Someone's cooking *riñones al jerez*."

"Are you sure?"

Felipe gave him a wide grin. "I've never been surer of anything in my entire life." He reached up, and slowly scratched his bulbous left ear with all the care and precision of a surgeon. "Would it be all right if I went off on my own for a while? To investigate, you understand."

"I understand," Paco replied.

He understood *very well*. All men needed food to fuel them, but there were some, like Felipe, who needed more than most – usually in a very rich blend – and the constable's brain would be a much more efficient machine after a bowl of kidneys in sherry.

Besides, it suited him to have Felipe disappear for a while. He had some serious questions he wanted to ask Cindy, and – given the way their last conversation had slipped so quickly into an argument – it might be wiser if he put them to her when they were alone.

He checked his watch.

36

"See you back here in about an hour, Felipe?" he suggested.

The fat constable licked his lips.

"An hour should be plenty of time to track those *riñones* down," he agreed.

Paco watched Felipe waddle across the square in the general direction of the tempting odor which he alone could smell, then turned his attention to Cindy.

"We need to talk," he said.

"What about?" Cindy demanded. "Your new friend *Doll?*"

"No. Not about her."

"Then what?"

"Sam Johnson. The moment I saw him, I knew I was out of my depth and that was going to need your help."

"My help!" Cindy repeated, unwilling to soften even a little. "That's rich, isn't it? You need my help! Well, I don't see how I *can* help. *You're* the Great Detective – *I'm* just your interpreter. And I'm probably not even as good at that as someone who's been brought up speaking Spanish and English from birth."

"I know nothing about Negroes," Paco pointed out softly.

"Say that again."

"I know nothing about Negroes. I never expected Sam Johnson to be black. It came as a shock."

"Why?" Cindy demanded. "Do you have some kind of prejudice against them? Have you decided that because the victim was only a *black* man, his murder isn't worth investigating?"

She was angry, Paco thought – but how he did or did not regard Sam Johnson was only a part of what was causing her to lose her temper.

"I'm not prejudiced against Negroes," he said, trying his best to stick to the subject.

Cindy put her hands on her hips.

"Well, it sure sounded like it from where I'm standing," she retorted.

"How can I be prejudiced?" Paco argued. "I've never really thought about them enough to have formed an opinion."

Cindy laughed disbelievingly.

"I find that very difficult to accept, Ruiz," she said.

"That's because you're not trying to look at things from my point of view," Paco said soothingly. "I have no feelings about the man in the moon either, because even if he exists, he's never played a part in my life."

"But you've never seen the man in the moon," Cindy countered. "You must have seen Negroes before."

"Not really," Paco replied. "I suppose there were a few of them in Morocco when I was doing my military service – traders who'd crossed the Sahara from farther south – but it was the Arabs they did their business with, and I only ever saw them at a distance."

"Samuel Johnson was a man like any other," Cindy said. "Blood flowed through his veins just as it flows through yours, and when someone shot him, he felt it drain away as you would have done. He's entitled to justice as much as anyone else would be."

"Of course he is," Paco agreed. "But that's not the point."

"Then what is?"

"I always need to form a bond with the victim of a murder," Paco explained. "Even if I know that I wouldn't have liked him when he was alive, I at least need to understand how he would have thought – how he would have reacted in any number of different situations. I can do that easily with most kinds of Spaniards. I've even started to understand white *yanquis*, through you. But a *black* man? I have no idea where to begin."

Cindy nodded thoughtfully, and he knew that – for the moment at least – her mind had turned away from the subject of Dolores McBride.

"Yeah, I can see how that might present some kind of problem for you," she admitted.

"So maybe you can help me with it?" Paco suggested hopefully.

"A couple of minutes ago, I might have agreed with you," Cindy told him, "but thinking about it, I've started to realize that I know as little about them as you do."

"But you're a *yanqui*," Paco protested.

"A *white yanqui*, as you've just clearly pointed out," Cindy said. "A white *yanqui* from way out in the boonies."

What did the fact that she had been brought up in a village have to do with it? he wondered.

He was village-bred, too – but they had both traveled, and if anyone had asked him about the *gitanos* of the south of Spain or the Basques in the north, he could have given a considered opinion.

Cindy reached into her pocket, fumbled for a cigarette, and lit it distractedly.

"Jeez, I never knew how ignorant I really was until now," she said.

"Ignorant?"

"Look, there were a few Negroes around in the area I grew up in, but they certainly didn't live anywhere near where the white people did. And if they came into town – which I suppose they had to do occasionally – they made pretty damn sure they kept well out of white folk's way."

"You're saying they didn't mix at all?" Paco asked incredulously.

"Shit, yes. Back home, the Negroes are expected to know their place. If they were being served in a store and a white person came in, they accepted it as natural that the guy behind the counter would abandon their order and deal with the new customer first. That's just the way things were."

"They didn't resent it?"

Cindy gave him a troubled frown.

"I don't know," she confessed. "Thinking about it, I expect they probably did. But they knew better than to complain. They were brought up understanding that if they ever stepped out of line – if they looked at a white woman in the wrong way, for example – they'd soon find themselves in serious trouble."

"What kind of trouble?"

Cindy shrugged awkwardly. "You know."

"No, I don't," Paco told her. "I have absolutely no idea what you're talking about."

"Well, look, nothing like this has ever happened in my town, you understand, but from the stories you read in the papers, it seems as if a couple of dozen Negroes get ... get lynched every year."

"Lynched!" Paco repeated, his incredulity growing. "You mean *hanged*. Until they're *dead*?"

Cindy nodded. "Hung from a tree – and *left* hanging there as a warning to all the others."

"And don't the police do anything about it?"

Cindy sighed.

"I imagine they could if they wanted to," she admitted. "But most of the lynchings seem to take place in small communities."

"So?"

"The local sheriffs probably know who was involved, but ..." she shrugged again, "... even if they have no sympathy with the killers, they still have to live in the town when it's all over, and I guess they think the best thing to do is to look the other way."

Paco found himself thinking back to his childhood – to the village where the landowners rode around on their grand horses and the peasants were expected to show the proper deference. In a way, he supposed, the Negroes in the United States must live under similar conditions. But there was one big difference – it didn't take wealth or a fine house to make you one of the aristocracy over in America, you only had to be *white*!

And what power over life and death that skin color seemed to give you. Though the Spanish *guardia civil*, acting in the interests of the landlords, had habitually beaten up peasants who were seen as troublemakers, not even that notoriously heartless band of men would ever have considered stringing one of those peasants up from a tree.

"What about when you went to college?" he asked Cindy. "There must have been black men there, mustn't there?"

"Not as students," Cindy told him. "There *are* a few colleges which admit Negroes, but they're *only* for Negroes. The only black men I saw were janitors and gardeners. And then, of course, there were the Georges."

"The Georges?"

40

"On the trains in the States we have what are called Pullman coaches. They're named after George Pullman, who was the guy who designed them. All the attendants on the Pullmans are black – I think it's considered quite a good job for a Negro – and they're all called George."

"You mean, you can't get the job in one of those coaches unless your first name is George?"

Cindy laughed.

"Of course not. But all the attendants are called after George Pullman, whatever their real names are." The smile turned into another frown. "I accused you of being racially prejudiced a while back, didn't I?"

"Yes, but as I explained ..."

"You know what? It's not you who's really prejudiced. It's me! Sure, I was horrified when I read about lynchings in the newspapers – but I've never questioned the idea that I should *make* the mess and some black guy should *clean it up* after me. So I'm not as bad as the son-of-a-bitch who puts the rope around some poor black sap's neck – but I'm bad enough. And it took coming to Spain, and talking to you, to make me even realize it."

Paco was realizing something, too. If his Cindy could have thought like that, how would other people – without her humanity – have looked on the Negroes?

"What about the army?" he asked.

"What about it?"

"Is there such a thing as a black soldier?"

"Sure there is."

"So they *do* mix with white men in the army?" Cindy shook her head.

"The Negroes have their own regiments. Of course, their officers are white ..."

"Of course," Paco said dryly.

"... but they don't really come into contact with any of the ordinary white soldiers."

41

"Not even in combat?"

"Negro soldiers don't go into combat."

"They don't?"

"I think maybe they did in the Civil War – and just after it, when we were fighting the Indians – but they certainly don't now."

"So if they don't fight, what *do* they do?"

"I … er… I'm not an expert on this kind of thing. I really don't know all the details."

"Can't you even give me an example?"

"I'm … er… pretty sure that they use them to dig the latrine trenches."

In other words, Paco thought, their sole function in this case, too, was to clean up other people's – *white* people's – messes.

He closed his eyes and tried to imagine what it must have been like to be Samuel Johnson.

To live in a world where insults could be heaped on you without your daring to retaliate – because any show of defiance could result in a lynching.

To be given the shitty tasks purely because of the color of your skin.

To know that however good you were at anything, a white man would always be hired in preference to you, simply *because* he was white.

Yes, that was the kind of background that Samuel Johnson must have grown up in. And yet somehow he had managed to rise above it – to find the strength and the courage to commit himself to fight to improve a world which, by and large, had always treated him like dirt.

As a police officer, Paco had always had a certain sympathy for the underdog. As a man, he prized courage above most other virtues. He had never met Samuel Johnson – and would probably never be able to completely understand him – but he was beginning to feel the man's loss, and he swore to himself that, whatever it took, he would find Johnson's murderer and make sure that he was punished.

Chapter Five

The town hall council chamber was an impressive room by almost any standards. The walls were paneled, and the ceiling carved with an intricate and complex geometric design. A dais stood at the front of the room, and the chairs which had been placed on it were elaborate enough to have been the thrones of minor royalty. Even the rows of wooden, high-backed benches which filled the rest of the chamber – though probably less comfortable than the seats on the dais – had a certain style about them.

Looking down from the platform, Paco found himself asking what these foreign visitors – these *yanquis* who came from what, he imagined, was a thoroughly modern country quite unlike his own – made of it all. Their first thought was probably to wonder how a modest town like San Antonio de la Jara – a town in which not even all the roads were paved – could boast such a sumptuous chamber. But though it might baffle the *yanquis*, it was no mystery at all to him.

The chamber, he was sure, would have been built at the expense of some *conquistador* who had returned from South America with his pockets weighted down with Inca gold, and had been determined to do something which would display his wealth to the whole world – or at least to the town in which he had grown up.

Ah, Spain had been a power to be reckoned with in those long-gone days of glory.

And now?

Now it was little more than a practice ground on which the bigger, more influential countries tested their new weapons – a rehearsal hall for the larger conflict which was bound to follow this bloody, but parochial, war.

Unless, Paco told himself … unless men like those in the Abraham Lincoln Brigade really *could* make Madrid the tomb of fascism.

The *brigadistas* began to file into the chamber. As Dolores McBride had explained earlier, they varied greatly in age, complexion and height. Even their uniforms were not, strictly speaking, uniform. Some of them wore the same type of jacket as the Spanish soldiers who Paco had fought side by side with in the Jarama Valley. Others were dressed in combat jackets which looked as if they were left over from the Great War – and probably were. A few even had on civilian clothes – worn tweed jackets and old camelhair overcoats.

But it was neither their physical differences nor their uniforms which really caught Paco's attention – it was the elaborate, almost choreographed, way in which they took their seats.

They had entered the room as a number of clearly distinct groups – the colored *brigadistas* had formed one, half a dozen men with Central European features had made up a second, and a third had consisted of broad men with weather-beaten faces and tattoos on their muscular arms. Yes, that was how they had entered. But then, instead of choosing to sit together, they had deliberately parted, so that one of the Central Europeans found himself with a Negro sitting to one side of him and a burly, tattooed man to the other.

It was almost as if they were putting on a show for him, Paco thought. Or perhaps it might be more accurate to say that it was as if they'd been *ordered* to put on a show for him.

"Are you ready to begin, Ruiz?" asked Cindy, from her seat next to his on the dais.

"I won't be talking to them."

"You won't?"

"No. Felipe's going to address them."

"Me!" the fat constable said, giving his ample thigh a thoughtful pinch. "Well, I must say, I'm very honored to he asked. But you're the *jefe* here. Shouldn't it be left up to you?"

"I can't speak to them *and* study them at the same time – at least, not properly. Whereas if you put them through the standard procedure, I can be watching them closely to see how they react to it."

"A good point," Felipe agreed. "One thing, *jefe*…?"

"Yes?"

"Since I'll be in charge, would you mind if I granted myself a temporary promotion?"

Paco grinned. "Why not?"

Felipe cleared his throat.

"Are you ready?" he asked Cindy.

"I'm ready."

The fat constable clapped his chubby hands together.

"Attention, all you men!" he said loudly, in a voice that a ham actor would have been proud to own. "My name is Felipe Fernandez – *Captain* Felipe Fernandez – and before the war I was a member of the Madrid police force."

While Cindy translated, Paco did his best to suppress a chuckle. It was typical of the fat man to have promoted himself to captain rather than being content to become merely a sergeant. Felipe's attitude to life in general mirrored his attitude to food – and he never did anything by halves.

"I am here to investigate the death of one of your comrades," Felipe continued. "Now we know where he was killed, when he was killed, and how he was killed. What we still have to find out is the 'who' and the 'why'. And we will – make no mistake about that."

He looked expectantly around the room, as if he were waiting for the murderer to instantly jump to his feet and confess. But apart from a few men who shifted their backsides in an effort to try and find a more comfortable position on the hard seats, nobody moved.

"It is most likely that Samuel Johnson was killed shortly after he left the Plaza Mayor," Felipe said. "Raise your hand if you saw him on the fateful night."

Several hands went up into the air. Felipe nodded his head in a manner which suggested he had been anticipating *just* that response – and that he considered them very wise men not to try and hide from him things he already knew.

"Now put your hands down again if you didn't actually see him leaving the square," he ordered the *brigadistas*.

All the men instantly dropped their arms to their sides.

"So nobody saw Johnson go," Felipe mused. "Which means that if the murderer was following him out of the square, nobody saw him, either." He ran a finger and thumb over his wobbly chins. "Very well, then, let me ask you all another question. Is there anybody here who has a reasonable suspicion as to who the murderer might be?"

No one raised a hand in response to Felipe's question, but the fat constable did not seem the least discouraged.

"I've investigated any number of murders in my time with the police," he said, "and I've never yet questioned anyone – a man or a woman, old or young, who didn't have *some* theory or other about the killer and his motive. So why don't you tell me what's on your minds?" He hooked his thick thumbs into the waistband of his pants. "Come on, boys! You'd be surprised how many theories – ones which have sounded crazy even to the men who were telling them to me – turned out to be a fairly accurate summary of what actually happened."

James Clay, the short, dark political commissar of the battalion, rose to his feet.

"Yes?" Felipe said.

Clay spoke for around two minutes, and though he couldn't understand a word of what the *yanqui* was saying, Paco could tell from his tone and gestures that he was making some kind of a speech.

"Mr. Clay says that everyone here knows why Samuel Johnson was killed," Cindy translated when the commissar had resumed his seat again. "It was because the enemy saw him as a danger."

Clay was doing no more than trotting out the Party line, Paco thought. But not everyone seemed willing to accept it – several of

46

the other men were actually shaking their heads, as if they disagreed with their commissar.

"You!" Felipe said, pointing to a middle-aged man on the front row who had been one of the head shakers. "Tell us what you think? What's your theory on the motive?"

The man hesitated for a second after Cindy had translated, then said, "It could have been the French."

The French? Paco thought.

The French!

What the bloody hell had they got to do with it?

Commissar Clay was back on his feet immediately. "The French *brigadistas* are our loyal and trusted allies in the great struggle which we are all waging against the forces of fascism and repression," he said hotly. "They would never have killed Comrade Johnson."

But the same men who had been shaking their heads before were nodding them now.

"Why should the French *brigadistas* have wanted Johnson dead?" Felipe asked.

"Because he'd hurt their pride," said the man who'd first raised the possibility of the killer being a Frenchman. "Because he made a fool of all of them – from Marty down – that day when we went into Albacete and ..."

"That particular incident was nothing more than a small misunderstanding," Commissar Clay interrupted hastily. "I have had a long and frank meeting with the French commander, and the whole matter has been cleared up to everyone's satisfaction."

Maybe to *Clay's* satisfaction, Paco thought. Maybe even to the satisfaction of the French commander. But as far as several of the men in the chamber were concerned, it was obviously still far from resolved.

"I'd like to hear more about why you suspect the French," said Felipe doggedly, ignoring the commissar's interjection.

So would I, Paco thought.

But not right at that moment – not as long as Commissar James

Clay was there, ready to smother any interesting spark of information with the thick blanket of Party dogma.

"Well, spit it out, man!" Felipe said impatiently. "Why do you suspect the French are behind it?"

Paco climbed quickly to his feet.

"Would you mind if I asked a few questions now, Captain Fernandez?" he asked, knowing from past experience that the only way to shut the fat constable up, once he'd got his teeth into something, was by direct intervention.

"I thought I was doing quite well on my own," Felipe muttered, almost under his breath. But more loudly, he said, "Please be my guest, Inspector Ruiz."

Paco surveyed his audience – the young faces and the relatively old; the black, the white and the brown; those who looked interested in the proceedings, and those who seemed as if they'd much rather be somewhere else entirely.

"You must appreciate from the beginning that Captain Fernandez and I know little or nothing about the country you come from," he said. "So please understand that any question I may ask comes from my own ignorance, rather than through a desire to trick you."

He paused to let Cindy translate, then continued, "I believe that relations between the whites and the Negroes in the United States are not always harmonious, and I was wondering if perhaps there could have been a racial motive behind the murder of Samuel Johnson."

Commissar Clay started to rise to his feet again, but he was beaten to it this time by one of the large men with tattooed arms.

The man started to speak in a powerful voice that would have carried well beyond the room, and punctuated his remarks with stabbing gestures from his big, thick fingers.

He'd probably been a street corner agitator at one time, Paco decided – a rabble-rouser who understood how to work his audience. There had been any number of men like him in Madrid before the military had revolted – before free speech had been abandoned in favor of survival.

The man had been talking for perhaps three minutes when one of the other *brigadistas* – a shorter man from the Central European faction – jumped to his feet as if he could bear to listen to no more.

Like the burly speaker he was interrupting, this man used his hands as he talked, but instead of a stabbing motion he waved them wildly – almost imploringly – in the air.

It was extremely frustrating not to understand what was going on, Paco thought – to get the tone of the words, but have no clue as to their meaning. A detective who did not understand the language of the people he was investigating had about as much hope of success as a blind man had of learning how to paint.

The small man was still shouting at the big one, and now the big one was shouting back. Several other *brigadistas* were gesturing to them both to sit down, but to no effect. Even Commissar Clay seemed to have abandoned any hope of trying to restore order.

A sandy-haired *brigadista*, who had been so quiet up to that point that Paco had not even noticed him, now rose to his feet. The effect of his action on the other two men was not instantaneous – but it was pretty damn close to it. Within seconds of the new man standing up, both let their arguments taper off, and turned expectantly to hear what he had to say.

The sandy-haired man spoke quietly, but with great conviction. As he made his points, the shoulders of the other two men drooped, and an expression appeared on their faces which could only have been called growing shame.

The sandy-haired *brigadista* had reached the end of what he'd wanted to say, and sat down again. The tattooed man and the Central European hovered uncertainly for a second, then followed suit.

An uneasy tension had enveloped the room. It was almost as if all the *brigadistas* were embarrassed – as if they felt they had let themselves down in front of strangers.

Paco turned around to Cindy, expecting her to be waiting eagerly to translate the exchange while it was still fresh in her mind. But she wasn't ready at all! Instead, she was gazing at the sandy-haired man

49

with a look of wonder – almost of hero-worship – on her face.

Was it the man's words which had had such a powerful effect on her? Paco wondered. Or was it something else entirely?

"Are you all right?" he asked.

Cindy kept her eyes glued firmly to the sandy-haired man.

"I asked if you were all right," Paco said, more sharply this time.

The edge to his voice seemed to snap Cindy out of her trance.

"I'm … uh … fine," she said unconvincingly.

"You look like you've seen a ghost."

"In a way, I have." Cindy shook her head, as if she were trying to clear her mind of thoughts which shouldn't have been there at that moment. "You want me to tell you what that brouhaha was all about?"

For perhaps half a minute he had been more concerned about Cindy than he had been about the job in hand, Paco realized. And in that short half minute, the focus of attention of the meeting had shifted. Before, the *brigadistas* had been watching each other and he had been watching them watching each other – which was just as it should have been. Now, however, the Lincolns' gaze had shifted to the dais, as they tried to understand just what was going on between the blonde translator and the ex-policeman.

In other words, Paco thought angrily, I've allowed myself to lose my grip on the meeting.

"The brouhaha?" Cindy repeated. "Shall I …?"

"Forget that for the moment. Tell the *brigadistas* they can go now, but as they leave I want them all to pick up a piece of paper from the stack on the table by the door."

"And what are they to do with it?"

"I want them to write their names at the top, and then give an account of where they were at just after midnight on Friday. They're to say who they were with, and whether they noticed anything that was even a little unusual. Most important of all, stress that none of them should discuss his account with anyone else."

"And when they've completed their reports?"

"They're to hand them over to Chief of Police Fernandez."

It wasn't much of a joke that he'd made at Fat Felipe's expense, but he'd expected to see at least a glimmer of amusement flash in Cindy's eyes.

But there was nothing. It was almost as if she hadn't heard – or had heard, but was incapable of accepting anything he said on any level other than a literal one.

Cindy turned to face the hall again. She translated Paco's request for information to the *brigadistas* in a flat, almost wooden, tone – and the whole time she was speaking, she kept her gaze firmly fixed on the sandy-haired man.

The Lincolns rose to their feet. By the time they'd reached the door, they had managed to re-form into the groups they'd been part of when they entered, so that even though they had kept separate during the meeting, Central European now left with Central European and colored *brigadista* with colored *brigadista*.

There was a lot of mistrust in the air, Paco thought. And possibly, also, a certain degree of fear.

He turned to his interpreter.

"You can translate the argument for me now," he said.

"What?" Cindy replied abstractly – almost as if she had forgotten that he was even standing there beside her.

"You can tell me what the argument between those two *brigadistas* was all about."

"Do you want a *full* translation?"

"No. Just give me the rough outline."

"You asked them if Samuel Johnson's death might have had anything to do with his race," Cindy said.

"Yes," Paco agreed. "I remember."

"The big man with the tattoos – his name is Ted Donaldson – said it sounded as if you suspected that one of *them* was the killer, and if that *was* what you were thinking, it showed that you have no real understanding of either the Communist Party or the International Brigade."

Maybe Donaldson was right, Paco thought. Maybe he didn't

understand the brigade and the Party. But he did understand murder – and he knew that very few killers were complete strangers to their victims.

"Go on," he told Cindy.

"Donaldson said that it couldn't possibly be a racial killing, because within the Party all men and all women are comrades in arms and discrimination on the basis of color isn't tolerated. As far as he and the other *brigadistas* were concerned, Comrade Samuel Johnson was their equal and as good as any man who was serving in the battalion."

"And did the other, shorter man – the one who looks like he might be a Pole or Czech – disagree with that?"

"Not exactly."

"Then what *did* he say?"

"Mannie Lowenstein – that's the short man's name – said that the situation Donaldson had outlined was how things *should* be, but since they've been in San Antonio, he personally has discovered that there's a big gap between theory and practice. Donaldson might, or might not, treat Negroes as if they were his equals, but it was certainly true that he – and the people like him – didn't extend the same courtesy to the Jews."

"And how did Donaldson answer that?"

"He said that none of them should ever allow themselves to forget that Leon Trotsky is a Jew."

And Trotsky, Paco thought, had committed the cardinal sin as far as the people who looked towards Moscow for guidance were concerned – he dared to contradict the beloved Comrade Stalin. And as a result of that disagreement, he was now living in exile, with the sentence of death – which Stalin had imposed on him – hanging over his head.

"What did your boyfriend have to say?" Paco asked, the words coming out harsher than he'd intended they should.

"My what?"

"The sandy-haired man who managed to quiet Donaldson and Lowenstein down."

"He said that by arguing as they were, the two of them were playing right into the fascists' hands. That by fighting among themselves, they were leaving the gates wide open for the enemy to enter. He said that every time they disagreed with each other, it was like giving the fascists a fresh consignment of bullets, and while he'd be a fool to deny that there *were* differences in the brigade, he was also absolutely convinced that the *brigadistas* had so many important things in common that those tiny differences didn't matter a damn."

"A very full translation," Paco said. "You seem to have hung onto his every word."

"And what – exactly – do you mean by making a snide little comment like that, Ruiz?" Cindy demanded, sounding suddenly angry – and possibly, he thought, a little *guilty*, too.

"I mean that he's no stranger to you, is he?" Paco asked, dodging the question. "Where do you know him from?"

"Where do you *think* I know him from? We were introduced on my last trip to Venus!"

"I didn't know space travel was one of your hobbies."

Cindy sighed. "For God's sake, Paco, isn't it obvious that I knew him back in the States?"

It was only when Felipe coughed uncomfortably that Paco remembered he was still on the platform next to them.

"All this standing in one place has made me a bit stiff," the constable said. "If you can spare me, *jefe*, I think I'd like to wander round the town for a while and stretch my legs."

Paco nodded, grateful that Felipe was excusing himself – however unlikely that excuse itself seemed coming from the fat man – but at the same time, he hated the fact that there needed to be an excuse at all.

Felipe stepped down from the dais, and headed for the exit. Paco's gaze followed his partner's progress.

All the *brigadistas* had already left the council chamber, he noted.

Except for one!

The sandy-haired man was loitering by the door, almost as if he were waiting for someone.

Which, of course, he was!

Paco turned back to Cindy and saw that her eyes were once more fixed on the quiet spoken *yanqui* who seemed to have a power over his comrades that even their political commissar lacked.

"So you know him from back in the States," he said. "How *well* do you know him?"

A warm smile came to Cindy's lips – but he didn't think that it was for him.

"I know him *very* well. We're old friends," she said. "Come on, I'll introduce you to him."

She stepped off the dais, and though she didn't really seem to care whether he followed her or not, Paco thought that he probably should.

The sandy-haired man had had a serious expression on his face – as if he had been re-playing the earlier disagreements in his mind – but as he saw Cindy approaching, his frown disappeared and was replaced by a broad grin.

The *yanqui* had a good four or five centimeters over him, Paco estimated, and despite the deceptively soft quality of his voice, he had a broad, hard body. But the most significant thing about him, as far as the ex-policeman in Paco was concerned, was that until he had stood up to have his say, he had pretty much blended into the crowd – which was no mean trick for a man as physically imposing and craggily handsome as he was.

The two *yanquis* spread their arms open wide, and enveloped each other in a tight bear hug. After a short time – though it seemed far too long to Paco – Cindy disengaged herself from the sandy-haired man, and giggled in what could only be called a girlish way.

"I couldn't believe it was really you when you first stood up," she said – and though they were both *yanquis*, she spoke to him in Spanish.

"I couldn't believe it was you, either," the man replied, also speaking in Spanish. "The last time I saw you, you were all dolled up in academic gown and mortar board, positively bursting with pride and self-congratulation, waiting to receive your degree. And now here you are in Spain, dressed like a soldier, playing your part in the most important struggle we've yet seen in the whole of the 20th Century." He stepped back, to take a better look at her. "My, but you've grown up, Cindy. You were always a pretty girl, but now you've developed into a beautiful woman."

"*You* haven't changed at all," Cindy said.

"I've got older."

"It's only improved you."

Listening to the exchange, Paco felt a strong desire to either throw up or hit somebody very hard. Instead, he merely coughed embarrassedly, as Felipe had done earlier.

The sound was loud enough to remind Cindy that he was still there, and she turned her attention back to him.

"Paco, this Dr Gregory Cummings. He used to be my instructor back in my college days," she said. "Greg, this is my friend, Francisco Ruiz. As you've probably already gathered, he used to be a policeman in Madrid."

Friend! Paco repeated to himself.

They had made love in his tiny flat in the center of Madrid, and in the fresh, crisp, open air of the Guadarrama Mountains. They had shared incredible danger when they were in the hands of General Castro's rebel army. When it had seemed more than likely that they would both be executed, their only wish had been that they should be allowed to die together. And this was how she introduced him to this man from her past – as her *friend*.

The *yanqui* stretched out his arm towards the Spaniard.

"I'm very pleased to meet you, Señor Ruiz," he said.

Reluctantly, Paco took the proffered hand. He would have gained some satisfaction from Cummings' grip being limp or slimy, but instead it was as firm and confident as a real man's grip should be.

"So what happens now?" the American asked. "Do you want to go for a drink or something?"

"That would be ni ..." Cindy began.

"Perhaps we could take you up on your kind offer at some other time," Paco interrupted her. "At the moment, as you may have noticed, we have a murder investigation to conduct."

He was sounding petulant, he thought – perhaps even childish. But he couldn't help himself. Though he had never fully realized it before, he had been looking for Cindy Walker all his life. And now, for the first time since they'd confessed they loved each other, it occurred to him that just as it had been possible to find her, it was also possible to lose her.

"I don't want to get in the way of your investigation, Señor Ruiz," Greg Cummings said, his tone as measured and reasonable as it had been when he'd rebuked the other two *brigadistas* earlier.

"Good," Paco said. "In that case, I'm sure you'll understand that since we have a number of …"

"On the other hand," Cummings interrupted him, "as little as I know about police work, it does seem to me that part of your investigation really should involve wanting to talk to some of the guys."

"It does involve talking to them," Paco said, surprised at just how defensive he sounded to himself.

"When I say 'talk' to them, I mean *really* talk. And that's never going to happen at a formal meeting like the one we've just had. It needs to be somewhere less structured – more relaxed – somewhere the guys will feel more inclined to open up to you."

Stop telling me how to do my job, you bastard! Paco thought.

But aloud, all he said was, "Go on."

"And correct me if I'm wrong here," Cummings continued, "but wouldn't the best place to have that kind of talk be in a bar?"

"Probably," Paco admitted.

"Well, then, why don't you let me take you to one of the places where the guys go to let off steam?"

Cummings grinned winningly. Despite his craggy features, it was an almost boyish grin, and Paco, who had never managed to appear boyish even when he *was* a boy, felt a stab of jealousy.

"Shall we go?" Cummings suggested, the grin still in place.

"Very well," Paco said. "But let us get one thing clear between us from the very beginning."

"And what might that be?"

"That I know how to conduct an investigation into a murder – and you don't."

The grin did not falter – even for a second. "That's understood," Greg Cummings agreed.

"If I want your help at any point, I will ask for it. But if I don't ask for it – and I probably won't – then keep out of my way."

Cindy let out a deep breath which could almost have been a gasp of astonishment.

"Paco …" she protested.

"Don't go getting all het up about nothing, Cindy," Cummings advised her. "You've been in my classes. You know I would never countenance any interfering in the way I do my teaching, and Señor Ruiz feels the same about *his* work. He's quite right to clearly draw the boundaries from the start. It avoids all kinds of misunderstandings later on."

He was being both reasonable and logical, Paco recognized, just as he had been when he was addressing his comrades. Furthermore, he was both a man who spoke excellent Spanish and one who knew the other *brigadistas* well. On any other case he'd investigated, the ex-inspector would have regarded Cummings' presence as a gift from heaven – and if he were being honest with himself, he'd have to admit that the sandy-haired American was a gift in *this* case.

Paco took a deep breath. As a policeman, he had only one concern – to find out who had killed Samuel Johnson – and everything else was irrelevant. Cummings' appearance on the scene might create complications in his personal life, but they could only be faced once the murder had been solved.

He felt himself slipping quickly back into his old, familiar role. He was once again becoming the dogged Madrid detective who was willing to sacrifice anything – even his own safety – if he thought it would bring him even a little bit closer to a solution.

"Take me to the bar, Señor Cummings," he told the sandy-haired man. "But remember …"

"I know," the American interrupted. "If you want my help, you'll ask for it. Otherwise I'm to mind my own beeswax."

Chapter Six

The house had once belonged to the biggest landowner in San Antonio de la Jara, and before the war its central hall had seen more than its share of dances and other entertainments. But such diversions were a thing of the past. The government had commandeered the whole building as the Lincolns' barracks, turning the upstairs rooms into dormitories and the elegant hall into the place where they ate their meals and played boisterous games of basketball.

It was to the hall that two or three score of the *brigadistas* had returned after the meeting in the *ayuntamiento*. Now, a few minutes later, they were spread around it, each group sitting at a table which it had taken care to ensure was not too close to any of the other tables. Some of the men were bent over the sheets of cheap blank paper they had been issued with, laboriously writing a few words, stopping to lick the tips of their pencils thoughtfully, then writing a few more. But most of the *brigadistas* seemed more inclined to talk than to write, and the sounds of a dozen muted conversations rose uncertainly and bounced off the carved ceiling.

"You hear what Ted Donaldson said?" one of the colored *brigadistas* asked his companions disbelievingly. "No way it was a racist killin'! That was what the man claimed. Any of you guys think of a time when a nigger got hisself kilt an' it *wasn't* racist?"

"You got to learn to put the past behind you, man," protested one of the others. "This ain't the Deep South we in. The men we's with now are our sworn comrades."

"You got that half-right," the first man countered. "There's some whiteys here I'd give my life for – an' I knows they'd do the same for me. But there's others that would slip on the hood an' plant a flamin' cross in front o' my door without even thinkin' twice about it."

The men who Paco had thought of as Central Europeans – but who thought of *themselves* as American Jews – sat at a table closer to the door.

"You made a big mistake in that meeting tonight. Mannie," one of them, an ex-tailor called Jake Millburg, said worriedly.

"And what big mistake was that?" Mannie Lowenstein asked.

"Taking on Donaldson in the way you did. You've made an enemy out of him now. You should have just kept quiet."

Lowenstein sighed exasperatedly. "The Jews have kept quiet for far too long! For *hundreds of years* too long! Every other race is willing to stand up for what it believes in. And so were we – *once*. Remember what happened at Masada? Over nine hundred Jews held out against the might of Imperial Rome for five years. And when they were finally overwhelmed, did they surrender? No, they did not! Rather than fall victims to the Romans, they took their own lives – as men should."

His companion groaned. "Ancient history!"

"Perhaps," Lowenstein agreed. "But it's *our* ancient history – the history of a time when we were prepared to stand up for ourselves. And what have we been since then? Sheep who have stood by and let the countries of Europe either expel us or massacre us."

"This is not good talk for a communist," warned a third member of the group. "Our identity is defined not by what we might once have been, but our membership of the Party."

Mannie Lowenstein bowed his head. "I forgot myself for a moment," he agreed contritely.

"We must write our reports for the policeman from Madrid," Jake Millburg said, taking advantage of Lowenstein's unexpected surrender. "We must prepare them carefully, making sure that we all provide alibis for each other."

"Even if we weren't really together?" Mannie Lowenstein demanded, a dangerous edge creeping back into his voice.

"You were right when you said that even here there are those who are against the Jews," Millburg replied. "You are right to believe that there are those who will always suspect a Jew just *because* he is a Jew. We know that we had nothing to do with Samuel Johnson's death. What can be the harm in making sure that no one else suspects us?"

"So we are not Jews any longer – except when we are!" Lowenstein said angrily. "Would a *goy* ever have spoken as you just have, Jake? No! Never! He would not even have considered the possibility that just by being who he was, he would automatically fall under suspicion. And neither will I! I am as good as he is – and I refuse to lie. I was not with you when Johnson was killed, and nothing you can say will make me claim that I was."

Lowenstein was wrong about what the Gentiles would, or would not, say. His companions knew it, and at a table at the far end of the room Ted Donaldson – well out of their earshot – was about to prove their point.

"Now lemme see, where exactly were we at midnight Friday?" he said, making a great show of thinking about it. "I guess we must have been at the end of the square closest to the town hall, mustn't we?"

His friends, who were all – as he was himself – ex-longshoremen from the New Jersey docks, exchanged awkward glances.

"*We* were all at the other end of the square," one of them, a bald man, said, after some seconds had passed. "But you weren't with us."

Donaldson laughed easily. "Hell, Curly, you were so drunk that if President Roosevelt an' the Pope had been standin' next to you – and givin' each other hand-jobs – you'd prob'ly have forgot all about it by the mornin'."

"You weren't there," Curly said, with conviction. "Sure, we were all drinkin' together till around eleven, but then you disappeared."

"So what are you sayin'? That I went to the church an' shot the

61

nigg … an' shot Sam Johnson?"

"Hell, course I ain't sayin' that."

"So what's the harm in puttin' down in the statements that we were all together?"

"I'll tell you what the harm is," Curly replied. "You write down what really happened – that you went off 'cos you'd had too much to drink – and that cop from Madrid is gonna *think* that maybe you ain't tellin' the truth, an' …"

"That's the point!" Ted Donaldson interrupted. "You've stood on the picket line, just like me. You *know* how cops think. If that son-of-a-bitch from Madrid is down here lookin' for somebody to frame for Sam's murder, he ain't gonna choose a rich man like Jim Clay or a college professor like Greg Cummings – he's gonna try an' pin the rap on an ordinary workin' man."

"…an' if he *thinks* you ain't tellin' the truth, then he's gonna put you somewhere on his list of suspects," Curly continued, as if Donaldson had never spoken. "But if we say you was with us – an' then somebody else says they noticed you leavin' the square, the cop's gonna *know* that you were lyin', an' that's enough to put you right at the *top* of his list. An' not only that – he just might start thinkin' that the rest of us had somethin' to do with the murder, too."

"Remember that strike back in '34?" Donaldson asked, with just a hint of panic in his voice. "Remember how that Pinkerton would have busted your head if I hadn't gotten in the way?"

"An' I'd have done the same for you. But this is different – this is a murder investigation."

"So you'd sell me down the river?"

"Only if you deserved it," Curly argued. "Listen, Ted, we ain't dealin' with the New Jersey Police Department here. This cop from Madrid is not workin' in the interest of the fat-cat landlords an' property developers. He's part of the new system of revolutionary justice – of the people's justice. So if you didn't kill Sam Johnson – an' nobody here thinks for a minute that you did – then you got nothin' to fear by tellin' the truth."

"I liked Sam Johnson," Donaldson protested. "I was with him when we took that truck to Albacete an'..."

"An' a couple of days before he got himself killed, you came damn near to gettin' in a fight with him."

"I didn't look for that. He was the one askin' for trouble. I don't need *nobody* to tell me how talk to the Yids, especially some ni ..."

"Especially some *nigger*?" Curly suggested.

"Especially some down-home boy who don't know squat about the way that the Hebes ..."

"When you write your statement, just put down the truth, Ted," Curly said firmly. "Do that, an' you're gonna be all right."

"You still gonna be sayin' that when they line me up in front of a firin' squad?" Donaldson asked bitterly.

And so it went on. A dozen tables – a dozen small islands of argument and discussion, of fears and suspicions. There were those who mourned the loss of Sam Johnson as a friend, and those who mourned for the feeling of solidarity which seemed to have all-but disappeared since his murder. There were a few men who – despite the Party's avowed policy – couldn't see that the death of one Negro was such a big tragedy, but many more who felt that they had been deprived of a man who they would willingly have followed into battle, and into death. Yet whatever they believed, there were few of them – if any – who were willing to accept James Clay's assurances that the murderer, whoever he was, was long gone. Perhaps he would be found, and perhaps he wouldn't, but they were certain – deep within themselves – that Sam Johnson's killer was still in San Antonio.

Chapter Seven

It had been chilly enough earlier in the day, but now that night had descended, covering the town in its thick black cloak, the air had acquired real teeth.

Greg Cummings led Paco and Cindy down a series of narrow twisting streets, finally coming to a halt in front of a bar which nestled in the lee of the crumbling town walls.

"This is where Sam did most of his drinking," Cummings said. "He liked the philosophy behind the place."

"The philosophy?" Cindy repeated.

Greg grinned. "A couple of the bars in San Antonio are still owned by the guys who they belonged to before the revolution. But not this one. This is a *colectivista* bar. Like a lot of the land, it's owned by the commune, and any profit it makes is for the benefit of everybody."

Cummings opened the door, and they stepped into the bar. At the far end was a zinc-topped counter cutting the rest of the room off from the rough stone back wall which formed part of the town's ancient fortifications. Two large barrels – one containing white wine and the other red – stood, like sentries, at either end of the counter. A leg of smoked mountain ham hung from a metal spike on the wall, and stuffed olives bobbed around in a large tin can filled with brine.

The bar would have looked equally at home in Tordesillas, Olivenza, or any of a thousand other small towns throughout the length and breadth of Spain, Paco thought – but its customers certainly would not have. They were, on the whole, taller than Castilian Spaniards, and most of them were much paler. They sat awkwardly on their stools, as if they did not feel they belonged there.

As, indeed, they didn't – Paco reminded himself. Though he knew nothing of their backgrounds, he'd have been willing to wager that a few months earlier they would never even have dreamed they'd be spending the following February in a place as alien to their experience as this.

"What are you guys going to have to drink?" Cummings asked, acting the host.

"The drinks can wait until later," Paco said brusquely. "Who do you think I should talk to?"

The sandy-haired *yanqui* looked slightly puzzled. "Excuse me?"

"You suggested that we went somewhere for a drink, and I told you that we had no time for socializing because we were involved in a murder investigation," Paco replied. "You said it might help the investigation if we came here to talk to some of the *brigadistas*. Well, we're here. Which of the *brigadistas* would be useful for us to start with?"

"It's all business with you, isn't it?" Cummings asked, giving him a disarming smile.

"I take my work very seriously," Paco replied, refusing to let the smile affect him.

"Sure you do," Greg Cummings agreed. "And so you should." He sighed. "Look, I'm sorry if I sounded flippant just now. I guess that seeing Cindy completely out of the blue like this has kinda knocked me off track for a second. But I do appreciate the importance of your task here, and I fully accept that the sooner you get started, the better it will be for all of us."

Paco said nothing.

"In case you didn't recognize that for what it was, Greg was making an apology, Ruiz," Cindy said, with a warning edge to her voice.

Yes, that was exactly what Cummings was doing, Paco accepted. And he, himself, should respond to the man's apology in the same spirit as it had been offered.

"This is a difficult situation we find ourselves in here, and we all make mistakes when we're under pressure," he said, trying to sound conciliatory. "Shall we wipe the slate clean, and begin again?"

"Sure," Cummings said, with an easy graciousness. He glanced around the bar. "If you want to get down to business, then talking to those guys at the table in the corner is probably as good a place as any to start."

Paco's gaze followed the *yanqui's*. There were three men sitting at the table. One was little more than a kid, the second a black man, and the third the middle-aged man who had suggested back in the town hall that the French might, in some way, be behind Samuel Johnson's death.

"That's strange," Paco said pensively.

"What is?" Greg Cummings asked.

"That three men who are so obviously different in so many ways should be sitting together."

"Ah, so you've seen through the charade that our worthy commissar ordered us to put on for you in the council chamber," Cummings said.

Despite himself, Paco felt another stab of dislike for the man.

"It's my job to see through things," he said.

"The fact of the matter is that if you'd been here a few days ago, it wouldn't have been a charade at all," Greg Cummings told him. "It's true that since Sam's death, all the guys have been sticking to their own kind, but until last Saturday morning, everybody in the battalion pretty much mixed with everybody else without even thinking about it."

"So what makes these three carry on like they used to – as if the murder had never happened?" Paco asked.

"Interesting question. I guess it's probably because out of all of us, they were the closest to Sam, and so, naturally, they're taking his death the hardest. Look at the young guy – Bill Turner. He's doing his best to hide it, but you can tell he's real cut up."

Paco examined the boy. He had blond, straw-like hair, and eyes as big and innocent as a puppy's. And Greg Cummings was right – his pain was there for all to see.

"You want me to take you over and introduce you to them?" Cummings suggested.

"No, we'll do that ourselves," Paco replied. "You're here for a drink – go over to the bar and get yourself one. Tell the barman I'll pay for it later."

It was a clear dismissal, and Cummings recognized it as such. He gave a good-natured shrug, and headed for the bar.

"What the hell's the matter with you, Ruiz?" Cindy hissed, as soon as Cummings had left them.

"The matter with me?" Paco repeated, as if he had no idea what she was talking about.

Cindy stamped her foot in exasperation.

"Greg's going out of his way to try and help you, and in return you're treating him as if he's something that's just crawled out from under a stone."

"Have I embarrassed you?" Paco asked. "I didn't mean to. Tell me what I said which was wrong, and I promise I won't make the same mistake again."

"That's bullshit, and you know it," Cindy told him. "It's not the words you use, so much as the way you use them. Even when you say the *right* things, you sound like you're on the attack."

"We're looking at the man from two completely different perspectives," Paco pointed out.

"Is that right?"

"Yes, it is. To you, Greg Cummings is an old friend. To me, he's just like any other suspect."

"Any other *suspect*!" Cindy said, her anger mounting. "Do you really believe – even for a moment – that Greg could ..."

"They're *all* suspects," Paco cut in. "Every last one of them. All the *brigadistas*, all the villagers, people we don't even know about yet but who could have got in and out of San Antonio without being noticed."

"But, as far as you're concerned, some men are more suspicious than others," Cindy said bitterly. "Especially if they happen to be friends of mine."

She was right – and he knew she was right. If he was not actually strongly suspicious of Greg Cummings, he was at least actively hostile to the man – and Cummings had given him no real reason for that. He was sure that once they got back to their room, they would have a flaming argument, and that – because he *was* in the wrong – he would end up apologizing.

Might it not be best to short-circuit the whole process and apologize now? he asked himself.

Yet though he could form the words in his mind, they refused to come out of his mouth the way he had intended.

"You think I'm acting in the way I am just because you knew Cummings at college?" he asked, going on the offensive, even though he was sure it was the worst thing he could possibly do.

"I'm certain you are."

"It doesn't work like that. Not with me. When I'm involved in an investigation, my private life doesn't exist. Out here in San Antonio, we're not the lovers we were back in Madrid. We're not even the *friends* that you introduced us to Greg Cummings as."

"So just what are we?"

"I'm a policeman and you're my translator, and we've both got a job to do. Do you still want to do your job – or should I ask Señorita McBride if she will be willing to take your place?"

Cindy looked at him as if – at least for that moment – she really hated him.

"I'll do it," she said, in a voice that was almost a hiss.

Chapter Eight

It was only a minute or two since Greg Cummings had left them and gone over to the bar, yet in that short time Paco felt as if he and Cindy had somehow managed to put a million miles between them. But now was not the time to mourn the loss, he told himself angrily. Now was the time to act like the hard, dedicated policeman he had just bragged to Cindy that he always became when he was wrapped up in a case.

He headed for the table in the corner where Sam Johnson's three best friends were sitting, aware that, as he and Cindy negotiated their way between the other tables, all the eyes in the room were following their progress – some with interest, but many with suspicion.

"Would you ask them if it would be all right if we sat down?" Paco said.

Cindy spoke a few words in English, and the three men nodded. Paco pulled out a stool for her to sit on, but she pointedly ignored the offer and reached for one herself. It was going to be awfully cold in the bed they'd share that night, the ex-policeman thought.

"So now that we're here, what do you want to know?" Cindy asked coldly.

"We could start with their names."

The young white man with the straw-colored hair was – as Cummings had already told him – called Bill Turner. The older white man was Sean O'Brien. The black man said his name was Nat Johnson.

"Johnson!" Paco repeated. "Is he any relation to the victim?"

"Not that he knows of," Cindy told him, when she had listened to the black man's answer. "He says that his great-grandparents probably worked on the same plantation as Sam's great-grandparents, and the name they both ended up bearing belonged to the man who owned them all. We did that, you know," she added, a guilty note creeping into her voice. "We robbed the Africans of their own names – names that meant something to them – and we gave them ours instead."

Paco shook his head wonderingly. He had thought he'd begun to get some picture of the United States through Cindy, but the more learned, the more he realized that his ignorance was even vaster than the country itself.

Bill Turner was talking to Cindy. Paco understood none of the words, but he could tell that Turner's accent was far less clipped and far less precise than Greg Cummings way of speaking.

"Mr. Turner would like to know what they can do to help you," Cindy translated.

"I need to get a clear impression of what kind of man Samuel Johnson was," Paco said.

"He was a great man," Bill Turner replied. "If he'd only lived longer, he could have been a *very* great man."

"Ask him how they met," Paco said.

"I met him while we was waitin' on the dock in New York to board the ship that brung us to Europe," Bill Turner explained to Cindy. "We got to talkin', an' we found we got on just fine." He paused, and shook his head. "I'm not explainin' things well. It was more than just us gettin' on – meeting Sam made me look at the world in a whole new way."

"How do you mean?"

"Well, I'd always thought *nigras* didn't have the same kinda brainpower we had – but Sam, now, he was sharp as a knife. An' he was funny too. For instance, take what happened when we was boardin' the ship ..."

* * *

70

The FBI agent stands at the top of the gangplank, his eyes burning with contempt at the sight of the approaching traitors. If it was up to him, he would arrest them on the spot, throw them in jail and lose the key. But it is not up to him. He has been told the procedure and – like it or not – he must follow it.

As the two men – one an obvious hayseed, the other a black man – draw level with him, he holds out his hand to halt him.

"Passport," he snarls.

The hayseed hands it over, and agent reads that his name is Bill Turner.

"Why are you going to France, Mr. Turner?" he demands.

The hayseed gazes at his shoes and mumbles something.

"Say that again," the agent says.

"Lookin' for work,' Bill Turner replies.

"Why did you say that?" Cindy asked. "Why didn't you just tell him you were coming to join the International Brigade?"

Turner laughed. "If I'd done that, ma'am, he'd never have let me board the ship. The government wants to pretend that what's goin' on here in Spain ain't nothin' to do with the good ol' USA. An' it would sure be one hell of a lot easier to do that if there wasn't no American volunteers here. That's why our passports was stamped, 'Not valid for travelin' in Spain'."

"But President Roosevelt is a *Democrat*," Cindy protested. "He should be doing all he can to support the democratic government of Spain."

"That's the way I see it, too, but it seems like he don't. I guess he thinks he's got other fish to fry, ma'am. Anyways, as I was tellin' you…"

The agent does not believe Bill Turner – Europeans come to America in search of work, not the other way round – but he has no choice but to talk the hayseed's word.

He turns to the black man.

"And what about you, boy? Are you looking for work in France, too?"

The black man does not stare down at the ground, as Turner has done. Instead, he looks the agent straight in the eye and says, "No, sir. I thought I might just try a spot of skiin' in the Alps."

Bill Turner chuckled. "Imagine that! A *nigra* from Mississippi, who'd never even seen snow till he moved up north – a colored guy who'd had no more than a couple of bucks in his pocket at any one time – lookin' that Fed straight in the eye and tellin' him he was goin' to try a spot of skiin'. It sounded real funny – but you have to understand that he didn't do it as no joke."

"So why *did* he do it?"

"Cos he knew he had to lie to get on that boat, but he wanted to make it clear to the Fed that they both *knew* it was a lie. That story about goin' skiin' was an act of … of … what's the word?"

"Defiance?" Cindy suggested.

"Yeah, defiance. It said, 'Screw you!' And I was proud to be standin' beside him when he said it."

"Why don't you tell 'em about what happened when we docked at Le Havre," Nat Johnson suggested.

"Yeah, I will," Bill Turner agreed.

They have crossed the Atlantic in steerage – in the very bowels of the vessel – but now that they have docked in France, they are all herded into a stateroom on one of the upper decks.

They look around them – at the chandeliers and the heavy drapes – and find it hard to believe they are still on the same ship. But the luxury which surrounds them does not hold their attention for long, and they are soon focusing on the three men who are sitting at a table at the far end of the stateroom.

Two of the men – both from the subtle cut of their suits and from the aura of old world weariness which seems to hover over them – are clearly Europeans. The third – a solid man whose jacket is fashioned on aggressive lines, and whose expression is as black as a thundercloud, is clearly American.

72

The American consults a list which lies on the table in front of him.

"Jack Anderson!" he calls out.

"Yes, sir," Anderson replies.

"Get your butt over here.'

Anderson detaches himself from the crush and walks over to the table.

"How much money have you got on you, Jack?" the Fed asks – and there is no doubt in anybody's mind that he *is* a Fed.

Anderson reaches into his pocket and pulls out his total wealth.

"Five dollars, sir."

"And how do you expect to survive in France on that?"

The truth – and they both know it – is that once he is in France, Anderson won't need money, because the Party will take care of him.

But Anderson daren't say that, so instead he replies, "I'm expecting a money order to be wired through any day now."

"Are you indeed?" the Fed asks. "Well, I think we'll just hold onto your passport until that money order arrives."

"But I can't leave the ship without my passport," Anderson protests.

"Exactly," the Fed agrees. "Go through to the next room and wait there, Anderson." He looks down at his list again. "Fred Bartlet?"

Bartlet only has four dollars, and he is sent into the next room, too.

"Now most of us were panicking over what the hell we were goin' to do when our turn came round," Bill Turner said. "But not Sam. See, he wasn't just thinkin' of himself – he was thinkin' of the whole group. An' he'd worked out somethin' – some-thin' real simple, but somethin' none of the rest of us had cottoned on to."

"And what was that?" Cindy asked.

"That they was callin' us up in *alphabetical* order, so it was real easy to work out which of us was goin' to be next. Anyways, Sam reached into his pocket, took out all the money he had, and passed it on to me. 'Jeb Bradley's standin' at the end of the row,' he whispered. 'See he gets this money. And tell the rest of the comrades to give him some of theirs as well.' Well, by the time the Fed called Bradley's name,

Jeb had over forty dollars on him. The Fed was real surprised, but he didn't have much choice but to give Jeb his passport back. And the second Jeb was back in line with the rest of the comrades, he passed the money along, so that the next guy who was called up could flash a wad of greenbacks too."

"Didn't the government man work out what was going on?" Paco asked.

"Sure he worked it out – in the end," Bill Turner agreed. "But I guess when he did, he realized that he'd either have to go through the whole business again or give up on it. And I don't think he had the stomach to go through it all a second time, especially since the Frenchies were already laughin' at him behind their hands. So what he did instead was, he tried to bribe us."

"How?"

"If any of you men are thinking of traveling to Spain, you should be aware that the French government has got the border shut down so tight you'll probably never get through," the Fed said. "And that's lucky for you, because if you did manage to cross the border, you'd really be in trouble. The rebels have got all the guns and all the manpower, and going up against that would be like signing your own death warrants."

The Fed paused, and let his eyes sweep slowly over the recruits.

"So why don't you do something sensible, instead?" he asked. "This ship's going back to the States in a couple of days, and if you're on it, the government will pay your fare for you."

Another pause.

"I think, deep in your hearts, that's what most of you want to do, but you're afraid of what the others will think. Well, let me to tell you, it'll only take one brave man to step forward and say he's going home and the rest will follow."

"Did anyone step forward?" Paco asked.

"No. We all just stood there thinking about it, an' I could tell some of the guys were giving it serious consideration. Then Sam broke ranks – and I guess some of the comrades, them who didn't know him as well as I did, thought he was volunteerin' to go back.

Johnson stands in such a way that can address the Fed and the comrades at the same time.

"I'm overcome by your kind offer, sir, I really am," he says, and he looks both humbled and almost on the point of tears. "If I'd known, way back when I was starving, just how generous Uncle Sam could be,' he continues, and now it is regret at his own failing to grab opportunities while they were there which fills his face, "I'd have asked him for some money then. But the thing is, you see," he concludes, his expression changing again to one of almost ecstatic anticipation, "this is now – I can hear the call of the mountains, an' I just got to get me some skiin' in."

"That set all the other comrades laughin' their heads off," Bill Turner said. "He'd made the government's offer seem comical – not worth even thinking about. An' that was just what Sam had intended. Twice, in the space of half an hour, he'd shown us that we might be weak as individuals, but we couldn't be beat if we stuck together."

It was easy to say that before you'd been to the front, Paco thought – but he *had* been there, and knew that while solidarity might do many things, it wouldn't stop a bullet.

"Did you have any more trouble when you'd disembarked from the ship?" he asked.

The young American shook his head.

"Just the opposite. The guys workin' in French customs knew who we was and where we was goin', so they didn't even look at our baggage. An' the railroad men had held up the train for us, so we could get to Paris as quick as possible. The French government might not be on our side, but the French people are with us, sure enough."

Paco turned to Sean O'Brien. "And yet you think the French might have had something to do with Sam Johnson's death?" he asked.

The other man scowled.

"When I said that, I wasn't thinking about the people we met in France," he said. "I was talking about the bastards who are based in Albacete."

"The head of the brigade is a Frenchy called Andre Marty," Nat Johnson explained. "He's the guy who decides who gets the supplies – an' who don't. An' guess what? The Lincolns might be short of stuff, the Germans an' the Italians might not have what they need, but the French battalion never goes short."

"If it was just a question of food, we wouldn't give a damn," Sean O'Brien said. "I'm used to going hungry, an' so are most of the other lads. But when it comes to essential equipment – the tools of the trade, as you might say – that's another matter entirely."

"Essential equipment?" Cindy repeated. "You mean, like rifles?"

Sean O'Brien laughed bitterly.

"Oh, rifles were no problem at all," he said. "The ones they gave us had been around since Adam was a lad, but they'd still fire bullets. Except that there weren't any bullets to fire." He lit a cigarette and inhaled deeply. "Have you ever fired a rifle?" he asked Cindy.

"No."

"The first time you pull the trigger, you feel like you've been kicked by a bad-tempered donkey. You get used to the kick with practice. You learn to compensate for it. But how the devil are you supposed to get that practice when you've no ammunition?"

"You sound like you didn't need the practice," Cindy said.

"Me? No! I've been shootin' at rabbits – an' a few two-legged targets – since I was a kid. But half the lads had never handled a gun before, an' for the first few days all they could do was point the bloody thing and shout 'bang!' It was enough to make you weep."

"We went to Jim Clay an' Matt Harris an' said we had to have ammunition," Bill Turner said. "An' do you know what they told

76

us? They told us to be patient." He picked up his glass of wine, and knocked it back in a single swallow. "If it had been left up to Clay an' Harris, we'd still have been waitin' for ammunition when we were finally shipped out to the front."

"But it *wasn't* left up to them?"

"Nope. It surely wasn't. While the rest of us were just sittin' around and bitchin' about the fact that there weren't no ammunition, Sam was turnin' his mind to solvin' the problem…"

It is early morning, shortly before the brigadistas are to go out on maneuvers, when Bill Turner sees Sam Johnson standing outside the barracks and swinging a bunch of keys in his hand as if he were a magician and they were a rabbit he'd just pulled out of his hat.

"What you got there?" Bill Turner asks, curious.

"These is the keys to a truck," Johnson tells him. "An' not just any truck – a truck with a tank full o' gas."

"An' what you gonna do with them?"

"Thought I might drive over to Albacete. Any of you guys want to come with me?"

Once he has explained why he plans to go to Albacete, there are volunteers enough – and Johnson picks five of them. He drives the truck along the bumpy road to the city and parks it in front of the warehouse where the brigade's stocks are being stored.

"Remember them men inside are our comrades," he tells the others, as they climbed down from the truck. "We don't want no trouble with them. But still an' all, we ain't leavin' until we got what we come here for."

There are three men in the reception area – a couple of guards, and a thin faced clerk with a *pince-nez* balanced on his nose.

"'Ow can I 'elp you?" the clerk asks.

"We need a few cases of bullets," Sam Johnson replies.

"An' you do, of course, 'ave the proper forms?"

Johnson shakes his head. "We ain't got the time to wait around till they come through."

"Wizout the correct forms, it is impossible," the Frenchman says, turning back to his paperwork.

Sam Johnson puts his hand on the clerk's shoulder. It is a friendly gesture, but at the same time it could not but help remind the Frenchman what a big man Johnson is.

"Impossible, you say?" Johnson asks. "I'll tell you what's impossible, comrade. It's impossible that a few thousand men with nothin' more than a just cause on their side could stop a fascist army from takin' over Madrid. But that's what's happened, ain't it?"

"You must leave now," the clerk says, dismissively.

"Friend o' mine back in San Antonio is havin' a birthday party later today," Johnson said, "an' I don't feel I can rightly go to it, lessun I take him a present – like a few boxes of ammunition. An' I am goin' to that party, Comrade."

"Do not make me use force," the clerk threatens.

"You do what you gotta do," Sam Johnson tells him.

The clerk nods his head towards the guards, and they pull back the bolts on their rifles. Another nod and they have hoisted the butts to their shoulders so that the barrels pointing at Johnson.

Sean O'Brien reaches down for the knife he carries in his boot. Bill Turner looks frantically around the room for something he might use as a weapon.

A third brigadista stepped quickly into the space between Johnson and the guards.

"You want to shoot Sam, do you?" he demands. "Then you're just gonna have to shoot me first!"

Everyone was losing their heads – everyone except Sam Johnson.

"There'll be no shootin'," he says calmly, over his shoulder. He turns his attention back to the clerk. "Say I showed you I had the right paperwork? Would you give me the ammunition then?"

The clerk shrugs. "But of course."

"OK. Say I told you I has the paperwork in the truck, and I'd bring it to you once we'd loaded the ammunition – an' you believed me? Would you give me the bullets?"

"It would be 'ighly irregular."

"Perhaps, but say you trusted me. Isn't possible you'd give me the ammunition?'

The clerk shrugs again. 'I suppose it is possible.'

"An' say I betrayed your trust an' just drove off. That would look bad, wouldn't it?"

"Yes, it would look bad."

"But who would it look worse for? The honest clerk? Or shifty black man? We both know the answer to that. And wouldn't it be better do things that way," Johnson pauses and looks around the room, "than to follow a course of action that ends in blood bein' spilled?"

"You 'ave the necessary paperwork?" the clerk asks.

"Sure," Johnson agrees, winking at him. "It's right there in the truck."

"Then I will release the ammunition," the clerk says.

Sean O'Brien chuckled at the memory of their raid on Albacete.

"All hell was let loose when Monsieur Marty an' his Frogs found out what we'd done," he told Paco and Cindy. "But by then it was too late to do anythin' about it – because we'd already used up half the ammo."

"And you really think that might have been a motive for killing Sam Johnson?" Paco asked.

O'Brien shrugged. "When your pride's hurt, you want to lash out at whoever it is that's hurt it. In peacetime, you use your fists, but when there's a war goin' on, that sometimes doesn't seem like quite enough."

"You sound as if you've had personal experience."

"I've seen men die under mysterious circumstances before, yes," O'Brien said enigmatically.

"In Ireland?" Cindy asked.

"That's right," O'Brien agreed.

"How did you know that was where he'd have seen it?" Paco asked Cindy.

"Just a guess – based on his Irish accent."

79

So he was Irish, Paco thought. And I didn't know it. Worse, it hadn't even occurred to me that he might be.

How could he possibly conduct an investigation under these circumstances? While O'Brien's origins had been obvious to Cindy, to him the Irishman's words had made no more sense than the words of any of the others had. If these men had been Spaniards – talking in a language he understood – he would have built up a complete mental picture of each of them by now. As it was, he had only the vaguest notions – and even they might turn out to be totally wrong.

The depth of his ignorance was staggering, he realized. Not only were there so many things he did not know, he didn't even have a clear idea of what he *should* know – what was important to know and what wasn't.

Watching Cindy talk to these men was like watching another man make love to a woman and trying to convince yourself that you were playing a vital part in the process. It was hopeless!

"Ask him what an Irishman's doing in the Abraham Lincoln Battalion," he said to Cindy.

O'Brien smiled wryly as he spoke.

"He started out with the English battalion," Cindy explained. "They fought on the Cordoba front."

"And ...?"

"A number of his comrades were killed in action. They were listed in the *Daily Worker* – which is the newspaper of the British communists – as part of the English dead."

"So what?"

"He says they fought as Irishmen, and they died as Irishmen – so it was only right that they should be listed as Irishmen. After that, he and his comrades decided that they didn't want to be part of the English battalion any more. When they were told they had no choice, they mutinied rather than stay where they were. They got their way in the end, and were transferred to the Lincolns."

Paco shook his head frustratedly. The Irish refused to serve with the English. The Americans accused the French of treating them

80

unfairly. There was at least *one* Jew in this battalion who felt that some of his fellow *yanquis* were prejudiced against him. How could an ex-policeman who didn't even speak their language ever manage to untangle the threads which would lead him to a murderer, when there were so many other threads – leading God knew where – mixed up with them?

"Thank them for their help," he said to Cindy. "Tell them that I may want to talk to them again."

While Cindy was translating, Paco glanced quickly around the bar. A few of the *yanquis* who had been drinking there earlier had left, but Greg Cummings was still standing by the zinc counter, sipping at his glass of wine as if he had all the time in the world.

And waiting! Paco thought.

Waiting for Cindy!

They had both had a long and tiring day, and it would have been natural – under most other circumstances – for him to suggest to Cindy that they turn in for the night.

But Paco couldn't do it!

He simply couldn't bring himself to say that they should leave now, only to be told in return that he could go if he wished, and she would join him later, after spending some time catching up on things with her old and dear friend, Greg Cummings.

As he rose to his feet, it felt as if his legs had turned to lead.

"I think I'll go and see what's happened to Felipe," he said. "He might have some useful thoughts about the case."

"That's probably a good idea," Cindy replied. "I'll see you back at the widow's house."

And he noticed that even as she was speaking to him, she could not resist glancing across the room at Cummings.

Paco stepped out of the stuffy bar and into the cold night air. Why did this have to happen, he wondered? Why should the one thing which was right about his life suddenly start to disintegrate before his eyes?

* * *

Though he had told Cindy that he needed to talk to Felipe, he now decided that was the last thing he wanted to do. The fat constable knew him so well that he would soon sense that something was wrong, and Paco didn't feel strong enough to explain it all to him. So, instead, he would go back to his room in the widow's house, and try to suppress his feeling of self-pity just long enough to be able to fall into some kind of sleep.

He had walked perhaps twenty meters up the street when he heard the sound of footsteps behind him.

And not just any footsteps – not ordinary, *innocent* footsteps.

Whoever it was behind was matching his pace, slowing down when he did, putting on a burst of speed when that was necessary to maintain the same gap between them.

Paco felt a chill run down his back which he knew had nothing to do with the air temperature.

Could the unseen presence be the murderer?

It would certainly not be the first time that a killer who was worried that he was getting far too close to a solution had stalked him.

It had happened during the investigation into the headless corpse at Atocha railway station.

It had happened in the mountains outside Madrid, when he'd been trying to solve the case of the general's dog.

He had survived on those occasions – but there was a good chance that, this time, he might not be quite so lucky!

There was a cross street looming just a few meters ahead of him, and seeing it, one part of his brain began to formulate a plan, while another part regulated his speed and made sure his body gave no indication he was about to make his move.

He approached the corner as if he had no interest in doing anything but going straight on, then suddenly veered to the right, disappearing up the side street. He had taken two steps when he came to a halt, pulled his pistol out of his overcoat, and flattened himself against the wall.

The footsteps continued to click-click along the street he had just left, then slowed as they reached the corner. There could no longer be any doubt that he was being followed.

A dark shape turned the corner. With one hand he reached forward and grabbed it, slamming it against the side of the house. He raised the other hand – the one which was holding his weapon – and jammed the pistol's barrel against his shadow's neck.

"What do you want?" he demanded roughly. "Why are you following me?"

"Christ, you play a rough game, don't you, Inspector?" said an obviously female voice.

Paco stepped back and lowered his gun.

"Señorita McBride? Is that you?" he asked.

"Damn straight, it is."

"You were following me, weren't you?"

"Obviously."

"Why?"

"Because I wanted to buy you a drink."

"That's the only reason, is it?"

"Sure. I wanted to buy you a drink, and since your Miss Walker has singularly failed to take a shine to me – for some reason I don't even begin to understand – I thought it might be diplomatic to wait until she wasn't around before I issued the invitation. So what do you say? You want a drink or not?"

"I want a drink," Paco told her.

Chapter Nine

In purely physical terms, the bar which Paco allowed Dolores McBride to lead him to was almost the twin of the one he'd left Cindy and Greg Cummings in possession of. The room was more or less the same shape and size, the zinc counter and barrels of wine almost identical, and even the tin of olives had probably come from the same canning factory in Andalusia. The customers, however, were weather-beaten peasants and mechanics who were still wearing their oily overalls – men who belonged, rather than men who had merely been uneasily transplanted there from their homes across the ocean.

Several of the drinkers greeted Dolores by name, and as soon as she and Paco had sat down at a free table, the barman placed a bottle of Fundador brandy and two glasses in front of them.

"You're a regular, are you?" Paco asked.

"Yeah, I've been here a few times before," Dolores agreed.

"Did Sam Johnson drink here?"

"No, he didn't approve of the place."

"Why not?"

"It's an *individualista* bar. It belongs to a guy called Pepe – not to the collective."

"Then I'm a little surprised *your* principles allow you to drink here," Paco said.

Dolores grinned. "Comrade Stalin wouldn't mind."

"He wouldn't?"

"Hell, no! This isn't Russia, and Comrade Stalin doesn't expect it to be a communist state."

"So what does he expect?"

"Comrade Stalin's aim is to stop fascism, and he's decided that the best way to do that is by helping to establish a liberal democracy here. That's what America and the other Western powers should be fighting for, too – and they would be, if they had leaders who were geniuses like the General Secretary."

Dolores uncapped the bottle, poured out two very generous shots of brandy, then knocked most of hers back in one gulp.

"It ain't as good as the bourbon we can get back home," she continued, licking her lips, "but it's sure as hell better than nothing."

"Have you always drunk so heavily?" Paco asked.

Many women would have been offended by such a question, but Dolores merely shrugged.

"Not always," she said. "I've only gotten like this since I've been in Spain. This is a goddamn awful war, you know."

"But a necessary one?"

"Yeah, it's necessary – but that doesn't make it any easier to bear." Dolores topped up her glass again, but did not take a drink. "I've been here for two months – since the first batch of American *brigadistas* arrived," she told Paco. "I got to know some of the early guys really well. Half of the ones I made friends with in the first month are dead now, and I wouldn't give the rest of them much of a chance of survival. Why is it always the good men who have to die?"

"Because they *are* the good men?" Paco suggested.

Dolores threw back her head, and laughed heartily – though not without bitterness.

"My God, a philosopher as well as a cop," she said. "So how's the investigation going? Have you come round to the idea that Sam was killed by somebody from outside San Antonio yet?"

"No, I haven't," Paco replied. "I still don't know enough about the case to make any kind of judgement." He took a sip of his brandy. "I met a man called Greg Cummings at the town hall," he continued, forcing himself to sound casual. "Do you know him?"

"Yeah, I know him."

"What's your opinion of him?"

"He's a liberal."

It wasn't what Paco had been expecting – or hoping for. He'd wanted some detailed information on the man he was coming to see as a rival, and instead Dolores had just slapped a label on him.

"What's wrong with liberals?" he asked.

"Hell, you're Spanish, so you should know the answer to that better than anybody," Dolores replied. "Who was it who managed to keep General Mola's troops out of Madrid? Was it the liberals? Or was it the communists and their comrades in the socialist party?"

It was an easy question to answer, Paco thought. When the army had revolted, the liberal government had done little more than issue a few stern-sounding decrees, which, without any force whatsoever to back them up, had been nothing but hot air. Even when that same government had finally decided to arm the workers, it had given them rifles without bolts, and it had been workers themselves who had led a brave and bloody attack on the Montaña barracks – which was then being held by the fascists – in order to capture the bolts they needed.

"See, the liberals think that the system's basically sound as it is, and all they need to do in order to make it run more fairly is to find the right way of tinkering with it," Dolores said, warming to her theme. "I've never met a liberal yet who didn't believe that due to his efforts, he'd leave the world in a whole lot better state than he found it in."

"And the communists?"

"We know that the system is rotten to the core, and the only way to deal with it is to sweep it all away and start over again. But what makes us *really* different from the liberals is that we're not necessarily expecting to see things change in our lifetimes. We know that we're all nothing more than very small cogs in a very big machine. We're totally expendable, and we're willing cannon fodder. And the most we can ever hope for is that our personal sacrifice will help move the inevitable collapse of capitalism just one tiny step closer."

"So the individual doesn't matter? Not at all?"

"Damn straight."

"Then why does the thought of your dead comrades make you want to hit the bottle?"

Dolores McBride grinned ruefully.

"You've got me there," she admitted. "I guess that however much we tell ourselves we believe in scientific socialism, they'll always be a bit of bourgeois sentimentality lurking in some dark corner of us – at least, until the Revolution comes."

"How well did you know Sam Johnson?" Paco asked.

"We talked together quite a few times. He's going to be one of the subjects of my book."

"What book?"

"The one I'm writing about the *brigadistas*."

"Tell me about it," Paco said.

"I think these guys are real heroes," Dolores said seriously.

"So do I."

"But that isn't the way the American government – or a lot of the American people for that matter – see them. They're simply *Reds* as far as most folk back home are concerned. And to them, that's almost as bad as being a child molester. So that's why I have to write the book – to tell the truth, to get it all down on record while there's still the chance. It's going to be the *brigadistas'* memorial – probably the only one they're ever likely to get."

More bourgeois sentimentality emerging from her dark corners, Paco thought.

And why the hell not?

"What did Sam Johnson tell you about himself?" he asked.

Dolores laughed again.

"He told me a lot of things. Like, for example, how difficult it had been for him to get hold of a passport when he didn't have a birth certificate."

"Had he lost his birth certificate?"

Dolores shook her head.

"Never had one to lose. In Mississippi, where he grew up, they didn't issue Negroes with birth certificates. Or death certificates, either."

"Why not?"

"The state didn't register the birth and death of animals – why should it have treated blacks any other way?"

"What else did he say?"

"He told me about walking twelve miles each way to a shack of a school, to be taught by a teacher who hadn't even graduated from high school himself. And how, even then, the law only allowed the school to stay open for five months of the year, because for the rest of the time, the niggers – even the young ones – were needed for picking and chopping cotton. Incredible, isn't it? And don't forget, I'm not describing a dark, distant past – this is our century I'm talking about."

What Cindy had told him about the lynching had been horrifying enough, Paco thought – but, in a way, this was worse. Because it was not the work of a few individuals who had gone off the rails, in much the same way as some people had done in Madrid during the first few, mad weeks of the war. This was institutional repression!

The Spanish State of his childhood had not – God knew – done much to help the children of the *pueblos*, but at least it hadn't gone out of its way to keep them down in the dirt.

"I'm surprised that growing up in a place like that, Sam Johnson ever managed to find his way to Spain," he said.

"He wouldn't have, if he'd stayed back home in Mississippi. But he didn't. He moved to New York City. Do you want to know what it was that made him move to New York?"

"Yes."

"He had this cousin who'd lived in New York for years, and who'd gone down south to visit his family. He was in Mississippi for a few weeks, and all through his stay he did his best to try and persuade Sam to go back with him. Sure, life was tough on Negroes on the other side of the Mason-Dixon Line, he said. It was tough on Negroes *everywhere.* But New York was one hell of a lot better on them than Mississippi. Sam wouldn't be persuaded, but he did agree to go to the railroad station with his cousin to see him off.

All the way there, and right up the time they were standing on the platform, the cousin was urging him to just get on the train and at least give the big city a try. Still, Sam wouldn't say yes. Anyway, it was a boiling hot day in July, and the train was delayed. Sam was getting thirstier and thirstier, but there was nothing he could do about it, because the blacks-only water fountain had broken down months earlier, and nobody had bothered to fix it."

"The blacks-only fountain!" Paco repeated, not quite sure whether or not he had heard correctly.

"That's right," Dolores agreed. "There was one fountain for the blacks and another for the whites. So, they were standing there, and the cousin must have been getting thirsty too, because he said, 'I sure could use a drink of water,' and he started to walk towards the fountain which was reserved for the white people. Sam grabbed hold of his arm, and asked him if he was crazy. The cousin had been away from the south so long that at first he didn't understand what Sam was saying. And Sam couldn't understand why his *cousin* didn't understand *him*. 'What happens if you drink water from a whites-only fountain in New York?' he asked. And his cousin told him that there *were* no whites-only fountains there. That's what made Sam decide to go with him – because New York was a place you could always get a drink of water when you needed one."

"And was life better for him there?"

"As his cousin had promised him, it wasn't easy, but it was easier than what he'd been used to. Negroes had to take the jobs the whites wouldn't touch – or else did the same job as the whites and got paid less – but at least Sam could stand next to a white woman on a street car without worrying about being lynched."

"What job did he have?"

"He was a busboy on the railroad dining car at first, but eventually he worked his way up to being a waiter. It wasn't a great job. The waiters got fed, but not the diners' leftovers – that was considered too good for them. They weren't allowed to leave the dining car at night, either – can't have niggers running around on their own, now can you? – so after they'd been locked in, they put the tables together and slept as best they could. It wasn't even a steady job – they were taken on for one trip, and after that, if they were unlucky, they might not work for weeks. But like I said, it was a hell of a lot better than Mississippi, and most Negroes would have given their right arms to have taken his place."

"Did he work there right up until the time he came to Spain?"

"He could have, if he'd kept his head down and just got on with the job. But that wasn't Sam's way. Unions were legal by then – President Roosevelt had seen to that – but they weren't exactly *encouraged*. Still, there *was* a union for white railroad employees, and Sam didn't see why the blacks shouldn't have one, too, so he set about organizing a local branch."

"It cost him his job?"

"It almost cost him his life. He got beaten up real bad on the way home from a union meeting. The railroad company said it had nothing to do with the attack. And maybe it didn't. There are plenty of other people in the States who hate unions. Anyway, when Sam came out of hospital, he had no job to go back to. That's when the Party took him on. For the next three years he traveled all round the country helping to organize strikes and pickets. He was beaten up a couple of times more, but never as badly as the first time. Then Mussolini invaded Abyssinia, and Sam decided he would be more use there than he was back home. But the war in Africa was over before we even had time to do anything about it – so he came to Spain instead."

It all sounded so straightforward, Paco thought – a life sketched out in a few sentences. But it couldn't have been as simple as that.

Or as easy.

Every step Samuel Johnson had taken must have required a tremendous amount of both effort and courage. And now he was dead – killed by some bastard who probably wasn't worthy of licking his boots.

"I want Sam's murderer caught as much as you do," Dolores said, "but like I told you before, he'll be long gone by now."

"And what if he isn't?" Paco asked. "What if he's still somewhere in San Antonio?"

"You check on the *brigadistas* movements at the time of the murder, and you'll find they've all got alibis."

"How can you be so sure of that?"

Dolores looked suddenly uncomfortable – as if he'd noticed a vulnerable spot which she hadn't even known was visible.

"The Party believes that unity is strength," she said, choosing her words carefully. "Apart from when they're out on specific individual missions, it encourages its members to stay together at all times."

"So that it's easier to keep tabs on them?"

"We're fighting a war," Dolores said, managing to sound both fierce and defensive. "Not just in Spain, but throughout the Western world. We're up against huge odds – and if we don't maintain strict discipline, which is all we've really got going for us, we'll go under."

"So all the *brigadistas* will have alibis?"

"Yes."

Paco shook his head.

"It doesn't work like that. Even the most sociable of people have times during the day that they can't account for. Do you have an alibi, for instance?"

"Do I need one?"

"If we are to prove your theory that the murderer is no longer in San Antonio, it would certainly help."

"As a matter of fact, I do have an alibi," Dolores said, smiling to show that her outburst of temper had dissipated itself. "But unless it becomes strictly necessary to reveal it, I think I'll keep it to myself."

"You sound mysterious," Paco told her.

"A woman – even a good communist like me – should always sound mysterious. It's part of her attraction."

Was she flirting with him? Paco wondered. It certainly sounded as if she was.

91

Dolores drained the last of her brandy.

"Time to turn in for the night," she announced. "Wanna join me?"

"What!"

"I said, do you want to join me?"

"I have my *novia* here with me," Paco exclaimed.

"Sure you do," Dolores McBride agreed. "That's why I wouldn't expect you to stay with me all night."

She laughed at his obvious perplexity.

"I don't want to steal you away from your precious Cindy, if that's what you're worried about," she continued, "but you're a man and I'm a woman, and maybe for an hour or so we could help each other to forget what a shitty place this world we live in really is. So what do you say?"

She was a strikingly beautiful woman, Paco thought, and he was tempted to accept the offer – if only to help assuage his battered ego after the way Cindy had made him feel earlier.

"Most men wouldn't take so long to decide," Dolores said. "Most men wouldn't take any time at all."

"I'm sure they wouldn't," Paco agreed. "But I just can't do it."

Dolores shrugged.

"Well, that's the way it goes," she said philosophically. "You don't blame a girl for trying, do you?"

"No," Paco said. "On the contrary, I'm flattered."

Dolores stood up.

"Do you want to see the notes on the *brigadistas* that I've made for my book?" she asked.

"They might be useful," Paco agreed. "When can you give them to me?"

"Let me think about that for a moment. I have to go into Albacete tomorrow morning to file my report for the paper, and given the state of the roads in this goddamn country, that could take most of the day. Tell you what. Why don't you come round to my place – Calle Mayor, Number 26 – at about six o'clock tomorrow evening, and I'll have them ready for you?"

She read the expression on his face a second time, and laughed loudly.

"The notes do exist, you know. I'm not just using them as bait for a trap in which I end up having my wicked way with you."

"I never thought you were," Paco protested.

"Sure you did," Dolores answered. "But if you're still worried about my intentions, bring Miss Cindy with you as a chaperone. Then maybe all three of us can go out for a coffee and practice being civilized with one another. OK?"

"OK," Paco agreed.

"Then it's a date. Six o'clock at Calle Mayor 6." Dolores kissed her index finger, placed it lightly on his forehead, and headed for the door.

Paco watched her leave. And he was not alone in that – the eyes of all the farmers and mechanics hungrily devoured her every step.

Chapter Ten

For a full five minutes after Dolores had left the bar, Paco sat staring at the doorway. A beautiful woman had offered him the chance to forget how shitty the world was for an hour or so, he reminded himself – and he'd turned her down. He was still not sure whether he was a man of honor, or the biggest fool in Spain.

"You are the one in ... investigating the death of *El Negro*?" asked a nervous voice which cut through his thoughts.

Paco looked up at the speaker. The man was about forty years old, and had a thin, pinched face, narrow shoulders and very long, gangly arms. There was evidence of intelligence in his right eye, but the left one was flickering so rapidly that it was almost impossible to read anything in it at all.

"Yes, that's me," Paco admitted.

The man gave the brandy bottle a hungry, hopeful look.

"Do you mind if I sit down?" he asked.

"Be my guest," Paco replied and, because it would have been cruel not to, he added, "Why don't you have a drink?"

With trembling hands, the man quickly filled Dolores' empty glass, and immediately took a slug of the Fundador.

"He was a g ... great man," he said.

"El Negro?"

"Th ... that's right. The others – his *compañeros* from the United States – are here to fight for the Republic, and we welcome them with open arms. But Samuel Johnson wanted more. He was not the

94

kind of man who could be content to wait until he was sent to the front to do something useful. He wanted to help immediately – right here in this town."

Paco took a sip of his brandy.

"How did he want to help?"

"The government in Valencia tries to pretend that all of us behind Republican lines are united against the fascists. But w …we are not. There is more than one kind of revolution in this country, and the kind of revolution that s…some people are trying to impose is as bad as the thing it is trying to replace. D…do you understand what I'm saying?"

Paco nodded. He knew only too well. On the rebel side, there was a unified command which crushed all opposition with the bullet. On the Republican side there were many groups with their own power base – socialists, anarchists, communists, liberals … the list was endless.

"T…there are those in this town who would be more at home on the o…other side of the front line," the man continued. "People who are not yet rich at the expense of others' sweat – but would like to be."

"What does this have to do with Samuel Johnson?"

"He h…helped us fight for what was right. He argued our cause better than we could argue it ourselves."

"But I thought he didn't speak Spanish."

"He didn't – not much. But where there are m…men who speak words of wisdom, there will always be m…men to put those words into a language which others can understand." The thin-faced man poured more brandy, as if he needed it to give himself the courage to carry on. "B…besides, it was not just his words which carried weight – it was the man himself. He knew what it was like to be one of the oppressed, and he had risen above it. He was an example to us – a shining beacon of what we could achieve if only we believed in ourselves."

"Fine words," Paco agreed, "but what do they mean?"

"They m … mean that …"

The bar door swung open, and the thin-faced man turned towards it with an expression on his face which could almost have been called panic. Two new men had entered the bar. They were around the same age as he was, but they had the squat, broad bodies of men well used to toiling on the land. They scowled at the thin-faced man, then went over to the bar to order their drinks.

"You were saying …?" Paco prompted.

"I … I am n…not the man you should be talking to, señor. If you really wish to learn the truth about what is happening in this town, you should speak to Juan Prieto."

"And where will I find him?"

Though he still had half a glass of brandy left, the thin-faced man rose to his feet.

"A…ask anybody – anybody at all," he said, in a voice which was almost a gasp. "E…everybody knows Juan."

He lurched from the table to the door, and disappeared into the dark street. No sooner had he gone than one of the broad peasants – whose scowl had probably driven him away – was sitting down in the seat he had just vacated.

"A man who is so far away from his home should be careful who he chooses to talk to," the peasant said, in a thick voice which had the slightest trace of menace in it.

"A man should be careful who he talks to wherever he is," Paco replied noncommittally, noticing that the other man had a long, jagged scar above his left eye and that – from its slightly askew angle – his broad nose had probably been broken at least once.

"And more than that, he should be careful who he *listens* to – who he *believes*," the peasant continued, as if he had not spoken. "The man who works hard from dawn to dusk – who cares for his land as if it were his own child – has a greater right to decide the future of his *pueblo* than a wastrel who could not lift a bale of hay, even if he was willing to."

Paco grinned.

"If a hedgehog can curdle milk, why then may a queen not visit her own pantry?" he asked.

The peasant scowled again, waited a few seconds for Paco to explain. Then – when it was plain he wasn't going to – said, "What does that mean?"

"I've no idea," Paco confessed. "But if you're going to talk in riddles, I see no reason why I shouldn't as well."

The peasant slammed a big fist down on the table.

"I didn't sit down to be made fun of," he growled.

"Then why *did* you sit down?" Paco asked. "It certainly wasn't because I invited you to."

"In the old days, your kind might have had some power over us," the peasant told him. "But those times, thankfully, have gone. We are in control of our own destinies now."

"More riddles," Paco answered. "When are you finally going to get to the point?"

"You want to find the man who killed *El Negro*," the peasant said. "Very well – do all you can to bring him to justice. But if you know what is good for you, you will search for your killer far from this town."

"Because that's where I'll find him?" Paco asked. "Or because it is inconvenient to you – personally – to have me here?"

The peasant stood up.

"I have said all I intend to say," he told Paco. "A wise man will take a warning when it is offered."

"And a frog will never ride a bicycle while it still has a spring in its legs," Paco responded.

The peasant gave him one last threatening scowl, then returned to the bar. His companion looked at him questioningly, and Scar-brow shook his head, as if to imply that in talking to the man from Madrid he had been doing no more than wasting his time.

Paco took another swallow of his Fundador brandy. The three men – the government official he'd met on the front, the political commissar of the Abraham Lincoln Battalion, and the burly peasant with the scar – were about as different from each other as any three men ever *could be*, he thought. Yet they had one thing in common – they all wanted him to believe that whoever had killed Samuel Johnson was long gone from the town of San Antonio de la Jara.

Paco was not drunk by any means, but by the time he'd reached his new lodgings, the brandy he'd imbibed had worked its way well into his system. He looked up at his bedroom window from the street, and saw that the oil lamp was burning.

So Cindy had left the bar, and was now waiting for him. He wondered what kind of reception he could expect from her.

He climbed the stairs and opened the door. Cindy was sitting up in bed, reading. The look she gave him was far from welcoming.

"So you've managed to finally drag yourself away from your old friend, have you?" he said, before he could stop himself.

"What is it with you?" Cindy demanded. "Aren't I entitled to have known anyone before I met you?"

Paco shucked off his overcoat and then his jacket, and let them both slide onto the floor.

"Did you sleep with him?" he asked, and when she didn't answer, he said, "Did you sleep with *Greg Cummings*?"

"I knew who you meant the first time. There was no need to elaborate."

"Well, *did* you?"

"Did I sleep with him *tonight*? Is that what you're asking?"

"No, not tonight," Paco replied, feeling a cauldron of anger starting to bubble up deep inside him. "Before! When you were a student – when he was supposed to be nothing more than your teacher."

"And what if I did sleep with him then?"

"Does that mean 'yes'?"

"It means, 'And what if I did?'"

"Then I want you to stay away from him."

"Even if I had slept with him – and I'm not saying whether I did or not, because I refuse to be interrogated like this – it was a long time ago," Cindy said.

And he could tell that she was getting angry, too.

"Not so long ago," Paco said.

"A *very* long time ago. But whatever happened, that was then, and this is now. If I want to see him as a friend, I will – whether you like it or not. You're not my husband to order me about, and you couldn't be, even if you wanted to – because you already have a wife in Burgos."

It was all true, but *she* was his real wife, he thought – if not on paper, then in his heart. Or at least, she had been until that afternoon. Now he was no longer sure of either himself or her.

If he was about to lose her to the sandy-haired *yanqui*, might it not be wisest to just accept it – to harden his heart to her before the inevitable blow fell?

And he was growing increasingly certain that the blow *would* fall, because Cummings was one of her own kind, and he himself was nothing but a foreigner.

He took off the rest of his clothes, and climbed into the lumpy feather bed. He did not reach out to caress Cindy in case she repulsed him, and she made no move to come to him. So they lay stiffly side-by-side – together, yet farther apart than they had ever been before.

Slowly Paco drifted off to sleep. He dreamed, but not of the blonde woman next to him. Instead his visions were of the dark-haired beauty who seemed to appreciate what it was like to be a Spanish man much more than Cindy did, and who, if he'd taken her up on her offer, would not now be lying next to him with all the animation of a sack of potatoes.

Chapter Eleven

Below in the street, a donkey brayed obstinately as its hooves clacked on the smooth cobblestones. Above, on the roof, a few birds chirped miserably at the thought of another cold, miserable day. And in the distance there was a faint hum of an ancient tractor making its way complaining to the fields.

The sounds of morning, Paco thought, as he looked out of the attic window down onto the street – the signals that a troubled night's sleep was over, and another day of hunting down a cold-blooded killer was about to begin.

Behind him, he could hear another of the sounds of morning – the swish of cloth as Cindy dressed. At another time he would have turned round to watch her, getting almost as much pleasure from seeing her put her clothes on as he did from seeing her taking them off.

But this was *not* another time.

He felt as if he were sharing a room with a complete stranger. No, he told himself – it was worse than that. A stranger would have been easier to handle. Certainly, there would have been a sense of embarrassment and discomfort – a desire not to intrude or be indelicate. But with Cindy, who was anything but a stranger, there was something stronger – and much more unpleasant.

He could feel the hostility emanating from her. He was almost smothering in the blanket of reproach she had heaped upon him

Yet was it *she* who should be reproaching *him*? Though Cindy did not know it, and *could* not know it, he had – *almost* without a second's thought – turned down the chance of going to bed with a beautiful woman. And this despite the fact that an hour earlier he had seen her throw herself, with absolutely no restraint at all, into the arms of a man who was probably her former lover!

There was a small cafeteria directly across the street from his new lodgings – from *their* new lodgings, he reminded himself – and even from that distance Paco could smell the aroma of freshly ground morning coffee and the slightly greasy odor of bacon cooking on the *plancha*.

"I'm going down to have breakfast," he said, still not looking at Cindy. "Do you want to come with me?"

He was not so much issuing an invitation as giving her an opportunity to refuse, he thought.

"I'm not hungry," Cindy replied, grabbing the opportunity to decline with both hands – and making no effort to sound even the least convincing.

Still avoiding eye contact, Paco descended the stairs and crossed the street. The only customer in the bar at that moment was Felipe. The fat constable sat at a table by the window. He had placed a cup of hot chocolate and a huge plate of *churros* to his right, and had a pile of papers stacked on his left.

"You're making an early start," Paco said, trying to inject a note of cheerfulness into his voice.

Fat Felipe looked up.

"But of course I'm making an early start," he said. "That's me all over – as keen as mustard." He glanced past Paco onto the street. "Where's Cindy?"

"She's still in our room," Paco replied awkwardly. "She said she didn't feel hungry."

"Didn't feel hungry!" Felipe repeated incredulously. "That's strange. She may only be a slip of a girl to look at, but she's normally got the appetite of a horse and …"

He trailed off, as if suddenly remembering the scene he had witnessed in the council chamber the previous day.

"Yes, well, it's probably the change of air that's affected her," he finished lamely.

The owner of the bar came over to them, and Paco ordered a coffee and a *sol y sombra* – sun and shade – a drink which had earned its name from the fact that it was made by pouring a pale anis on top of a dark brandy.

"Don't you want anything to eat, *jefe*?" Fat Felipe asked.

Paco shook his head. After a night's drinking, his brain knew that he *should* eat, but somehow it couldn't talk his stomach into accepting the fact.

"I was drinking in one of the local bars last night," he said – and wondered why he had chosen to omit the fact that he had not been drinking alone.

"You?" Felipe said, pulling a comical face. "Drinking in one of the local bars? I find that very hard to believe."

The fat constable was acting as if this were just a normal case and his boss were his normal self, Paco thought – so perhaps the uncertainties which were churning up his guts didn't really show on the outside.

"I talked to two of the customers," he continued. "Or perhaps it would be more accurate to say that *they* talked to *me*."

Felipe reached for another strand of *churro* and dipped it in his chocolate.

"Did they have anything especially informative to tell you?" he asked.

"The way one of them spoke about the late Samuel Johnson, you'd have thought he was a saint."

"And the other?"

"He only mentioned Johnson in passing – most of what he said was actually aimed at intimidating me – but I got the distinct impression that he's more than happy to see the *yanqui* in his grave."

Felipe sucked the chocolate noisily off his *churro*.

"No two men will ever have exactly the same opinion of a third," he said, "but it's when they hold widely differing views that things really start to become interesting. Do you have any idea why one of them should mourn his passing and the other seem to be glad he's dead?"

"None at all. But perhaps things will become clearer when I've talked to some of the locals – which is what I intend to do while the *brigadistas* are out on their training exercises."

"And what about me, *jefe*?" Felipe asked. "Do you want me to come with you?"

"No." Paco looked down at the sheaf of papers stacked next to Felipe's left hand. "Are those the accounts of the *brigadistas* movements on the night of the murder?"

"Yes. Sergeant Cummings brought them round to me half an hour ago. He said there are two or three still missing, but he should get those to me by the end of the day. He seems a very efficient man, don't you think?"

"All the reports will need to be thoroughly checked and cross-referenced," Paco said, ignoring his assistant's last comment. "That should take you all morning at least."

Felipe looked instantly despondent.

"But that's *paperwork*," he protested. "You know I've never been any good at paperwork. Anyway," he added, brightening a little, "most of the statements are written in English. I won't understand a word of them."

"Cindy will help you."

"Cindy? Won't you be needing her yourself?"

Paco shook his head.

"As I said, I intend to spend the morning talking to the locals, so I won't need a translator. In fact, having a foreigner with me might actually inhibit them from talking freely."

Besides, he thought, though he was not willing to admit it to Fat Felipe, it would be something of a relief to get away from Cindy for a while.

Paco picked up the pile of statements, and flicked through them. He stopped when he came to one which had GREG CUMMINGS written at the top in bold letters. He read the first sentence, then handed it to his assistant.

"Just as I suspected. The bastard couldn't resist the temptation to show off by writing his statement in Spanish."

"Maybe he was just trying to make things easier for us," Felipe suggested quietly.

"I want you to check Cummings' statement very carefully indeed," Paco continued. "But be subtle about it – I don't want Cindy to know we're paying him special attention."

Felipe nodded, perhaps a little sadly.

"And when we've finished going through all the statements?" he asked. "What do we do then?"

"Follow up on any inconsistencies which might emerge. For instance, if X says that he was with Y, but Y doesn't mention anything about being with X in *his* statement, then you must find out which one is telling the truth. And whatever you do, don't give them the opportunity to talk to *each other* before you've interrogated them *both*, because the last thing we want is to give them time to iron out any kinks in their stories."

"Keeping a couple of suspects apart sounds like a job for two policemen, rather than one," Felipe grumbled.

"You're nearly big enough to be two policemen all on your own, Felipe," Paco joked.

But the fat constable was not prepared to see the humor. Instead, he shook his head from side to side.

"We've worked together for a long time, you and me, *jefe*," he said.

"You don't need to tell me that."

"And during the time we've been partners, I've had to put up with listening to a lot of complaints about you – both from the general public and from other police officers."

It was not the first time Felipe had said something like that, but there was usually a teasing element to his tone which was totally lacking now.

"Go on," Paco said.

"I've heard you called rude, impulsive, and even reckless," Felipe told him. "And a lot of the time, I've secretly agreed with the criticisms. But I've always stood by you. Do you know why?"

"Because we're friends?"

Felipe shook his head so vehemently that all his chins wobbled at once.

"No, not because of that. I've done it because *I admire* you."

"Enough of this hero worship," Paco said offhandedly.

But Felipe was not to be diverted.

"I admire you because, whatever your faults – and there are enough of them to fill a very thick book – you've always been true to two guiding principles."

"And now, I suppose, you're going to tell me what those two guiding principles are," Paco said sarcastically.

"Yes, I am," Felipe replied, unruffled. "The first is that you're determined to see justice done. And the second is that you'll follow an investigation through to the end – whatever it costs you personally."

"Get to the point," Paco snapped, feeling his anger start to rise.

"You've abandoned both those principles in the last couple of minutes," Felipe said. "I saw the first one go out of the window when you picked out Cummings' file for special attention. You'd no reason to do that – except that it would suit you very well if we could find him guilty of something, even if he didn't do it."

"Now listen …" Paco began.

"No, you listen," Felipe interrupted, sounding fiercer than Paco had ever heard him before. "You dropped your second principle when you decided to leave the interrogations up to Cindy and me. You *know* it needs two cops to do it properly, but for that to happen, you'd have to spend more time with Cindy than you want to. Well, tough! If that's what the case demands, then that's what we need to give it. I shouldn't have to tell you that. I *wouldn't* have had to tell the *jefe* who I agreed to come down to Albacete with – but you're not that *jefe* anymore."

"Any time you find it's starting to make you sick in the stomach to work with me, you've only to tell me, and I'll see to it personally that you're put on the next train back to Madrid!" Paco said hotly.

"*Jefe…*" Felipe said mournfully – and it was obvious that after the tremendous effort it had taken him to say what he felt needed to be said, the fight was completely drained from him.

"Don't you *jefe* me, you bitching bastard," Paco told him, homing in mercilessly on his partner's new sign of weakness. "In case you've forgotten, I am your superior officer, and I have given you a set of orders. In our present circumstances, I can't force you to obey those orders, as I could have done in the old days back in Madrid – but if you choose not to, then I want nothing more to do with you. Have I made myself clear?"

Fat Felipe bowed his head with the resignation of one who has tried his best, and now accepted the inevitable failure.

"Sí, señor," he said.

"I shall expect your report by this evening," Paco said. "And I shall expect it to be a *fair* report, not simply one designed to please the kind of man you seem to think I have become. Understood?"

"Sí, señor."

"Very good," Paco said.

His coffee and *sol y sombra* sat untouched before him, but he had no interest in drinking them now. He stood up so suddenly that he knocked his chair over, and without bothering to pick it up again, he marched towards the door.

Once he was outside in the street – once the cold air of La Mancha had hit him in the face like a bucket of icy water – the regrets began to set in. Felipe had only spoken the way he had out of a sense of friendship – Paco knew that – and he'd had no right at all to attack the fat constable in return.

And perhaps … only perhaps … there was a germ of truth in what Felipe had said. Maybe, because of what had happened between him and Cindy, he was *not* being *quite* as objective about this case as he had been about the other investigations he'd conducted.

106

Now was not the time to think about that, he told himself angrily. He had a lot of investigative work to get through that morning. To conduct his inquiries properly he needed to keep his wits about him – and attacks of self-doubt would only serve to get in the way.

He lit up a Celtas and strode resolutely towards his first port of call.

Chapter Twelve

The house stood on the very edge of San Antonio, even beyond the remains of what had once been a section of the town wall but was now no more than a few large stones poking out of the ground like rotting teeth. It was at the end of a terrace of similar houses, and the owner had used the gable end as one wall of the rough barn he had constructed. The barn aside, there was nothing to distinguish this dwelling from its neighbors – nothing to suggest that the man who lived in it was particularly important. Yet it was this house that the gangly nervous man in the bar had advised Paco to visit if he wished to learn more about what was really happening in the town.

Paco knocked on the front door. The woman who answered his knock was twenty-three or twenty-four. She was not pretty in the conventional sense. Her eyes were perhaps a little too narrow, her nose a mite too ungainly and her lips just a shade too thin. But there was something about her, Paco decided – perhaps an aura, perhaps the strength of character so evident in her features – which made her almost beautiful.

"Yes?" the young woman said abruptly.

She seemed like someone who could normally see the humor in both herself and the world in general, Paco thought, adding to his picture of her, but yet there was tightness about her which suggested that she had not found much to laugh about for quite some time.

"My name is Francisco Ruiz," he said. "I am – or at least, I was, an inspector of ..."

"I know who you are, and why you are here, señor," the woman interrupted him.

Of course she did. San Antonio de la Jara might be a little bigger than the average Castilian village, but it still had the true village mentality, and everyone in it would know everything there was to know about a stranger within a few hours of his arrival.

"I would like to talk to Don Juan Prieto," Paco said. "Could you please tell me in which part of town he is working in today?"

The woman laughed, though without much amusement.

"He is not working anywhere. He only wishes he could."

"Is there something wrong with him?"

"Why don't you come inside and see for yourself?"

The young woman gestured him to follow her. Paco found himself – as he'd expected to – in a large room which occupied the entire lower floor of the building. At the back of the room was a range on which the family meals were cooked, and next to it was the sink in which the pots would be washed after the meal had been eaten. Closer to the front door was a large scrubbed-wood table, and against one wall there was a horsehair sofa, on which lay a broad man with his right leg in plaster all the way from the ankle to the hip.

The man smiled welcomingly.

"I am Juan Prieto. Forgive me for not getting up to greet you," he said.

"What happened to you?" Paco asked. "Did you have an accident?"

"An accident? Well, that is certainly what some people would like us to believe it was," Juan Prieto said darkly. "Why have you come to see me, Inspector Ruiz? Did someone send you?"

"I met a man in a bar last night," Paco explained. "He suggested it might be useful to talk to you."

"And who was this man?"

"He didn't give me his name, but I'm sure you would know him. He was thin, and he had a nervous twitch in his left eye."

Prieto nodded.

"I thought if anybody sent you it would be Angel. He has a big

109

heart, but he also has the courage of a field mouse – and if anything needs to be said, he would much rather someone else said it." He turned his head towards the woman. "Fetch a glass of wine for our guest, Concha."

The woman nodded, and walked over to a carved wooden cabinet set against the wall. With her back to the two men, she opened the cabinet and took out a bottle of wine.

Concha! Paco thought. Concha Prieto! Why did that name sound familiar to him?

And then he had it!

"You were the one who found Samuel Johnson's body, weren't you?" he asked.

"Yes, I was the one who found him," the woman agreed, still facing away from him.

"What were you doing in a burnt-out church at that time of night?"

The woman shrugged her shoulders, but did not turn.

"I just went there. I can't explain why."

"Do you often go there? Do you still worship?"

"No one in this family has paid homage to the god of the landlords for the last twenty years," Juan Prieto said.

"Then why…" Paco began.

"I've just told you, I can't explain it," the woman said, with an edge to her voice which could perhaps have been exasperation – or may have been something else entirely.

Why doesn't she face me? Paco wondered. She must have finished pouring the wine by now, so why won't she look me in the eye?

"Pull up a chair and sit down, Inspector," Juan Prieto said.

Paco walked over to the table, picked up one of the straight-backed chairs, and placed it close to the sofa. Behind him, he heard Concha Prieto finally move away from the cabinet, but even as she handed the glass of wine to him, she was staring at the ceiling.

"Samuel Johnson was a good friend to this family," Juan Prieto said. "But he was more than just a friend – he was an ally as well."

"An ally in what?" Paco asked.

"In our struggle for social justice." Juan Prieto paused. "Before I talk about the part Samuel played in our lives, I should perhaps tell you a little of our recent history."

"Perhaps you should," Paco agreed.

"Until last July, there were only two large landowners in this area, but there were many small farmers, just struggling to get by," Prieto said. "The landlords were also the local money lenders, and though we owned our land, many of us were heavily in debt to them. Do you understand?"

Paco nodded. Prieto's story was – so far – a familiar enough one, and could have been told by most peasant farmers in most parts of Spain.

"We knew that there was going to be trouble long before it actually happened. Who didn't? The signs were there for all to see. When the bloody military rose in Morocco, we were ready to deal with our enemies closer to hand. We had guns hidden in our barns and buried in our fields, and we took to the streets to defend ourselves against the fascists. It was not a long struggle. The *guardias civiles* – who had decided to support the rebels – quickly saw they were outnumbered, and surrendered. In some towns, they were killed whether they surrendered or not, but here I insisted that once they had handed in their weapons, they should be allowed to leave San Antonio unmolested." Prieto paused again. "I am quite proud of that."

"You have a right to be," said Paco, who had been sickened by all the unnecessary killing he had seen for himself in the early days of the war.

"We let the priests and the landlords leave under the same conditions," Prieto said. "And suddenly we were free. Free from debt. Free from the church. I can't fully describe how wonderful that felt. We had been given a new life."

"I can imagine."

"But once the excitement had died down, we had to ask ourselves what we would do with this new life we had been given. We held a meeting of all the farmers and artisans of the town. There were those of us – especially anarchists like me – who said we should collectivize

111

everything. From now on, no one would own the land – and yet *everyone* would own it. Each family would put what they had into the collective, and would be paid a wage for its labor. We would all be equal at last."

"But there were objections," Paco guessed, remembering the big peasant with the scar over his eye, who had threatened him the night before.

"Yes, there were objections," Juan Prieto agreed. "There were those who asked how the collective could work without leaders. We told them that there would be leaders – *delegados* – each responsible for one area of work. One for the cattle, another for the vegetable oil, a third for the agricultural machinery, and so on. But these *delegados* would not be leaders in the traditional sense because they'd be elected by the whole commune. The objectors said that it did not matter whether they were elected or not. Human nature being what it is, once they had some power they would use it to their own advantage. We argued that that would not happen. The *delegados*, in addition to their new duties, would work in the fields alongside everyone else – doing exactly the same work – but would receive nine pesetas a week *less* in wages than the rest of the collective. In other words, they would work harder but not earn as much. Surely no man would accept such a job unless he really believed in what the collective was trying to do."

"You put yourself forward as a *delegado*, did you?"

Juan Prieto grinned ruefully.

"There were those in the village who wished me to serve," he admitted. "But to go on with the story – the majority of people in the assembly were in favor of forming a collective, but there was quite a large minority of *individualistas* who said that it would not work – that men who farmed their own land themselves would be far more successful than any collective could possibly be."

"If you were in the majority, you could have forced them to join – at gunpoint if necessary – whether they wanted to or not," Paco pointed out.

Juan Prieto sighed.

"True," he agreed, "but we had not turned our guns on our enemies, so how could we now turn them on people who we considered no more than misguided friends?"

"That has happened in other places," Paco said.

"But not here," Juan Prieto said fiercely. "Instead of fighting each other, we reached a compromise. Those who wished to join the collective could do so immediately. Those who wished to remain *individualistas* could continue to farm their own land – in addition to extra *parcelas* which we had confiscated from the landlords. Then, when the spring came and we could see the results of the two systems, we would decide by a vote which was in the best interests of the Republic. If the vote were to go against the collective, then any member who wished to could leave it, taking out exactly what he put in. But if there was still a majority *for* the collective, then the *individualistas* would have no alternative but to join us."

"Spring is not so far away," Paco said.

"Not so far at all."

"And how do you think the vote will go?"

"We have lost a little of our initial support," Juan Prieto admitted, "but if we can just hold on to what we have left, we will win easily."

"You sound as if you think there is a possibility that you *won't* hold the support," Paco said.

"I think that there are men in this town who will do all they can to ensure that we fail."

"Tell me about your accident."

Juan Prieto smiled.

"You are a clever man."

"I am a man who has learned to distrust convenient coincidences," Paco told him.

"My 'accident' happened late one evening. Everyone else had gone home, but I was out with the tractor in the fields, trying to make up some of the time I had lost doing my *delegado* work. The tractor turned over. I was trapped under it, and my leg was crushed. It's a good thing that my son came looking for me, or I would probably have frozen to death."

"What made the tractor turn over?" Paco asked, though he suspected that he already knew the answer.

"I was driving over some bumpy ground, and the bolts which held on one of the wheels suddenly sheared off. It could have been a genuine accident – such things do happen – but the collective's chief mechanic swears that he had checked the tractor over thoroughly only the day before."

"Are you saying that someone tried to kill you?"

"I would not go so far as that," Prieto said. "But it certainly suits those who are against the collective that I should be unable to campaign for it."

"I think I'm beginning to see how Samuel Johnson fits into all of this," Paco said.

"Are you?"

"Yes. After you were injured, you needed someone to replace you. Someone with the same power to persuade as you have yourself. And even though he could not speak our language, Johnson had that power."

"Samuel believed in strength through unity," Juan Prieto said. "Believed in it enough to fight for it at every opportunity which presented itself. When he addressed the members of the collective, they did not understand his words – but not for a second could they doubt his sincerity."

"With him on your side, you would have won?"

"Yes," Prieto agreed. "With him on our side, I do not see how we could have failed."

"And you think *that's* why he was killed?"

"I don't want to believe it – and perhaps the fact that I've even considered the possibility shows I have a jaundiced view of my fellow man – but, like you, I distrust convenient coincidences."

"Which of your opponents is ruthless enough to contemplate such an act?" Paco asked.

Prieto hesitated for a second.

"I told you that I argued for releasing the *guardias civiles* and the landlords unharmed."

"Yes, I remember."

"And I won the day – but not without a struggle. One man, in particular, was eager to spill our enemies' blood. His name is Iñigo Torres."

"Is he, by any chance, a big man with a broken nose and a scar over his right eye?"

"How could you possibly know that?" Prieto asked, surprise evident in his voice.

"We met last night, in the same bar where I talked to your friend Angel," Paco said. "He told me that if I insisted on trying to find Samuel Johnson's murderer, I'd be well-advised to focus my search somewhere a long way from San Antonio de la Jara."

"And will you follow his advice?"

Paco shook his head. "I still can't see someone coming in from outside the town to do the killing," he said. "And I can't see Samuel Johnson being inside the church by accident, either. I think he'd arranged to meet somebody – though whether it was a friend or a foe, I've no way of guessing. Does he strike you as the kind of man who would deliberately put himself in danger?"

"If he thought it would benefit a cause he cared about, he would do so without a second's hesitation."

There was a click as the front door opened. Paco swung around to see who was entering the house.

A young man stood in the doorway. He was about twenty or twenty-one years old, and dressed like every other peasant farmer from the area. The resemblance to both the man lying on the couch and to the young woman standing near the window was obvious – almost as obvious as the expression of anger which spread across his face when he saw that the family had a visitor.

The young man looked first at his father and then Concha, who had been so quiet while Paco had been talking to Prieto that the detective had almost forgotten she was there.

115

"What's he doing here?" the young man demanded.

"Luis …" Concha said, her tone both tentative and warning.

"I asked what he was doing here, Papa," the young, man said, ignoring his sister.

"He's here because he wants to find out who killed Samuel," Juan Prieto said quietly.

"And does he think *we* did it?"

"Of course not. But he wants to know if we can tell him anything about Samuel that might …"

"If he doesn't suspect us of the murder, then he should leave us alone," Luis said.

"Be reasonable, son," Juan Prieto pleaded.

"Why should I be reasonable?" Luis demanded. "These foreigners have brought us nothing but bad luck."

"They are here to fight side by side with us. They are here to defend the Republic."

"They have no *right* to be here." the boy said fiercely. "They should have stayed in their own country, instead of coming over to Spain and meddling in our affairs. I've been told what happens to black men like Samuel Johnson in the United States. If he'd tried to do there what he did here, they'd have strung him up from the nearest tree. And a good thing it would have been, too."

"You will apologize," Juan Prieto said sternly "both for being so rude in front of our guest and for saying such terrible things about a man who had become a good friend of the family. You will apologize immediately."

"No, I won't apologize to him," the boy replied defiantly. "He has no more right to be here than the *brigadistas*."

And then he turned his back on them, and stepped quickly out into the street again.

Even before Luis had slammed the door behind him, Concha was crossing the room to follow him.

"Leave him alone, Concha," Juan Prieto said.

"I can't. He's too upset."

"He'll calm down, given time. You stay here."

The look which Concha gave her father managed to both plead his forgiveness for disobeying him and to show her determination to do what she felt she must. Without another word, she opened the door and followed her brother out onto the street.

Juan Prieto was silent for a while.

Then he said, "I know what you are thinking. You are wondering what kind of man it is who is so weak that he cannot control his own children in his own home."

"Having talked to you even for a few minutes, I would never accuse you of being weak," Paco said.

But he *was* wondering how a man like Juan Prieto – a man who obviously exerted considerable moral influence over his community – could have so little effect on his son.

"My wife died many years ago," Prieto explained, reading his mind. "Concha was still a child at the time, Luis was little more than a baby. My daughter had to become a mother to her brother. As for myself, I ... I tried to give him more than a father should, in order to compensate for the fact that his real mother was no longer here. As a result, perhaps, he does not always show the respect to his father that others might expect him to. But that does not mean he loves me – or his sister – any less. He is a good boy."

"I believe you," Paco said.

But what he really meant was, "Because I have learned to respect you, I'm prepared to accept your judgment of your son – at least until I know enough to reach one of my own."

"I want you to find the man who killed Samuel," Juan Prieto said. "I would like it to be one of my enemies – a fascist from beyond the front line, or the man who arranged my accident – but that is not the important thing. What really matters is that you get the *right* man – so that Samuel can be properly avenged."

Paco looked Juan Prieto squarely in the eyes.

"Would you hold to that view even if the right man is someone close to you?" he asked.

"If you could prove to me that I had done it myself while sleep-walking, the answer would be the same," Prieto said, staring straight back. "If Samuel had lived, he could have done great things, both for us and for his own people. And if life is to make any sense, then those who deprive us of men like him must be punished."

"I'll do my best to find his murderer," Paco promised.

"I'm sure you will," Juan Prieto said. "But learn to tread cautiously, Señor Detective."

"Why do you say that?"

"Because in many respects you remind me of Samuel yourself – and men like the two of you have a way of making enemies."

Chapter Thirteen

Paco stood in the middle of the unpaved street outside Juan Prieto's modest house and looked around him. To his right was the vast Castilian Plain, which seemed to stretch endlessly – monotonously – to the very edge of the world. To his left was the street which would lead him to the Plaza Mayor, where Samuel Johnson had stood to watch the start of the *fiestas,* before making his way to the ruined church to meet his lonely death. But the ex-detective's mind was not focused on the town itself – he was thinking instead about Luis Prieto.

Why *did* the young man seem to have so much hatred in him for the foreigners who had come all the way to Spain to offer their help without any expectation of reward?

"But perhaps it isn't all foreigners that he hates," Paco speculated. "Perhaps he only hated Samuel Johnson."

Could it be that Luis Prieto, who would never have seen a black man before the *brigadistas* were unexpectedly billeted in his town, had suddenly discovered an instinctive racism lurking deep inside himself? And if that were the case, was he alone in his feelings – or were they shared with others in San Antonio?

Cindy had already explained to him that when a black man was lynched in the southern United States, it was not always necessary to look for any reason other than that he *was* black. So was it possible, therefore, that the same was true in San Antonio – that Samuel Johnson's murder had nothing to do with war or politics at all. Could it have been no more than an act of violence carried

119

out by men who were striking out blindly at someone who was so different from them that he either frightened them or disgusted them beyond endurance?

Paco looked up the street again. A couple of skinny dogs lay in the wintry sunshine, dreaming of bones, or perhaps just waiting for a stray cat to wander by so that they could chase it. An old man, leaning heavily on his walking stick, hobbled towards some bar where his fellow domino players would already be waiting for him. A small group of young children were crouched over the hard ground, engrossed in what was, to them, an all-important game of marbles. But there was no sign anywhere of Concha Prieto or her younger brother, Luis.

Paco tried to picture what they would be doing at that very moment. In his mind's eye, he saw Luis making angry gestures with his hands as he explained to his sister that his view of the world was absolutely right, and everyone else's was absolutely wrong.

And Concha – the girl who had been forced by circumstances to be like a mother to him for most of his life?

Concha would be listening patiently, waiting for a break in his fury so that she could quietly explain to him that sooner or later he would have to go back and face his father.

If he wanted to find out what was on the boy's mind, Paco thought – and he *did* want to find out – then he should do it soon, because once the boy had returned home and listened to his father counseling moderation and caution, he might start to sing a very different song.

He lit up a Celtas, and greedily inhaled the acrid smoke. Yes, talking to Luis Prieto immediately was an excellent plan, and the only flaw in it, as far as he could see, was that he had no idea where the young man was.

The village bars seemed as good a place as any to start his search, and Paco checked the two closest to Juan Prieto's house without any success. He did not find Concha and Luis at the third, either, though this bar's only customer was not a complete stranger to him.

The big peasant with a scar over his right eye was standing at the counter, a *copa* of anis looking tiny in his large callused hand. He looked far from pleased to see Paco standing in the doorway.

"I thought I'd made it clear that I didn't expect to see your face in this town again," he growled.

The man was looking for trouble, Paco thought – and suddenly realized that after all the emotional turmoil of the previous twelve hours that was exactly what *he* was looking for, too.

"Did you hear what I said, you piece of human offal?" the big peasant demanded.

Paco glanced quickly over his shoulder, then turned to face Iñigo Torres again.

"Oh, you were speaking to me, were you?" he asked innocently.

"So you're a comedian, as well as a cop, are you?" the big peasant demanded. "Well, your clever ways will do you no good down here. We're real men in San Antonio, and we can crush you city boys with no more effort than it would take us to crush a troublesome ant." He turned to the barman who was standing on the other side of the counter. "Isn't that right, Jose Antonio?"

"Whatever you say, Don Iñigo," the other man answered worriedly.

"So what are you doing here?" Torres asked Paco. "If it's a drink you're after, you've come to the wrong place, because this is an *individualista* bar, and unlike the *colectivista* bars, it doesn't have to serve scum like you if it doesn't want to."

"I don't want a drink," Paco said. "And even if I did, I'd go somewhere I liked the company better, Señor Torres."

"So you know my name, do you?" the big peasant asked.

"That's right. I got it from a friend of yours."

"Which friend?"

"A friend who's recently had a rather nasty accident with his tractor."

"Accidents happen," Torres said. "Juan Prieto had one, and so could you, if you're not careful."

"But I *am* careful," Paco told him. "I can see trouble coming long before it happens."

"You wouldn't see me!" Torres boasted. "Before you'd even started to know what was going on, I'd have broken every bone in your body."

Enough of just trading *insults*, Paco decided. He sniffed the air ostentatiously.

"Just as I thought," he said.

"What do you mean?"

"I wouldn't need to *see* you coming. The stink of cow shit you carry around with you would have tipped me off before you'd got within a hundred meters of me."

Torres slammed his glass down on the counter. "I could beat you to a pulp right here and now," he said angrily, "and there's not a man in this whole town who'd dare say he'd seen me do it."

"Shall we step outside?" Paco suggested.

"What?"

"You want to beat me to a pulp – and *I* want to see you try. There's no point in smashing up the bar, so why don't we step outside?"

Torres ran his eyes assessingly over Paco's frame. The man from Madrid was several centimeters shorter than he was, and at least twenty kilos lighter. Any fight they had should be a walkover for him. So why, he wondered, was he hesitating? Could it be because the other man seemed to welcome the thought of a fight even more than he did himself?

"Do you want to stand there all day, trying to kill me with your hard stares, you *maricón*?" Paco asked.

"You're a policeman," Torres said, amazed to discover a fear growing inside him. "Policemen aren't allowed to fight."

"I'm an ex-policeman," Paco told him. "And ex-policemen can do what they like."

Torres raised his hand to his mouth, and hit one of his chipped fingernails.

"Why should you want to fight me?" he asked wonderingly.

"It can't be to impress your fancy *yanqui* whore – because she isn't here."

Paco moved with a speed which took even a seasoned street brawler like Torres by surprise. One second he was standing by the door, at least a meter and a half from his target, the next his fist had buried itself in the big peasant's stomach.

Torres gasped, and would have doubled up had Paco had not followed through with a blow to the jaw which forced him to jerk his head back.

Two blows would not normally have been enough to fell such a hard man, but the anger and passion behind them was such that two blows were all it took. The peasant's knees buckled, and he collapsed into a heap on the floor.

Paco reached down, grabbed the fallen man's hair, and yanked his head a few centimeters off the ground. "Can you hear me?" he demanded furiously.

Torres groaned.

"I asked you if you could hear me," Paco repeated, tugging on the hair so that the head swung from side to side.

"Yes, I can hear you," Torres gasped.

"If you *ever* refer to Señorita Walker in that way again, I will kill you," Paco said. "No threats, no warnings. You'll just be dead. Do you understand what I'm saying?"

"I understand."

Paco let go of the hair, and Torres' head sank back to the floor.

"You – Jose Antonio – pour the man another drink," Paco said to the barman. "And you – *Don* Iñigo – get back on your feet."

Jose Antonio poured the drink and Torres – using the counter as support – struggled back to a standing position.

Paco took a deep breath.

"I have some questions I need answers to," he said. "Are you prepared to co-operate now – or will you need some persuading?"

"I'll co-operate," the big peasant grunted. "What do you want to know?"

"Tell me what you can about Samuel Johnson."

"The Negro?"

"Yes."

"I … I don't know what to say."

"Tell me how you and the other *individualista* farmers felt about him."

"I can't speak for them."

"Then speak for yourself."

"I have no opinions about him – or about any of the other *yanqui* monkeys."

"An interesting choice of words," Paco said. "So Johnson was a monkey, was he? Didn't it bother you, then, that the monkey should drink in your bars and talk to other white men almost as if he were white himself?"

Torres gave a cautious shrug.

"General Franco has his Moroccan monkeys fighting for him. Why shouldn't we have monkeys of our own? And if it offends me to see them drinking in our bars and sniffing around the local women, well, that is a small price to pay for them taking a bullet instead of us."

This man would have been right at home in a lynch mob, Paco thought disgustedly. But he could not really bring himself to believe that Torres had had anything to do with Samuel Johnson's death. If he had, a drunken bully like him would not have bothered to hide the fact – just as he had not really bothered to conceal his involvement in Juan Prieto's 'accident'.

"You might think of the *Negro* as a monkey," he told Torres, "but he was more of a man than you'll ever be."

Then he turned his back contemptuously on the big peasant, in much the same way as a matador turns his back on the bull, and left the bar.

Paco visited the rest of the bars in San Antonio with no more success than he had encountered at the first. Concha and Luis Prieto had simply vanished into thin air. Or, more likely, they had gone home again, and by now Luis had been persuaded by his father to curb his frankness.

So what did he do next? Paco wondered. How could he fill his time until another lead presented itself to him?

He knew what he *should* do. He should go and find Cindy and Felipe, because Felipe had been quite right – going through the statements and interviewing the Lincolns *was* a two-man job. Yet even the *thought* of seeing his best friend and his *novia* before he absolutely had to was enough to make him shudder.

He was ashamed of the way he had spoken to the fat constable that morning. In the face of Felipe's cogent argument, he had chosen to take shelter behind his rank. It had been a cowardly act, made all the more ludicrous because they both knew that rank was something neither of them really gave a hang about.

And how did he feel about Cindy? He still loved her. His fight with Iñigo Torres had assured him of that, because, though it was a fight he had sought, the depth of his rage when Torres had insulted her had frightened even him. He had only hit the man twice, but he had wanted to do more, and it was only by drawing on all his reserves of self-discipline that he had avoided killing him.

He still loved her, then – but he was already half-reconciled to losing her. Why *should* she stay with him, when she was so obviously still attracted to Greg Cummings, a fellow countryman, a fellow academic? A man, in other words, with whom she had so much in common – a man so very, very different from the simple Madrid policeman who had temporarily infatuated her?

Paco wandered aimlessly through the village for quite some time. He told himself he was doing something useful – that getting a feel for the place was vital to his investigation – but secretly he accepted the fact that he was doing no more than wasting his time.

The *brigadistas* returned from their exercises out on the plain at just after five o'clock. They entered the town in full marching order, but as Paco stood observing them it was obvious to him that apart from a few of the older men – who had probably served in the Great War – none of them had really mastered the art of moving like real soldiers.

As the *brigadistas* disappeared up the street towards their barracks, he checked his watch. It was still an hour before he was due to put in an appearance at Dolores McBride's house. Since he could think of nothing more constructive to do, he decided he might as well go to one of the collective's bars and have a drink.

Chapter Fourteen

The church was no more than a blackened shell, but by some miracle – if such things were still permitted to exist in Republican Spain – the clock on the tower had managed to survive, and as Paco made his way up the Calle Mayor to Dolores McBride's house, it was just striking the hour.

Six o'clock.

The exact hour at which he had agreed to meet the *yanqui* journalist.

Dolores had suggested that he take Cindy along as a chaperone, but given the strained relations which now existed between the two of them – and the fact that seeing Dolores would probably only make them worse – Paco had decided that it might be wiser to come alone. Now, he was not so sure it was such a good idea after all. Because if Cindy had slept with Greg Cummings the night before, as he was more and more coming to believe that she had, and if Dolores McBride were to offer to sleep with him now...

He laughed aloud. Why *should* a highly desirable woman like Dolores – who could have virtually any man she wanted – give him a second chance? And even if she did, would he want to take her up on her offer? Could he bring himself to betray Cindy without knowing for certain whether or not she had betrayed him? And what would be the point, anyway? He had seen too much of revenge in the previous few months to still believe that the avenger came away from it unscarred.

He came to a halt in front of Number 26. Like all the other

127

houses in the street, it was tall and narrow, and sandwiched between its neighbors. Someone – probably Dolores herself – had nailed a large red flag over the front door lintel. The blind was down over the barred window, but through the gaps in the slats Paco could make out the light shining inside the living room. He was a policeman on duty he reminded himself, and Dolores McBride was nothing more than a witness who was assisting in his inquiries. He raised his fist and knocked loudly – and officially – on the door.

If the door had been properly latched, it would have stayed closed. But it wasn't, and the moment his knuckles made contact with the old wood, it swung wide open.

Paco instinctively looked inside – and immediately wished that he hadn't. He saw the fire blazing away in the fireplace, the sheepskin rug which lay in front of it – and two naked bodies writhing around on that rug.

The door banged heavily against the inside wall, sending a noise through the room which seemed to Paco to be as loud as a cannon-blast.

The effect on the two lovers was instantaneous.

The black-haired woman – who was straddling the sandy-haired man – swiveled her trunk round to locate the source of the noise.

The sandy-haired man – lying supine beneath her – twisted his head to the side in an attempt to do the same thing.

The woman detached herself from her lover, and climbed to her feet. She appeared to be completely oblivious to the fact that she was standing there stark naked in the presence of a man she'd only met the day before. Her companion was much more self-conscious. He reached for his pants, which were lying on the floor nearby, and spread them hurriedly across his groin.

Paco wondered whether he should quickly close the door again, and then beat a hasty retreat down the street. But it was already too late for that, he was beginning to realize, because – however much he wanted to – he couldn't unsee what he had just witnessed.

"For God's sake, don't just stand there, Paco!" Dolores McBride said, her voice – under the circumstances – remarkably controlled.

"So what should I … what would you like me to…?" he heard himself asking uncertainly.

"Come inside! And close the door behind you, before we either catch our deaths of cold or get arrested for scaring the horses."

Paco obeyed, more on instinct than for any other reason. Once inside the room, he found himself faced with the choice of either staring at what he had already seen was a remarkable body – or of looking away. He raised his eyes and focused them on the ceiling.

Dolores – still naked and still apparently unconcerned by the fact – walked over to the coat rack, unhooked her trench coat, and slipped it over her shoulders. Only when he was sure she was decent did Paco allow his eyes to travel down to room level again.

"What are you doing here?" Dolores asked, almost accusingly.

"We had an appointment."

"I know we did – and you're early."

"We agreed to meet each other at six o'clock," Paco pointed out, in his own defense.

"So what?"

"So it's after six now."

Dolores threw back her head and roared with laughter.

"After six!" she repeated. "Christ, I didn't realize we'd been at it for so long. How times does fly when you're having fun."

Her lover had gathered all his clothes together, and was beginning to get dressed again in as inconspicuous a manner as possible.

"If you'd like me to go away now and come back later …" Paco suggested tentatively.

"Hell, no! What would be the point of that?" Dolores asked, brushing the suggestion aside. "We've pretty much finished here, and I've never been one for the lingering cigarette afterwards." She turned to her lover. "Wouldn't *you* say we'd pretty much finished, Greg?"

Cummings nodded, and mumbled what may have been agreement. Then he cleared his throat.

"If you'll excuse me, Dolores, I have duties to attend to."

In the previous few minutes Paco had first been shocked, and then embarrassed. Now, he was merely amused.

If you'll excuse me, Dolores, I have duties to attend to! Cummings had said, almost as if he were at one business meeting and had realized he was running late for another.

Cummings crossed the room, somehow managing to avoid looking at either Dolores or Paco, fumbled with the latch, opened the door and stepped out into the street without another word.

There were a few seconds of silence after he had left, then Dolores McBride said, "Let me guess what's going through your mind, Inspector Ruiz. When I offered to sleep with you last night, it did your ego one hell of a lot of good. But now you've seen me with another man, and you're starting to feel vaguely cheated – because if anybody who has the urge can easily get me into bed, there's nothing special in the fact that you had the chance. In fact, you're very close to thinking that I'm nothing but a whore. Isn't that right?"

"No, it isn't!" Paco protested.

But he had to admit to himself that it was close enough to the truth to make him feel uncomfortable.

"I have standards," Dolores said, "but they're not the standards of the bourgeois moralist society. I won't go to bed with just *any* man, but I will go to bed with any man who I find attractive and who I think will give me pleasure. And Greg Cummings falls right into that category. Sure, his wishy-washy politics make me sick, but there's nothing wishy-washy about him once he's in the sack. In fact, the man's a positive tiger."

"I see," Paco said.

And he found himself wondering if Cummings had been a *positive tiger* with Cindy, back in the days when she'd been his student in the States. Wondering, too, if Spanish language and literature had been the only thing the craggily handsome sandy-haired man had taught her.

"You're trying to figure out just how long our affair's been going on, aren't you?" Dolores said.

"Yes, I am," Paco agreed – because to agree with her was much easier than admitting what had *really* been on his mind.

"Well, strictly speaking, what we have going together isn't an affair at all," Dolores said. "We've slept together seven or eight times – and we've hit some great highs between the sheets – but there's no emotional attachment involved. On either side. When Greg's sent to the front line, I won't sit around here moping – I'll find myself another man to take his place. And God knows, there'll be plenty of them to choose from. The new guy may even be you – if you can ever bring yourself to abandon your feelings of guilt over your blonde princess for long enough to really let yourself go."

She was naked under her trench coat, Paco thought. And if he asked her to, he was sure that – despite the fact she'd just had sex with Greg Cummings – she would open that coat for him and let him do whatever he wanted to her. But only a small part of his mind was mulling over this possibility. The rest of it – the part which usually dominated his life – was considering something else entirely.

When Greg's sent to the front line! she'd said, almost as a throwaway line.

But it was not a throwaway line to him! Once the *brigadistas* had left San Antonio de la Jara, he suddenly realized, the trail would go cold. Even if the murderer wasn't actually one of the Lincolns, without them around to question, his chances of tracking down the man who had put a bullet in Samuel Johnson's head would be, at the very least, halved.

"You said you'd give me the notes you'd taken on Johnson's life," he reminded the journalist.

Dolores McBride smiled mockingly.

"So despite the display I've just put on for you, you still haven't forgotten why you came here," she said. "Are you really such a cold, hard man, Inspector?"

"Yes," Paco replied, then, a little more truthfully, he added, "… at least I am most of the time."

"The notes are upstairs," Dolores McBride said. "I'll go and get them for you."

The trench coat only reached down as far as her calves, and as she climbed the stairs he couldn't stop his eyes from following her slim ankles. She offered relief without strings, and – whatever he'd told himself earlier – if his relationship with Cindy continued to deteriorate further, relief without strings might be just what he needed.

There was a frantic hammering on the front door.

Could it be yet another of Dolores McBride's army of lovers in desperate need of instant gratification? Paco wondered.

But it wasn't some eager young man who was standing there when he opened the door. Instead, it was a fat middle-aged police constable, very red in the face and looking as if his heart had been broken.

"I've … I've been searching for you for over a quarter of an hour," Felipe spluttered. "If I hadn't run into Señor Cummings out on the street, I'd still have had no idea where you were."

"Calm down," Paco said soothingly. "What's the matter? Has something happened?"

"Cindy!" Felipe gasped.

"Cindy!" Paco repeated, as he felt a sledgehammer slam into his stomach. "Has there been an accident? Is she hurt?"

The fat constable nodded, and Paco found that he was suddenly fighting for breath.

"Is it serious?" he managed to croak.

"Very serious," Felipe said gravely. "The doctor's not sure if she'll last out the night."

Chapter Fifteen

The old, iron-framed bed stood next to the dining table in the house on Calle Paz. It had only recently been hastily erected there, and it still seemed out of place – an intruder which had forced its way into the world of the shabby, familiar furniture.

"We thought it best not to take her all the way upstairs," the bald-headed doctor said in hushed tones. "In cases like this, it's always better to move the patient as little as possible."

Paco looked down at the blonde woman lying on the bed. Her eyes were closed, and her breathing was shallow. It would almost have been possible to mistake her for a sleeper, had it not been for the roll of bandage wrapped around the top of her head.

"She will be all right, won't she?" he asked, the realist in him giving way to a self full of blind hope.

"It's far too early to say *what* will happen," the doctor replied softly.

"It can't be as serious as it looks," Paco declared. "She's young! She's fit! It should take a lot more than a knock on the head to ..."

The doctor put his hand reassuringly on Paco's shoulder.

"She's in a coma," he said.

"Do you think I can't see that for myself?"

"It's certainly not beyond the bounds of possibility that she'll come out of it in the next few hours, and be left with no more than a nasty headache."

"But if she doesn't?"

The doctor shrugged.

"Sometimes it can take years for patients to regain consciousness. And – I have to be honest with you, Señor Ruiz – sometimes they *never* come round again. Whatever happens, you can take comfort from the fact that she's in no pain."

But *I* am, Paco thought. I'd never have believed it was possible to hurt so much.

"Shouldn't she be in a hospital?" he demanded.

"The nearest one to here is in Albacete. If I didn't even want to run the risk involved in moving her upstairs, I'm not likely to advise you to move her all that way, am I?"

"We could travel slowly," Paco said desperately. "We could take care not to do anything which might do her more harm."

"Even if you managed to get her there without further harm being done, there's nothing they could do for her there that we aren't doing here. We just have to let nature take its course."

Why *Cindy*? Paco asked himself anguishedly. If the bastards wanted to hurt somebody, why didn't they hurt me?

"My niece and I will take good care of her," said a voice to his left. "We have both nursed the sick before."

Paco turned towards the woman. This was her house. This was where Cindy had been found bleeding on the doorstep.

"Thank you, Señora Munoz," he said. "And thank you, Señorita Prieto," he added, speaking to Concha Prieto, the niece.

"Perhaps you should go now," the doctor suggested to the ex-policeman.

"Is there nothing I can do to help?" Paco asked.

"No, not at the moment. But come back later. Sit and talk to her for a while."

"Will that do any good? Will she even be able to hear me?"

"We can have no way of knowing that for certain, but it's possible that some of what you say may perhaps get through to her brain."

That was something at least. Paco told himself. It might be no more than the desperately thin straw which a drowning man was said to clutch at, but it *was* a straw, nevertheless.

Fat Felipe had been standing by the door, but now he walked over to Paco.

"Could you use a drink, *jefe*?" he asked tentatively.

"Use one?" Paco replied. "I *need* one – like I've never needed one before in my entire life."

In his panicked haste to see Cindy, Paco had noticed nothing when he entered Senora Muñoz's house. Now, as he left it again, he saw the stain by the doorstep for the first time.

It was a darker brown than the almost-frozen earth it had itself spread over. Even without prior knowledge of what had occurred there. Paco would have recognized it for what it was.

It was blood!

Cindy's blood!

He felt a lurching sensation in his stomach, and it was as much as he could do to prevent himself from doubling up and vomiting beside it.

"Don't look at it!" Felipe urged. "Don't even think about it."

"I … I…" Paco gagged.

"Let's go and get that drink you said you wanted so badly," Felipe suggested, grasping his boss's arm firmly with his podgy hand, and steering him away from the obscene reminder of what had happened to the woman he loved.

It was a short walk up the side street to Calle de las Murallas, but with every step a fresh needle of anguish stabbed at Paco's brain.

Cindy had been seriously hurt.

Perhaps she was dying.

Perhaps she was already dead.

And it was all his fault – because he was the one who had brought her to San Antonio.

Felipe shepherded him into the bar he'd visited the night before in the company of Dolores McBride. As on the previous evening, the place was full of peasant farmers and mechanics. They were all talking animatedly when the door opened, but the moment they saw who the new arrivals were, they fell silent.

So they all knew! Paco thought. But of course they knew! Why would he ever have imagined that they wouldn't? In a town the size of San Antonio news spread faster than if it had been broadcast on the radio.

Felipe glanced around the room at the frozen, pitying faces.

"What's the matter with you lot?" he demanded roughly. "Is the sight of two old mates out for a drink together so strange that it stops you arguing about the price of potatoes? Get back to your business, and leave us alone to get on with ours."

The peasants and mechanics turned away. Conversations started again, beginning as hushed whispers but slowly climbing back up to level they were at when the two *madrileños* first entered the bar.

Felipe turned to the waiter.

"We'll be sitting at the table in the corner and we'll be drinking Fundador brandy," he said. "Bring a full bottle, because we'll probably want it all."

He led Paco over to the table, and the two men sat down. When the waiter brought the brandy, Felipe watched him pour it, and did not nod for him to stop until his boss's glass was filled almost to the brim.

"Tell me how it happened," Paco said hoarsely.

"Where do you want me to start?"

"At the beginning."

"Cindy and I spent most of the day going through the *brigadistas'* statements. We'd just finished the job when we heard the tramping of their feet as they marched back into town. We had a list of the ones we wanted to talk to by then, so I suggested that we should start the interrogations straight away."

"But you didn't?"

"No."

"Why not?"

"Cindy said the Lincolns would be exhausted after their maneuvers, and we'd get much more out of them if we allowed them the time to take a short rest." Felipe paused, as if debating whether to say more, then added, "Besides, she said there was something she had to do first."

"Did she say what it was?"

Felipe looked down at the table.

"She said she needed to find you."

"Did she tell you why?"

Felipe closed his eyes and concentrated.

"She said that you're a clever man – probably even as clever as you *think* you are – but that when you get things wrong, you get them wronger than anyone else she's ever met. And you were wrong this time – so it was about time she put you right."

"What was it that I was supposed to have gotten wrong?"

"Cindy didn't say, *jefe*. But whatever it was, she seemed to think it was important."

Important to them? Paco wondered.

Or important to the case they were working on?

Would he ever know the answer to that now?

"What happened next?"

"We agreed to meet outside the *brigadistas'* barracks at six o'clock. Cindy went off looking for you, and I thought I'd use the time to go down to the nearest bar and order a few snacks."

"When did all this take place?"

"It must have been around about a quarter past five."

"Go on."

"About fifteen minutes later, Señora Munoz rushed into the bar where I was eating and told me that Cindy was lying in the alley outside her house with blood pouring from her head. I got there as quickly as I could. It was obvious what had happened. Somebody had hit her from behind. I knew she wasn't dead or she wouldn't have still been bleeding, but I checked her pulse anyway. Then I told Señora Munoz to fetch a doctor as quickly as she could. You know the rest."

Why would anyone attack Cindy? She was a stranger in San Antonio. She knew no one, and no one knew her. There was absolutely no reason why anyone should wish to harm her. Unless…

Unless Samuel Johnson's murderer was afraid she had uncovered some clue which could put him in danger!

"When you were going through the statements together, was there any point at which Cindy seemed particularly excited?" Paco asked.

"Not really what you might call excited," the fat constable replied cautiously. "But she did seem a bit abstract – as if something was preying on her mind – almost from the start."

But did that abstraction she'd displayed have anything to do with the murder – or was it more concerned with what had passed between them the previous evening? Perhaps she had merely wanted to tell him that Greg Cummings posed no threat to their relationship – because she'd already learned that her ex-instructor was involved in a passionate affair with Dolores McBride.

So why *had* someone attacked her? Why had someone run such a risk simply to prevent her from telling him something which could have nothing to do with the murder?

Because the killer didn't know that! He saw her on the street, noticed the look of determination on her face, and assumed, possibly wrongly, that she was on to him. Looked at in that way, it didn't matter a damn what she knew – only what the killer *thought* she knew.

Paco took a generous gulp of his brandy. Whichever angle he examined the situation from, he was forced back to the same conclusion. If he wanted to find the man who had hurt Cindy, he needed to find the man who had killed Samuel Johnson – because they were one and the same.

The door of the bar swung open, and Dolores McBride entered. The journalist glanced around the room, then made straight for the table where the two detectives were sitting.

"Do you mind if I join you?" she asked, with none of her usual confidence evident in her voice.

Paco nodded wearily. "Why not?"

Dolores sat down opposite him, reached across the table and took his hands in hers.

"I just can't find the words to tell you how sorry I am," she said, with a catch on her throat. "When I think that the poor girl was being attacked while I was … I was …"

While you were sating your sexual appetite, Paco thought viciously, pulling his hands free of hers. While you were rutting with Greg Cummings like a sow in heat!

He was being both illogical and unfair, he realized. However questionable Dolores McBride's morals were, it wasn't her fault that Cindy was teetering on the verge of death – and at least she'd been decent enough to come and express her sympathy.

"Will you be going back to Madrid now?" the journalist asked.

"No. The doctor thinks that it would be dangerous to move Cindy for the moment. Besides, I still have a case to investigate."

"You're going on with the investigation despite what's happened?" Dolores said, shaking her head in admiration. "Well, I'll say one thing for you, you've got some kinda *cojones*."

Yes, in that respect he had nothing to reproach himself for. But would he ever be able to look in the mirror again without blaming the face which was staring back at him for what had happened to Cindy?

"Look, I feel a bit awkward saying this, but if you're still intent on tracking down your murderer, you're going to need a new translator," Dolores McBride told him.

She was right about that, of course. He could never run his investigation without one.

"Are you volunteering for the job?" he asked.

"Yeah, I'll do it. Unless, of course, you can think of anybody else you'd rather use."

But there was nobody else – except possibly Greg Cummings.

"I'd appreciate your help," he said.

Dolores turned to Felipe.

"Would you excuse us for a few moments?" she asked the fat constable.

"Of course," Felipe said, raising his huge bulk from his stool and lumbering over to the counter.

"Is there something you wanted to say that you'd rather he didn't hear?" Paco asked, when Felipe was well away from them.

"No, but there's something I want to say that he'd probably *prefer* not to hear."

"Go on."

Dolores lit up an American cigarette.

"There are several reasons why I've volunteered to be your translator. The first is that somebody has to do it, and I've got more free time on my hands than most of the Yanks round here. The second is that I want to track down Sam's killer – probably even more than you do. But it's the third reason that made me ask your fat friend to leave. I like you, and I want to do anything I can – and I mean *anything* – to make your life a little easier."

"You're propositioning me again," Paco said.

"Hell, no. I'm just saying that if you want some physical relief – and a lot of men find that makes things easier to bear – then I'm available. It doesn't have to mean anything to either of us. I don't even have to enjoy it myself. Don't look on it as betraying Cindy – think of it just as a way of helping you to get through."

"You're very kind," Paco told her.

Dolores reddened.

"Oh Jeez, don't start going all appreciative on me – I'd find that very hard to handle. Just *use* me anyway you think might help. And I mean that, Paco."

It was one of the few times she'd ever called him by his given name, and he was very uneasy about how comforted it made him feel.

"I won't ask you to sleep with me," he said.

"OK," Dolores replied easily. "But I won't hold you to that promise if you change your mind." She took a long drag on her cigarette, and blew the smoke out of her slim nose. "So when do we roll up our sleeves and get to work? First thing in the morning?"

Felipe and … and … Cindy… had spent most of the day going over the *brigadistas* statements, and but for the dreadful thing which had happened to her, they would already have begun the interrogations.

"Could you start right now?" Paco asked.

"Sure," Dolores agreed. "Why not?"

Chapter Sixteen

The logs in the fireplace were now no more than smoldering, though an occasional burst of flame would cast sudden shadows around the room and across the sheepskin rug.

Just over an hour earlier, when he had blundered into this house by accident, it had been a very different scene, Paco thought. Then the fire had been burning fiercely, though it was doubtful whether that blaze had been able to match the ferocity of the two people who were locked together on the rug.

He turned from the fire and looked across the table at one of those two people – Dolores McBride.

"If you're to do this job that you've taken on properly, you're going to have to know a lot more than just know how to translate words from one language to another," he said.

"Like what?" the journalist asked, sounding intrigued.

"It's the little details which often matter most in an investigation like this one," Paco explained, "and it's *just* those little details which might get lost during the translation, unless you, Dolores, know enough about the background to realize they could be important."

Dolores McBride nodded sagely.

"Seems as if your job's not that different from mine. I spend a lot of my time collecting the little details so that I can build up the bigger picture."

That was probably true, Paco thought.

"So let's get down to business," he suggested. "The reason I want you to listen in while Felipe and I discuss the case is so you'll understand not only what we're dealing with, but the *way* we deal with it." He turned his attention to the fat constable, who was sitting on Dolores' left. "What have you found out so far, Felipe?"

Felipe shuffled through the stack of papers in front of him.

"Most of the *brigadistas* have alibis for the half-hour each side of the time Samuel Johnson was probably killed," he said.

Dolores nodded again, this time to remind Paco that she'd already told him that would turn out to be the case.

"Not that we can automatically accept any of those alibis at purely face value," Paco said.

Dolores' eyes flashed with anger.

"Are you saying that my comrades will have lied to you?" she demanded.

"They don't necessarily have to have lied," Felipe told her diplomatically. "They could have misled us just as easily by not really knowing what the truth is themselves."

"You want to explain that to me?" Dolores asked – a little mollified, but *only* a little.

"There are a number of ways it can happen," Paco said. "Far too many to go into now. So let me give you just one example. You know what it's like to be really drunk, don't you?"

Dolores laughed.

"Sure, I do. Since I came to Spain, I've probably become one of the world's leading experts on the subject."

"Say you've had a lot to drink, and you're talking to your *compañeros* in a bar," Paco said. "You look at your watch, and you see that it's eleven o'clock. You continue arguing and joking for what seems to you like another ten minutes, then you check your watch again – and see that it's half past one. Hasn't that ever happened to you?"

"Yeah, I suppose so," Dolores agreed reluctantly.

"That's what booze does to people – it compresses time. Now imagine this. You've got a group of drunken *brigadistas* in the bar on the main square, and one of them says he has to go to the lavatory.

His friends probably won't even remember he's left them. Why should they? Every one of them will need to empty his bladder at one time or another during the evening. And even if they do remember him leaving, they'll probably believe he was only away for a minute or so."

"But he could have been away for much longer than that?" Dolores McBride interrupted him.

"Exactly. He could have been away for fifteen or twenty minutes – which is plenty of time to walk to the church, murder someone, and get back to the Plaza Mayor. Do you see what I'm getting at?"

"I see it, all right, but none of the brigade would ever have thought of killing Sam."

Paco sighed.

"You can't work with us if you have that kind of attitude," he said.

"What kind of attitude?"

"When you're investigating a case – or even if you're only translating for the people who are investigating it – you have to force yourself to rule *nothing* out. Because if you start closing off avenues without any reason, you stand a good chance of missing a vital piece of information. I can't have people who wear blinkers on my team."

Dolores thought over what he'd said for a few seconds, then grinned ruefully.

"I've been falling into the trap of my own rhetoric, haven't I?" she said. "I've been assuming that because a group of men are involved in fighting for a noble cause, there's not one of them who can have an evil bone in his body. Hell, somebody who's been round the block as many times as I have should know that's a complete load of bullshit."

"So you're prepared to accept the possibility that Samuel Johnson might have been killed by one of the *brigadistas*?"

"I guess so."

Paco turned back to Felipe.

"What about the *brigadistas* who don't have alibis?"

Felipe again consulted the notes which he'd written out in his large, childish handwriting.

"There are only a few of them. James Clay, the political commissar, says he was working late in the office and ..."

"You can't possibly suspect Jimmy," Dolores interrupted. "I don't particularly like the guy myself, but it's beyond question that he's a ..." She caught the warning look in Paco's eye, and shook her head in exasperation. "There I go again," she said. "Sorry!"

"The second is the very big man with the tattoos – Donaldson," Felipe continued.

"Ted used to be a shop steward for the New Jersey Longshoreman's Union. Most of them have got tattoos," Dolores supplied, as if she imagined that, as far as the two detectives from Madrid were concerned, having tattoos automatically made him a suspect.

"Donaldson? He's the one who hates Jews, isn't he?" Paco asked.

"What makes you say an awful thing like that about him?" Dolores wondered.

"You were at the meeting in the town hall ..." Paco began.

But she hadn't been. Cindy – Cindy again! – had seen to that.

For Dolores' benefit, he quickly sketched out the heated exchange which had passed between Donaldson and the small Jewish man in the council chamber.

"OK, there's always been an anti-Semitic vein running through the stevedores, and maybe Ted Donaldson's still infected by it, just a tad," Dolores admitted reluctantly. "But he's been in the Party long enough now for it not to have an effect on his actions."

However much she professed her willingness to be objective about the case, she couldn't help leaping to the defense of her comrades, Paco thought. Cindy would never have ...

He'd been able to keep thoughts of Cindy out of his mind for nearly half an hour, but suddenly she was filling it again. The last words they had spoken to one another had been cold – almost acrimonious. Now she was in a coma, and she probably couldn't even hear him if he were to tell her how much he loved her – how much she had become the cornerstone of his life.

"*Jefe*?" Felipe said.

144

And Paco realized from the anxiety in his partner's voice that he must have been wrapped up in his own misery for quite some time.

"If Donaldson doesn't have an alibi, where does he *say* he was?" he asked, trying to sound business-like.

"He claims to have gotten drunk much earlier than everybody else, and some of the other *brigadistas'* statements confirm that. According to two or three of them, he was almost legless by nine o'clock."

"So he left the *fiesta?*"

"That's right. He claims he went for a walk to clear his head. The next thing he remembers, he was lying on the ground near the edge of town. He heard the church clock strike, and realized it was three o'clock in the morning. He didn't know anything about Samuel Johnson's murder until he got back to the barracks."

Did racism know any limits? Paco wondered. How easy was it for a man who hated the Jews to also hate the Negroes? And how would a white man who had gotten used to being a leader of men himself feel about a black man who seemed to have even greater power to attract followers?

"Who's next?" he asked Felipe.

"The man that Donaldson had the argument with in the council chamber – Emmanuel Lowenstein – also can't account for his movements."

Dolores opened her mouth as if she were about to say something, then bit back the words.

"You were about to tell us that Lowenstein couldn't have killed Sam Johnson because he's such a good communist?" Paco guessed.

"Mannie Lowenstein ended up in hospital three times as a result of getting beaten up for union activities," Dolores said carefully. "But I accept that that doesn't rule him out as your murderer."

You might say it, Paco thought – but you don't *believe* it.

"Why wasn't Lowenstein with the others?" he asked.

"He doesn't say in his statement. Just claims that he stayed in the *brigadistas'* barracks."

"Is it just a co-incidence that two of the men without alibis were also the two men involved in the argument in the council chamber?" Paco wondered. "Or do you think there was an element of play-acting in it?"

"What do you mean, *jefe*?" Felipe asked.

"Say Donaldson did kill Johnson. He doesn't have an alibi, so he goes for the next-best thing – which is to try and establish firmly in our minds that he's unlikely to be the murderer because he's on the side of the Negroes."

"And Lowenstein?"

"If Lowenstein killed Johnson, then what he wants to do is to present us with another suspect. So by suggesting that Donaldson is a racist as far as the Jews go, he's also opening up the possibility that Donaldson could hate blacks, too."

"That's a bit deep for me," Felipe confessed.

"It's also very far-fetched," Dolores McBride said, unable to restrain herself any longer. "Killers simply don't think like that."

"Don't they?" Paco asked. "Well, obviously you've had more experience than I have, but ..."

"There I go again," Dolores interrupted. "Sorry."

"There is one more *brigadista* without an alibi," Felipe said.

"Who?"

"Greg Cummings. He says that he stayed in the barracks during the *fiestas*, too. But he doesn't mention seeing Lowenstein – and Lowenstein doesn't mention seeing him."

Paco looked quizzically across at Dolores McBride.

"Liberals!" she said contemptuously.

"What do you mean by that?"

"The one thing that the liberals share with us communists is the belief that they always know what's best."

"But they're wrong about that – and you're right?" Paco asked, a small smile playing in the corners of his mouth.

"Absolutely," Dolores McBride agreed. "We *do* know what's best, because we're scientific, and we only deal with the broad sweep of history – with unstoppable trends and historical inevitability. They, on the other hand, think that they know what's best for *individuals* – whether the individual in question happens to agree with them or not."

"Is all that just a long-winded way of saying that Cummings does, in fact, have a solid alibi, but he prefers not to produce it because he thinks it will harm someone else?"

"Spot on, Señor Detective. At the time poor Sam got himself shot, Greg and I were at my house – making the beast with two backs. See, that's another thing about liberals – they're not very perceptive. Greg probably imagines he's protecting my reputation – as if anybody who really knows me thinks I give a shit about that. Hell, I don't mind a guy who's slept with me talking to his buddies about how good I am in the sack. As far as I'm concerned, that's just free advertising."

"How long was he with you?" Paco asked.

"We started humping at about eleven o'clock, took a well-deserved break, had a second bout, and were still at it when we heard all the furor that followed the discovery of Sam's body."

"You didn't go to sleep between your … er … sessions," Paco asked. "There wasn't any possibility that Cummings could have slipped out and killed Johnson without you knowing about it?"

"No," Dolores said, stony-faced.

"Are you sure?" Paco persisted. "Sometimes, after having sex, we fall asleep without even knowing it."

"I didn't fall asleep!"

"Given where this house is, and where the church is, he wouldn't have had to be gone for long."

Dolores looked distinctly uncomfortable.

"Jeez, this is becoming embarrassing," she said.

"What is?"

"I know I didn't fall asleep, because after we'd done it the first time, we got into this big argument about politics, and I can remember every word we said." She smiled awkwardly. "Yeah, I know, screwing and politics aren't natural bedfellows, but that's what happened. And we ended up getting so furious that before we knew what was going on, we were off jumping on each other's bones again."

Paco remembered arguments with Cindy ... oh God, Cindy ... which had ended up with a passionate reconciliation in the bedroom.

But that was entirely different, wasn't it? And what made it different? The fact that he loved Cindy, and Cindy loved him!

Yet did he know for certain that Cummings *hadn't* fallen in love with Dolores? Could he even say for sure that despite her hard outer shell, Dolores hadn't even fallen a little bit in love with Cummings?

"Anybody else on your list?" he asked Felipe.

"No, that's the lot," Felipe said. "But as you pointed out earlier, *jefe*, *not* being on the list is no more of a guarantee of innocence than *being* on it is a guarantee of guilt."

"True," Paco agreed. "But we have to start somewhere – and the men who *are* on the list are as good a place as any."

"Or you could start by seeing if there were any strangers in the town that night," Dolores suggested hopefully.

But the theory that Johnson had been killed by an outsider – always tenuous at best – simply didn't really hold water any more, Paco told himself. Because not only did the killer have to have been in San Antonio on the night Samuel Johnson was killed, he'd also had to have been there no more than a couple of hours earlier that very day.

How else would he have perceived Cindy as a threat?

How else could he have followed her up an alley and brutally smashed in her skull?

"We start by questioning the *brigadistas* who don't have alibis," Paco said firmly, looking Dolores McBride right in the eye.

The journalist shrugged.

"Whatever you say," she agreed. "After all, you are the *jefe*, aren't you, *Jefe*?"

Chapter Seventeen

There were four of them in the room in the town hall which the political commissar used as his office. James Clay himself was sitting behind his big desk. The other three – the two policemen from Madrid and the *Moscow News'* Spanish correspondent – sat facing him.

The political commissar had begun to speak even before they had settled into their chairs. His voice was as flat and dull as if he were reading from a telephone directory, his hands stayed determinedly still on the desk – as though afraid to betray him with gestures – and his hooded eyes gave away nothing. He spoke for perhaps a minute and a half, then stopped abruptly and signaled with a brief nod that Dolores should translate his words into Spanish.

"The gist of all that speechifying is that he wants you to know he regrets what has happened to Cindy," the journalist said.

"He does, does he? Then why didn't I even hear him use her name once," Paco asked.

"That's because he *didn't* use it. What he actually said, if I'm being strictly accurate, is that he regrets what happened to your translator."

My *translator*! Paco thought bitterly.

They had been in San Antonio for less than two days, but surely most people had realized, even in that short time, that Cindy was much more than a translator to him. Certainly, the political commissar – a man who should have had his finger on the pulse of the place – ought to have known it. And he probably did, Paco admitted to himself.

He probably did, but was just too rigid and formal to acknowledge the fact. God, the man was a cold fish.

Clay spoke again.

"He says that he hopes I will turn out to be an adequate substitute for her," Dolores said.

She should be more than an adequate substitute from Clay's point of view, Paco thought – because she was one of his own, a disciplined, card-carrying communist.

From the change in Clay's voice, it was probable that he was no longer expressing his stilted condolences, but instead was asking a question. Dolores listened, hesitated for a second, then produced a slow, careful answer. Clay countered with a second question, and – without waiting for a response to it – added a third. He seemed to be growing angrier and angrier. Dolores McBride waited until she was sure he'd finished, and when she spoke again there was an uncharacteristically conciliatory edge to her words. Finally, when they both seemed to have said all they wanted to, Dolores turned to Paco.

"He wonders why you're here," she explained. "He had assumed that once you'd taken the statements from his *brigadistas*, the investigation would be over as far as they were concerned."

"And you told him that it wasn't?"

"What I actually said was that it wasn't quite as simple as that. He demanded to know why not. I told him that though the statements did, in fact, rule most of the men out of the investigation – sorry to stretch the truth a little there – there were still question marks hanging over a few of them. It was when I said that he was one of those men himself that he started to get really pissed off."

"So is he willing to answer my questions or not?"

"Willing isn't exactly the word I'd have chosen, but I pointed out that if he didn't co-operate with you, you'd complain to brigade headquarters in Albacete about it, and he'd soon be snowed under with the paperwork that would generate. So let's just say he'll answer the questions, but I'd be surprised if he's very gracious about it. What exactly do you want to know?"

"Ask him about his background," Paco said.

"If you need those kinds of details, you only have to talk to me. They're all in the notes for my book."

"I want to hear it from him."

"You won't understand a word he's saying."

"That's true," Paco agreed, "but at least I'll be able to see the *way* he tells it. Don't translate that last part, by the way."

Dolores grinned.

"I won't. I'm not an idiot."

Clay spoke in the same flat, lifeless tone as he had before.

"He says his father was one of the bloated American capitalists ..." Dolores began.

"Forget all that rhetorical crap and just stick to the basic facts," Paco interrupted.

"He had what you might call a privileged childhood – private schools, his own horse, an automobile as soon as he was old enough to drive. He went to Harvard Business School, and planned to join the family firm. Then the Wall Street Crash came along – and there was no family firm left to join. It was when he saw the lines outside the soup kitchens that he began to understand that capitalism wasn't just wrong – it was inefficient. Any system which failed to use the talents of the masses wasn't functioning properly. That's when he joined the Party."

"Ask him what he would have been doing now if Wall Street hadn't crashed," Paco said.

"That's a bit below the belt, isn't it?" Dolores said, sounding a little concerned. "Ask him anyway," Paco insisted.

A slight smile came to Clay's lips as he listened to Dolores' words. It was the first indication Paco had seen that the political commissar had any sense of humor – and even then it was a humor based on irony rather than amusement.

"He says the question is irrelevant," Dolores told Paco. "Capitalism was a sick beast, full of inherent flaws – even without the Crash it could not have gone on as it was for very much longer."

"But what if it *had* survived for another few years?"

Clay's ironic smile widened as he answered this question.

"He says that if that had been the case, then at this moment he would probably have been standing on the deck of his private yacht, sipping champagne and watching the sun set over the Hamptons," Dolores translated. "But that wouldn't have been his fault. He simply wouldn't have known any better. No man can really see things as they truly are until he's been swept up into the relentless march of history."

"Ask him if there's any way he can prove to us that he didn't kill Samuel Johnson."

The question was relayed, and Clay shook his head.

"He can't prove he didn't kill Sam, but why would he have?" Dolores translated.

Why indeed? Paco wondered. Why should any man want to end the life of another? Yet they often did.

"That's enough for the moment," Paco said. "Please thank Señor Clay for his time."

Instead of merely nodding an acknowledgement, Clay launched into another short speech.

"He says that you may have finished with him, but he certainly hasn't finished with you," Dolores McBride translated, when the political commissar had fallen silent again.

"What more does he want to say?"

"He understands that you have been questioning some of the local people about the murder."

"He understands correctly."

"He wants you to appreciate the fact that to accuse one of them of killing Sam would be just as bad for Spain, and for your cause, as if you had accused one of the *brigadistas*."

"And why might that be?"

"To accuse a *brigadista* of the murder would be to split the brigade between the majority who wished to see him punished, and the few who sought to find excuses for him. Even if only one or two men took the killer's side, it would seriously damage morale."

"And if the killer turned out to be a Spaniard?"

"To accuse a Spaniard *from this side of the front line* would be to alienate the brigade from the very people it is here to protect."

"Does Mr. Clay actually *want* Samuel Johnson's murderer found?" Paco demanded.

"Yes – but only if he is an *acceptable* murderer – an enemy soldier or well-known fascist sympathizer. Otherwise, it would be better for the general good if the killer remained free."

"Does he realize that whoever killed Johnson probably also attacked Cindy – and that she may die?"

"As he's already said, he thinks that what happened to Cindy was regrettable, but that in the great struggle we have embarked on, everyone must run the risk of becoming a casualty."

Paco turned away from Dolores and looked directly at Clay.

"The difference between you and Cindy, you *hijo de puta*, is that you chose to be a part of this, and she didn't," Paco exploded.

He saw that Dolores was about to translate, and shook his head violently.

"Don't bother," he told her. "The bastard may not have understood the words exactly, but I'm sure he got the general message."

Chapter Eighteen

Paco gazed across the Plaza Mayor at the church tower outlined against the dark night sky. How quickly things changed, he thought. Only a few months earlier, that burnt-out shell had stood as a solid, immovable symbol of the old order. Only a few *days* earlier, a black man called Samuel Johnson had been alive, and looking forward to playing his part in building a brave new world. Only a few *hours* earlier, his beloved Cindy had been searching the streets of San Antonio for him. And only a few *minutes* earlier, he had felt so much rage bubbling up inside him that he had come within inches of killing Commissar James Clay.

The rage was gone now – it had begun to drain from him the moment he had left the town hall – and in its place was only the weariness of a man who had been forced to run an emotional marathon while carrying a heavy sack of guilt on his tired shoulders.

He heard a discrete cough, and remembered that he was not alone – that his fat assistant and his beautiful Mexican-American translator were waiting for him to say something. Yet he could not bring himself to speak. He was sick of being the leader, the man who was turned to for guidance and instruction. Let others take the decisions from now on. Let others judge who was guilty and who was not – and who should be put in danger, and who should stay safely back in Madrid, nursing the wounded.

"Shall we go up to the barracks to talk to Donaldson and Lowenstein?" Felipe suggested.

What would be the point of that? Paco asked himself.

An investigator should never begin an important interrogation unless he was on the top of his form. And he was feeling so far below his form at that moment he doubted he'd be able to pick out the murderer even if the guilty man spilled his guts and gave him a full and frank confession.

"Why don't you go and get yourself something to eat?" he said to the fat constable.

Felipe shook his head.

"I don't think that's a very good idea," he said.

"You're not trying to tell me you're not hungry, are you?"

"No, I'm hungry enough," Felipe admitted. "But …"

"But what?"

"I think it would be best if I stayed with you."

Paco was deeply touched. Felipe was a good, true friend, he thought – but the burden of friendship was yet another emotion he did not feel he had the strength to handle that night.

"Greater love hath no man than this, that he will give up his food for his partner," he said, trying to sound as if he had already begun to pull back from the edge – and knowing that he was not fooling Felipe for a second. "But it won't do Cindy any good to have you waste away to a shadow. Go and find some food – and that's an order."

"Are you sure?"

"It's what I *want* you to do."

The fat constable nodded gravely, then waddled off towards a side street in pursuit of a cooking odor that only his keen nose could detect.

"What about you?" Dolores said, when Felipe had reached the edge of the square.

"Me?" Paco asked.

"You should eat something, too, you know. Come back to my place, if you like. I'm not much of a cook to be perfectly honest, but I might just be able to manage to rustle up a *tortilla francesa* and salad without completely destroying the kitchen."

If he went back with her, he would sleep with her, Paco thought. And if he slept with her, he would despise himself.

155

"I think I'll just go and see Cindy," he said.

"Do you want me to come with you?"

"No, I'd like to do it alone."

"Yeah, I expect that'd be for the best," Dolores agreed. "Anything else I can do for you?"

"You could go back into the town hall and ask that son-of-a-bitch Clay not to send Ted Donaldson and Mannie Lowenstein out on maneuvers with the rest of the brigade tomorrow," Paco said.

"I'll take care of that right now."

"If the bastard says it can't be done …"

"He won't," Dolores promised. "I can be very persuasive when I really want to be."

For a moment she stood on tiptoe, as if she were about to kiss him goodnight, then she turned suddenly and walked back towards the *ayuntamiento*.

Paco watched and waited until she had disappeared inside the building. He was glad he'd asked her to do that, he thought. Glad that despite his personal misery, he had not forgotten he still had a job to do. He could only pray that by the time the sun rose again, he would have somehow re-discovered, deep within himself, the strength to able to do it.

It was as he was lighting up a Celtas that he felt the tingle at the back of his neck. It was not something he had anticipated, but it was undoubtedly there. And it could only mean one thing. Someone was watching him!

He quickly scanned the square. There were lights still burning in some of the windows, but he was sure the watcher was not stationed at one of them. Wherever he was – *whoever* he was – he was at ground level.

Paco strained his ears. There were noises in the distance – the sound of men talking noisily as they left a bar, the creak of wheels as someone pushed a handcart along a nearby street – but the square itself was silent.

No footsteps.

No one whistling to give himself courage in the dark.

Even the gentle bubbling of the fountain had ceased as the cold had gripped and the water turned to ice.

He patted his chest automatically, and felt his fingers make contact with the reassuring bulk of his pistol. He listened again, and this time he did hear something – a slight movement coming from one of the arcades.

As he drew his pistol, he suddenly realized that he had come alive again – that the inner strength he had been hoping for was back in control of him once more.

He took a series of slow, steady steps towards the arcade, raising his gun so the barrel would be pointing at somewhere on the watcher's trunk.

Five meters from the edge of the arcade he came to a halt, and crouched down to make himself a smaller target. If there was a time to speak, then this was that time, he told himself.

"I don't know who you are, or what you want," he said, "but I'm going to count to five and if you haven't come out by then, I'm going to start shooting."

He had reached three when the figure emerged from the darkness of the arcade, his arms raised high in the air.

Paco straightened up, and lowered his weapon.

"What are you doing here?" he asked.

Chapter Nineteen

Greg Cummings lowered his arms slowly and carefully, until the palms of his hands were flat against his sides.

"Why were you watching me?" Paco demanded. "Or was it Dolores you were watching?"

"It was you," Cummings said. "And I wasn't so much watching you as trying to decide whether or not it would be a good idea to come and talk to you. Would it make you nervous if I were to reach for my cigarettes?"

"No, it wouldn't," Paco said, holstering his pistol.

Cummings lit up a cigarette then said, "Look, I realize I'm probably the last person on earth you want to see right now, but I wanted to tell you how very sorry I am about what's happened to Cindy."

Cummings *looked* sorry, Paco thought. More than that – he looked devastated. His face was drawn, his lower lip was twitching, and from the redness around his eyes, he had probably been crying.

"How are you handling things?" the sandy-haired *yanqui* asked.

"Not well," Paco admitted. "Not well at all. I should have been there to protect her."

"We should *both* have been there," Cummings said. "The difference between us is that at least you have the consolation of knowing you were involved in important work when she was attacked, whereas all I was doing was…"

He let the sentence trail off into nothingness – but they both knew what he would have said.

Paco was beginning to feel something he would never have imagined he could feel for Greg Cummings. He was starting to *pity* the man.

"You can't hold yourself responsible," he told the *yanqui*. "She's my woman. I should have been looking after her."

"Cindy and I go back a long, long way," Cummings said, almost to himself. "I haven't seen her for years, but there wasn't a day that went by when I didn't think about her at least once."

"Were you lovers?" Paco asked, before he could stop himself.

Cummings shook his head, but in wonder, rather than denial.

"Do you really think it'd make you feel any better to know one way or the other?" he asked sadly.

"No," Paco said. "It probably wouldn't."

"I wish I still had my faith in God," Cummings said. "I wish I could believe that praying for Cindy would do some good – because that's the only thing any of us *can* do for her now."

"Who do you think attacked her?" Paco asked. "Do you think it's the same man who killed Samuel Johnson?"

"I'm no detective like you," Cummings replied. "All I am is a half-way competent academic from a hick college in the Midwest. But if you're really asking my opinion ..."

"I am."

" ... then I don't think that Sam was shot by one of the enemy. I think he was killed by one of our own."

"What makes you think that?" Paco asked the first *brigadista* he'd met who'd been prepared to admit there was even a faint possibility that one of the brigade might be involved in Johnson's murder.

"I arrived at the theory by a process of elimination," Cummings told him. "Once we've ruled out the idea of a killer coming in from outside, we're left with the inevitable conclusion that we've been nurturing a viper within our own bosom."

"And can you really rule out a killer from the other side of the front line?" Paco asked.

"Yes," Cummings said. "Yes, I think I can."

"Would you like to explain why?"

"The popular theory is that Sam was killed by the enemy, because he was a natural leader and the other *brigadistas* would have followed him anywhere. But who, outside the battalion, knew that was the case? If the fascists really had sent a killer in to damage us, they'd have instructed him to eliminate the commander or the commissar."

Unless, Paco thought, they had *excellent* military intelligence – unless someone from the battalion was working for the enemy. But when Cummings had used the words 'one of our own', it hadn't sounded as if it were a spy for the fascists he was talking about.

"Why should one of the *brigadistas* have killed Johnson?" he asked. "Because he was black?"

"No, *not just* because he was black. Because he was black *and* he bowed his head to no man. Because he was what the racists would call an 'uppity' nigger. Have you ever heard of the Ku Klux Klan, Inspector?"

"No," Paco admitted. "I haven't."

"It's a racist organization which was founded in the southern states just after *our* civil war. Its original aim was to keep the Negroes in their place by whatever means were available. Sometimes it simply drove the 'uppity' niggers out of town, but if that didn't work, it had no scruples about resorting to beatings – or even lynchings. It had pretty much disbanded by the end of the 1860s, when what we call Reconstruction ended, but around fifteen years ago, the Klan began to raise its ugly head once again. And it had tremendous – almost unbelievable – success. By 1924, it was estimated to have five million members."

Paco whistled softly. Any organization with five million members had a great deal of power. But he still did not see where Cummings was leading him.

"In the old days, back in the last century, the Klan was solely against the colored people. Any Jews, Catholics or recent immigrants who wanted to join it were welcome to do so," the *yanqui* continued. "But the new Klan is a very different matter. It's anti-Catholic, anti-Semitic and anti-foreign as well."

"So if it's anti-foreign and anti-Semitic …" Paco said.

"I'm getting to that," Cummings promised him. "By the late '20s, membership had fallen off dramatically again, and that's when it realized it had to find itself a new enemy. And it has – the new enemy is the communists. It's so much against Joe Stalin and his henchmen that I half-expected it to send volunteers over here to fight for General Franco."

"Because even though he's a Catholic and a foreigner, he's still not half as bad as the Reds?"

"Exactly."

"But it didn't send any volunteers?"

"Not as far as I know. But say that it had decided to go about things in another way entirely."

"What other way?"

"Say it had decided to infiltrate one of its members into the Abraham Lincolns, with the aim of destroying the brigade from the inside. If it could pull that off, think what a great propaganda coup it would have on its hands! Politics is only about words, its leaders could claim, but the Klan is about *action* – striking a decisive blow against the Godless Commies would be proof of that. Membership back home would soar!"

"Yes, I can see it," Paco admitted.

"But how could they strike that blow? There'd be no better way to cause suspicion and division in the Lincolns' ranks than by killing somebody. And if someone had to die, who would it give a Klansman more satisfaction to kill than an 'uppity' nigger?"

"You're saying that one of these Klansman is actually here?"

"I'm saying it's certainly a *possibility*."

Maybe Cindy's mind had been working along the same lines. Paco thought back to other cases he'd investigated – cases in which a casual remark had seemed innocuous at the time, but later, when he considered it, had come to have great significance. Was it possible that the same thing had happened to Cindy – that while she was working with Felipe on the *brigadistas'* statements, she'd suddenly

161

realized that some word or phrase she'd heard in the council chamber could only have been uttered by a member of the Klan? And might not the Klansman himself have realized the same thing, and, knowing that he'd given himself away, decided to silence Cindy before she could relay her suspicions to Paco?

"If this man really exists, do you have any idea who he might be?" Paco asked.

Greg Cummings shook his head.

"You often fail to see things unless you're actively looking for them. I wasn't looking for a Klansman, because the idea that they might be involved in all this didn't even come to me until this morning."

"But now you *have* had the idea, would you be prepared to investigate further?"

"If I see a water pipe leaking, I call the plumber rather than trying to fix it myself," Greg Cummings said. "In this case, you're the expert, so wouldn't I be better leaving it up to you?"

"If your plumber was half-blind, he might still be able to fix the pipe, but he'd need leading to it," Paco countered. "I'm half-blind on this case. I don't speak your language – and even if I did, I have no idea what's a normal thing for a *yanqui* to say, and what isn't. Besides, the *brigadistas* don't trust me as they trust you. You can go where I can't. You can hear things that wouldn't be said when I was there. That's why I need your guidance."

Cummings turned the request over in his mind.

"I'll do what I can," he said finally.

"I'd appreciate it."

The American reached up with his hand and scratched his freckled nose.

"You don't like me much, do you, Inspector Ruiz?" he asked.

"I only met you yesterday," Paco said noncommittally. "I haven't really had time to form an opinion."

Cummings grinned disbelievingly.

"I might take a day or two to make my mind up about someone," he said. "That's the way I've been trained to think. But not you. You're a man of action. You form your opinions on the hoof. I admire you for that. In fact, there are any number of things I admire you for, and I'm not surprised that Cindy fell for you – though, I have to say, it seems as if it's still something of a surprise to you."

It was, Paco thought. He'd never quite got over how lucky he'd been – which was perhaps why it had been so easy for him to believe that she'd leave him for another man.

"Maybe now that I'm finally in Spain, I can become a man of action, too," Greg Cummings said reflectively. "Maybe the bookworm in me can finally throw off his yoke and know what it's like to be you."

"It's greatly over-rated," Paco told him.

Cummings grinned again.

"Perhaps you're right," he agreed. "Perhaps the grass always *is* greener on the other side of the fence." A somber expression came to his face. "I think I'll turn in for the night," he said. "And maybe before I go to sleep, I'll say a little prayer for Cindy – sort of give God one last chance to prove that He exists." He turned towards the barracks. "Goodnight, Señor Ruiz."

"Goodnight," Paco replied.

He watched the *yanqui* cross the square and wished he could bring himself to be fairer to the man. But he knew that he couldn't, because Cindy had been fond of Cummings long before she had been fond of him – and he would never be able to forgive the sandy-haired *yanqui* for that.

Chapter Twenty

Asuncion Muñoz and her niece, Concha Prieto, admitted Paco into the house and ushered him over to the bed. In the old days, this kind of work would have been left to the nuns, he thought. But now nuns were as scarce behind Republican lines as trade unionists were behind Nationalist lines – which was to say that if there were any there at all, they were in hiding.

He looked down at Cindy. She did not seem to have moved even a fraction of an inch since the last time he'd seen her.

"Has there been any change?" he asked in a whisper.

"No, but she looks very peaceful," Concha Prieto said, avoiding his eyes.

That was how they spoke of the dead, Paco told himself.

"It's hopeless, isn't it?" he asked.

And the moment the words were out of his mouth, he remembered that the doctor had told him comatose patients were sometimes aware of what was going on around them.

"I ... I didn't mean ... " he stammered. "Where there's life, there's always hope, isn't there?"

"Yes, whatever happens, we must never give up hope," Asunción Munoz said somberly.

Paco looked down at Cindy's pale face again.

Could she hear him? Had any of his words penetrated a mind which no longer had the power to order her limbs to move – or even her eyes to open?

"Would you give us a few moments alone, please?" he asked the two women.

Asunción and Concha nodded, and moved away from the bed. Paco knelt down and took Cindy's hand in his.

Why did it feel so lifeless and cold? he wondered anguishedly.

Was it because she'd already given up the struggle?

"Don't die, Cindy," he pleaded. "I know what I said earlier about it being hopeless, but that wasn't really *me* talking at all. Those were nothing but the words of a weak fool who had forgotten what a fighter you are. You *can* pull through if you really want to."

He studied her eyelids for even the slightest flicker which might show that she'd heard him, but there was none.

"I'm not asking for anything for myself," he continued. "If you want to leave me for someone else once you're back to normal – if you want a new life in which I have no part to play – that's fine. Just don't die."

There was still no reaction, and despite what the doctor said, he could not bring himself to believe that any of his words had got through to her. Wherever Cindy was – whatever thoughts and suspicions lay somewhere in her poor injured brain – there was simply no way she could be reached.

He felt like a man condemned to be shot at dawn, and who watches the sun slowly rising and begs it not to, even though he knows he is only wasting some of what little breath he has got left to him.

His legs felt as heavy as lead as he had to force himself to his feet. Asunción Munoz was standing by the door, waiting to let him out onto the street, but there was no sign of her niece.

"Has Señorita Prieto gone home?" he asked, more to have something to say than because he was interested in the answer.

Asunción Munoz shook her head.

"Concha's not feeling very well, so she's just stepped outside for a breath of fresh air. But she'll be back – don't worry about that. We'll look after your *novia* as if she were one of our own."

"And if there's any change, you'll tell me about it right away – even if it's the middle of the night and you have to wake me up?"

165

"Of course I will," Asunción Munoz assured him – but from the expression on her face she appeared to think it unlikely that his night's sleep would need to be interrupted.

A man who has just seen the woman he loves on the verge of death should not go back to his empty bed without a drink inside him. Paco thought as he entered the bar to which Greg Cummings had taken him to the night before.

As on the previous evening, there were a number of *brigadistas* sitting at the tables, but it was the young Spaniard at the bar who immediately caught Paco's attention. Standing so close to a group of older men, Luis Prieto at first gave the impression of a child pretending to be an adult. But there was nothing childlike about the work-hardened muscles which bulged from under his overalls, nor did the troubled expression on his face suggest he still viewed the world through a child's optimistic eyes.

Paco walked over to the counter.

"You've nearly finished your wine," he said, glancing down at the young peasant's glass. "Can I buy you another one?"

"I don't accept drinks from policemen who go around poking their noses in where they're not wanted," Luis Prieto said aggressively.

Then, suddenly, the fire left his eyes, and was replaced by a look of pity which Paco was growing all too familiar with.

"I'm ... I'm sorry," the young man stuttered. "I forgot for a moment that you ... that your *novia* ... How ... how is she?"

"It's too early to say for sure how it will turn out, but it was good of you to ask," Paco said kindly.

"I ... I didn't mean ... I don't believe in kicking a man when he's down," Luis Prieto continued, still confused and embarrassed. "I ... Yes, thank you, I'll have another glass of wine."

Paco ordered a wine for Luis, and a brandy for himself.

"Do you know any of the other *brigadistas* – apart from Samuel Johnson?" the ex-policeman said, once the drinks had been served.

"What makes you ask that?" Luis Prieto replied, suspicion rapidly replacing embarrassment.

166

"No real reason," Paco said, telling a policeman's lie. "I was just wondering whether you disliked *yanquis* in general, or whether it was Sam Johnson in particular that you couldn't stomach."

"I used to like Sam," Luis Prieto muttered. "I admired him. But that was before …"

"Before what?"

"Just before."

"So *did* you meet any of the other *brigadistas*?" Paco asked, returning to his original question.

"Yes, Sam brought some of them to our house. He thought it was important that the villagers and the *brigadistas* should get to know one another."

"Why?"

"He said that was the only way we would really learn that wherever we were from, whatever the color of our skin, and no matter how rich or poor we were, we were all united in the fight for justice and humanity."

That sounded very like the Sam Johnson he was building up a picture of, Paco thought.

"Which *brigadistas* did he bring to your house?" he asked.

Luis Prieto looked around the bar.

"For a start, *they* came quite often," he said, pointing towards a table where Bill Turner, Sean O'Brien and Nat Johnson, the three men who had been Samuel Johnson's closest friends, were sitting.

"Anybody else?"

"There was a small, stocky man. I think he's Jewish."

"Mannie Lowenstein?"

"Yes, that's his name."

"Any others?"

"A very big man, with tattoos on his arms. He was called Donald-something-or-other. And a man with pale red hair called Greg Cummings. He speaks very good Spanish. When he came to the house, he would translate what the others had said for us."

"But he didn't always come with the rest?"

167

"No. He was only there two or three times."

"And the other times? Did you still try to talk, even though you didn't have a translator?"

"Yes. Sam said it would be difficult, since they spoke little Spanish and we spoke no English, but that we must make the effort. So we spoke with our hands, and with the help of the dictionary, and we did somehow manage to understand each other a little."

"What did you talk about?"

"Many things," Luis Prieto said, evasively.

"Such as?"

"The war. Farming. Our families."

"Did you ever talk to any of them about the way the Negroes are treated in the United States?"

The young peasant fixed his eyes on the far corner of the room.

"I don't think so."

"Yet you seem to know something about it."

"I don't know what you mean."

"The last time we met, you told me that Negroes who stepped out of line were lynched, and that you thought it was a good idea."

"I was upset. I didn't mean it."

"Not only that, but I got the impression that whoever told you about it thought that it was a good idea, as well."

"You're wrong!" Luis Prieto protested.

"Am I?" Paco asked. "Or could it be that I'm right – and you're ashamed to admit it?"

Luis Prieto made no answer, but continued to stare at the corner.

"Look at me," Paco said.

"Why should I?"

"Because that is what men do. We are not dogs who look away. When we talk to one another, it is done face to face."

Luis Prieto reluctantly turned towards him.

Paco waited until their eyes were locked, then said, "Did any of the *brigadistas* ever mention an organization called the Ku Klux Klan to you?"

168

Luis Prieto blinked, then picked up his glass and knocked back the remains of his wine.

"I have to go home now," he said.

"You have heard that name before, haven't you?" Paco persisted.

"My father will be waiting for me. He needs help to get up to his bed," Luis Prieto said.

And before Paco could press him any further, the young man had turned and fled the bar.

A man in his position was entitled to one brandy, Paco thought, but two would have been giving in to weakness, and when he had finished the glass he had bought to keep Luis Prieto company, he paid his bill and left the bar.

The streets were even quieter than they had been earlier, for though peasants liked to drink, they were also early risers.

Paco made his way up the steep street towards the Plaza Mayor. He did not hurry, because there was nothing to hurry for. All that awaited him in his lonely room was a bed which had seemed barely big enough for Cindy and himself, but would be a vast empty ocean without her.

He thought of the Prieto family – the father, the son and the daughter – and the different ways in which they had chosen to react to Samuel Johnson's murder.

He wondered if Greg Cummings' theory could be more than a theory – if a hateful *yanqui* racist organization really had managed to infiltrate the International Brigade with the sole purpose of destroying it. If it had – and if it succeeded – then it would also be helping to destroy the Spain that he long ago accepted he would probably eventually give his own life for.

More thoughts flashed through his mind in quick succession as he climbed the cobbled street.

Had Ted Donaldson really been as drunk as he claimed to have been on the night of the murder?

What possible reason could Mannie Lowenstein have had for staying in the empty barracks instead of celebrating the *fiestas* with all his comrades?

169

And was Commissar James Clay telling the truth when he said that he had no motive for killing Samuel Johnson?

Paco had almost drawn level with Dolores McBride's house, and he could see that a light was still burning on the upper floor, in what was probably her bedroom. The investigation had become more and more complicated as the day had progressed, and he felt a sudden strong temptation to knock on her front door and tell her that he wished to discuss it with her, as he would once have discussed it with Cindy.

But he knew that whatever he tried to persuade himself now, the complexities of the investigation would not be the real reason for his call.

If he did knock on her door, and she answered dressed only in her trench coat – as he was sure she would – then all thoughts of the murder would melt away immediately and he would seek nothing more than a brief escape from his misery which, even beforehand, he could only think of as cowardly.

He had carried on walking as he had wrestled with himself, and now that his feet had taken him beyond Dolores McBride's front door, he felt his desires slowly begin to ebb away. He stopped to light a Celtas, confident that danger was past.

Mankind was rarely given the choice of whether to continue existing or not, he thought. One man might decide to take another's life, a second might choose to end his own, but for most of humanity, death came when it – and it *alone* – was ready. He wished that were not so. He wished that he could be given the power over life and death for just one moment, so that if *someone* really had to die, he could decree that it would not be Cindy but himself.

Chapter Twenty-one

The watery morning sun hung uncertainly in the sky, as if it had only climbed so far through a tremendous effort, and now was wondering whether it could summon up the strength to go any farther.

Looking at it shining weakly through the cafeteria window, Paco knew just how the sun felt. A man should not have to begin an important round of interrogations after a night like the one he'd been through.

It had been a night in which he had prayed for sleep to come and numb his conscious mind, only to discover, when he did finally drift off, that his unconscious had been occupied by a malevolent demon bent on destroying what was left of his sanity.

Cindy had died a hundred times in his dreams. Each time her death had been more terrible than the last – and each time the demon had pointed the finger of guilt more surely in his direction. He had awoken with a blinding headache and a belief that even the simplest of tasks was beyond him. Yet he had eventually forced himself to climb out of bed because, like the sun, he was caught up in an inevitable process which he had no choice but to see through to the end.

He glanced around the cafeteria table at the three people who were waiting for him to speak. Dolores McBride sat at his elbow, her dark eyes alive with energy and sensuality. Next to her was Felipe, already enthusiastically attacking the plate of *churros* which lay in front of him. And directly opposite Paco was Mannie Lowenstein, sipping, almost birdlike, from his cup of coffee.

"Shall we begin?" Paco asked.

Even without waiting to be asked a question, Lowenstein started to talk, and as he spoke a slow smile began to play on his lips.

"He says that he's been interrogated by the police more times than he cares to remember," Dolores translated. "They've used rubber hoses and sleep deprivation, but they've never been so brutal as to offer him a cup of coffee before."

Paco forced a smile to his face. Suspects often made jokes, he reminded himself. They did it to convince their interrogators – and perhaps themselves – that they were not intimidated by their predicament. Or else they did it in an attempt to create a bond of friendship with the man on the other side of the table – on the other side of the fence!

But Paco did not think Mannie Lowenstein had made his joke for either of those reasons. The *brigadista* did not seem to be intimidated, nor eager that the others should like him. There appeared to be only one reason he had made his comment – and that was that he found his situation genuinely amusing.

"Ask Señor Lowenstein to tell us about himself," Paco said.

Dolores translated his words, then listened to his reply.

"He says that's a pretty tall order," she said when he'd finished. "He doesn't see himself as a particularly complicated man, but, even so, there is a great deal he *could* say. He suggests it would save us all a lot of time if you were to be more specific – if you were to spell out exactly *what* it is you want to know."

I want to know what makes people like him tick, Paco thought. I want to know what made him leave his home and family to come to a foreign country at war with itself – a country where, chances are, he'll be killed.

"Ask him why he joined the Communist Party in the first place," he said, using the question as a key to open doors to other areas, but aware that he was probably also opening the floodgates to a stream of ideological jargon and slogans.

"My parents both died in the big influenza epidemic of 1912, and

I was brought up in the Brooklyn Jewish Orphans' Asylum," Mannie Lowenstein said. "There are two basic lessons you quickly learn in an orphanage – at least there were in that particular institution. Would you like to know what they are?"

Lowenstein's outburst in the council chamber had been misleading. The *brigadista* was not the volatile and nervous man that he had appeared then. Quite the contrary, Paco decided – he was one of the coolest and most self-contained men he had ever met.

"What were the lessons you learned in the orphanage?" Paco asked, since this appeared to be what was expected of him.

"The first was impressed on us by the people who ran the orphanage – and it was to avoid self-pity," Lowenstein told him. "Sure, we'd lost our parents. But at least we ate well. At least we had decent clothes on our backs. And that made us luckier than a hell of a lot of other people."

"And the second lesson?"

"That one we *weren't* taught. It was just something we kind of picked up from the other kids. It was both the simplest and possibly the most fundamental lesson I'll ever learn. And it was this. We either all hang together or pretty damn soon we'll be hanging separately."

"So you became a member of the Communist Party as soon as you left the orphanage, did you?"

Lowenstein smiled. "No, it was a much longer spiritual journey than that. The orphanage got me a job in a clothing company. I was just a go-fer at first, but I took some classes in night school and soon became the chief clerk. From the start, I was involved in charity work – and there was plenty of that to do once the Depression had started to bite – but I voted on a straight Democratic ticket, because I believed that the Democrats were for the working man. It was the evictions which taught me how wrong I'd been, and got me involved with the Communist Party."

"The evictions?" Paco repeated. "What were they?"

* * *

There were thousands – perhaps hundreds of thousands – of families living in rented apartments in New York City in the late twenties. The accommodation was often mean and cramped, but at least it sheltered them from the elements – and as long as they had that basic protection, there was room for hoping for something better in the future. The Wall Street Crash destroyed that hope. Men lost their jobs, and without their jobs they could no longer pay the rent. The landlords called the sheriff's department, and the sheriff had no alternative but to throw the defaulters out onto the street.

Lowenstein would walk home from work and see them there – whole families sitting on the sidewalk, surrounded by their few pathetic sticks of furniture. There were few variations in their expressions. The men all looked crushed – they had strived to support their families, and they had failed. The women gazed bleakly into the road, seeing not the houses across the street but the impossibility of the task which lay ahead of them.

And the children?

The children played, as children will, but their parents' desperation was starting to infect them, too, and after a while, though they still ran and shouted, they were doing no more than going through the motions.

"Do you have any idea what I'm talking about here, Inspector'?" Lowenstein asked.

Paco nodded gravely. He remembered the evictions he had seen in his childhood, when poor peasant families were thrown off their handkerchief-sized pieces of property by the *guardia civil*, working at the behest of the village money lender, and he recalled how those families had been forced to wander the countryside looking for casual seasonal work and sleeping wherever they could find shelter.

"It used to break my heart to see them like that," Lowenstein said. "But what could I do? Maybe I could have gone short myself, and scraped the rent together for one family. But what about the rest? I couldn't support them all."

Then the day had come which had changed his life forever. He had seen yet another poor family cast out onto the sidewalk. The mother had been clutching a baby – with huge eyes and a hacking cough – to her scrawny chest, like so many had done before her, yet in her eyes there were signs of hope. And the source of that was the young men and young women who were taking their furniture back up the stairs. Cheerful young men and women! Optimistic young men and women! Purposeful young men and women!

"They were members of the local branch of the Young Communist League," Lowenstein explained to Paco, "and, unlike me, they were not just feeling pity – they were doing something to help these poor, oppressed people."

"But what did they achieve in the long run?" Paco asked. "Wouldn't the landlord just have the furniture taken out again?"

"That's exactly what they usually did. But the YCL would take it back into the house a second time! And a third! And a fourth if that was what it took! And eventually, the landlord would decide that, given the pitiful amount of rent he was losing, it wasn't worth his effort to push things any further. This was a fine example of the unity through strength I'd always believed in actually *working*! I went straight down to the Party's office and asked how I could join."

"How long had you been a member of the Communist Party before you were ordered to come to Spain?" Paco asked.

"Ordered!" Dolores McBride repeated. "I told you, they weren't ..."

"Just ask the question," Paco said firmly.

"No one from the Party ordered us to come to Spain," Lowenstein said. "It was a privilege that had to be won."

"Won?"

"Sure. The Party's not rich, and it simply couldn't afford to pay the expenses of sending *everybody* who wanted to fight the fascists. So it had to weed out the ones who would be least effective. There was a pretty tough medical for openers. Then we all had to appear before the selection board and convince it that we'd have more to contribute than some of the other volunteers. Usefulness, not belief, was the key to being accepted – which is why some very good communists were turned down, and why some guys who would never have joined the Party in a million years are here now."

Men like Greg Cummings, Paco thought – liberals who the Party normally held in contempt, but who would probably do a good job of fighting against Franco's army.

"As a matter of fact, I met quite a few of my old friends while I was being examined by the board," Lowenstein continued. "Kids I'd grown up with in the Brooklyn Jewish Orphans' Asylum. They'd come pretty much to the same conclusion that I had – that we have to fight fascism now, before it was allowed to get any stronger. Several of those guys are serving on the front at this very moment – including three who are brothers – and not more than half of them are communists."

"Ask Señor Lowenstein why he didn't join in the *fiestas*," Paco told Dolores. "Ask him why he's one of the few men in the battalion who can't produce an alibi for the time Samuel Johnson was murdered."

Dolores translated the question, and Lowenstein shook his head as he gave his reply.

"He says it's a personal matter," the journalist translated.

"Tell him that there's absolutely no such thing as 'a personal matter' in a murder investigation."

Another short exchange followed.

"He says that he liked Sam Johnson – more than that, he admired him – and that he would never have killed him. But if you want to believe that's what he did, then there's nothing he can do about it."

"Ask him about the argument he had with Ted Donaldson," Paco said.

Lowenstein's answer took two or three minutes. There was an earnest look on his face as he spoke, and several times he gestured with his hands.

"He says that the argument with Donaldson was nothing but a mistake," Dolores translated, when he'd finished.

"That's it?" Paco asked, wishing that he'd had Cindy, not Dolores, doing his translating for him. "All those words – all that explanation – and that's all he told you?"

Dolores sighed.

"You wanted to know what he said, and that's the essence of the message."

"And what's the *full* message?"

"He says that we all acquire prejudices as we're growing up, but hopefully, the longer we are members of the Party, the more we can learn to overcome them. We should tolerate our comrades' efforts to shed their past lives, and not be over-critical while they are going through what is often a difficult process. He says that what Comrade Donaldson was saying about the Party's attitude toward the Negroes was a perfectly accurate statement, and that he, himself, should not have clouded the issue by speaking about something else."

These people were almost like the Spanish clergy had been in the old days. Paco thought. They might argue furiously amongst themselves, but if anybody from the outside attacked one of them, they would soon close ranks and retreat behind a shield of dogmatism.

"Is he now claiming that Ted Donaldson isn't really anti-Semitic after all?" he asked.

"He is saying that there are no faults which cannot be corrected with the proper application of Party discipline."

"What does he know about the Ku Klux Klan?"

Dolores shot Paco an astonished look.

"The Ku Klux Klan?" she said. "Why the hell do you want to know about the KKK? I'm surprised you've even heard the name."

Nor would I have, if it hadn't been for Greg Cummings, Paco thought.

"Ask him," he said aloud.

Reluctantly, Dolores posed the question.

"Comrade Lowenstein says that the Klan is a hateful, hateful organization," the journalist translated. "He said it just like that – repeating 'hateful' twice. He says that all the water in the world could not wash the blood from its hands."

"Was he using the present tense, as you are?"

"Yes."

"So he thinks the Klan is still active?"

"In January last year, a Negro called Jerome Wilson was lynched in Franklington, Kentucky," Lowenstein said. "In March, Anderson Ward was lynched in Maringouin, Louisiana; Abe Young in Slayden, Mississippi; Reverend Brookins' daughter in Poinsett, Arkansas; the Reverend Allen in Hernando, Mississippi, and Mary Green in Mississippi County, Arkansas. Those are just a few of the names of the dead. I could produce many more. And though the Klan may deny it, its invisible hand was behind all those murders."

"And does it have an 'invisible hand' in the International Brigade?" Paco asked Dolores.

"This isn't just crazy!" Dolores McBride exploded. "It's also in incredibly bad taste."

"Most murders do tend to involve some degree of bad taste," Paco countered. "Please ask him the question."

Lowenstein listened to the translation, then, shook his head.

"That is impossible," he said.

"*Es imposible*," Dolores translated.

"I know what he said," Paco replied.

But he did not think that Lowenstein looked entirely convinced by his own answer.

"What was your impression of all that?" Paco asked Felipe, when they were alone again.

The fat constable leant back in his chair, rubbed his more than ample stomach, and burped loudly.

"I think that if you are questioning the chickens on the activities of the fox, it would be better to ask them about it yourself, rather than rely on another chicken to convey the information for you," he said.

Paco grinned briefly, then was serious again.

178

"You're saying that you don't trust Dolores."

"I am sure that Señorita McBride is an honest woman as far as she is able to be," Felipe replied. "But her interests are not the same as ours. Our duty is to catch the murderer. *Her* duty – as she sees it – is to protect the battalion."

Paco nodded. "And what she doesn't see – what none of them see – is that the best way to protect the battalion is to tackle its problems head-on, rather than pretend they don't exist. They all have their own suspicions – though they're not prepared to admit it – and the longer we take to solve the crime, the stronger their suspicions will grow, until, in the end, they tear the battalion apart." He lit up a Celtas. "What did you make of Lowenstein's reaction to my question about the Ku Klux Klan?"

"He doesn't seem to like it very much," Felipe said.

"No, he doesn't." Paco agreed. "But how much does he actually know about it?"

"He seemed very well informed to me."

"He had the statistics at the tips of his fingers, but that proves nothing. You're a city boy from Madrid, yet you talk glibly about foxes and chickens, when you've probably never seen a fox. And Lowenstein, who's from New York City, talks just as glibly about the Ku Klux Klan – and he's probably never seen one of those particular foxes, either. So what we need to do is talk to a real country boy."

"And where will we find one?"

"Dolores is bringing Ted Donaldson to talk to us right this minute."

"But he's a stevedore from New Jersey!" Felipe protested.

"He is *now*," Paco said. "But I don't think he always was. I used to be a country boy myself, don't forget – and however long it might be since we've all left the *campo* behind us, I can still pick other country boys out of the crowd."

179

Chapter Twenty-two

Dolores McBride was not a small woman by any means, but framed in the cafeteria doorway next to Ted Donaldson, she seemed almost tiny. Yet it was clearly Dolores who was in charge, and as she took Donaldson's arm and led him across to the table where Paco and Felipe were sitting, it seemed almost as if she were dragging him.

The journalist took the chair she had been occupying earlier, and indicated to the stevedore he should take the one Mannie Lowenstein had been sitting on.

"Señor Donaldson wishes to make a personal statement before the questioning begins," she said.

Paco sighed.

These *yanquis*! he thought. They saw themselves as being informal – and in many ways they were – but in some respects they were more bureaucratic than the most pedantic official in the most procedure-bound government ministry in Madrid.

"Let's hear this statement, then," he said.

"Comrade Donaldson regrets the remarks which he made in the council chamber," Dolores said. "He regards Leon Trotsky as a traitor to the world revolution, but the fact that he is of Jewish origin has no relevance to that fact. As Comrade Stalin has taught us, if a man or woman is prepared to dedicate himself or herself to the revolution, then background is immaterial."

To use Felipe's phrase, it was like a chicken talking for a chicken, Paco thought – with neither of them prepared to admit that one of their fellow chickens might just be a fox in disguise. However much Dolores might despise Greg Cummings as the liberal – though she apparently had no complaints over him as a lover – the sandy-haired man at least seemed capable of examining possibilities the rest of the *brigadistas* would prefer to shrug off.

"I'd like Señor Donaldson to tell us a little of his personal history, if he doesn't mind," Paco said.

"Ted has been a shop steward in the stevedores union for several years," Dolores said, without even looking at Donaldson. "He was one of the leaders of the last major dock strike. He's been arrested several times, and beaten up on three occasions – once by federal marshals and twice by the Pinkertons. He was accepted almost immediately when he volunteered to fight in Spain."

"Let him speak for himself," Paco said, irritatedly.

Dolores shrugged in an attempt to mask her own irritation.

"If that's what you really want," she said.

"It is."

"It's just that I know his history – he's going to be one of the people in my book – and I thought I'd save a little time by giving you the details myself."

"Ask him where he was born," Paco said firmly.

"Why should you want to know that?"

"Because I do."

Dolores asked the question, listened to the answer, then said, "He was born in Moultrie, Georgia."

"That's in the southern part of the United States, isn't it?"

"Sure it is. So what?"

"Is his home town close to the sea?"

The journalist laughed.

"Hell, no. I'd guess it must be well over a hundred miles from the ocean."

"So ask him how he became a stevedore."

"There was no work in his home town," Dolores said, when Donaldson had answered. "He drifted to New York. There was

181

employment going on the docks, and they like to employ big guys like him. It's as simple as that."

"Ask him what he knows about the Ku Klux …"

"Oh, for God's sake, not that again," Dolores interrupted, exasperatedly. "I don't know who put that crazy idea into your head, but it's going to lead you absolutely nowhere."

He was almost on the point of telling her that the information came from her lover, but at the last moment he held back. He needed Cummings' cooperation again, and he was likely to lose it if Dolores – because she was furious with him – refused to let the sandy-haired man into her bed.

"How do you know my questions won't lead anywhere?" he asked Dolores. "Have you suddenly become some kind of detective?"

"I know because I know *the Party* better than you do. We're not the bunch of amateurs that you seem to think we are. The guys who selected the *brigadistas* in New York knew their job. They would never let some Negro-hating Klansman slip through their net."

"You wouldn't have thought they'd have let anyone anti-Jewish slip through it, either," Paco countered. "But we're both well aware that Donaldson has said things against the Jews."

"And he regrets them."

"That won't make the words – or the thoughts that were behind them – go away."

"You don't understand us at all," Dolores told him. "You'll *never* understand us."

"You're saying that before you even ask him the question, you're sure he knows nothing about the Klan?"

"We're Americans! We all know *something* about the Klan," Dolores said, getting angry. "We all know something about the Red Indians and the California Gold Rush, too. But so what?"

"Did he talk to Luis Prieto about the Red Indians or the California Gold Rush, when he was at the Prieto house?" Paco demanded.

"I don't expect he did."

"Did he talk to Luis Prieto about the Klan?"

It had been a shot in the dark, but from the look on Donaldson's face when he heard the words 'Klan' and 'Luis Prieto' so close together, Paco knew that it had hit the target squarely in its center.

The big stevedore spoke.

"Comrade Donaldson says he did discuss the Klan with Luis Prieto – at least as far as was possible given the linguistic difficulties," Dolores said, the surprise evident in her voice.

"Why?"

"He wanted to make Luis aware that there is evil in the world far beyond the confines of Spain."

If that had really been his intention, he didn't seem to have had much success with Luis Prieto, Paco thought.

"What made him choose the Klan as an example of evil?" he asked.

"He saw it as a penance."

"A penance for what?"

The big stevedore spoke for some time, his voice low and his eyes fixed on the table.

When he had finished, Dolores said, "He wants to be honest with you, but first he wants your word that anything he tells you won't go beyond this table. He especially wants your assurance that it won't get back to the Party."

The Party! The Party! Wherever the journey started, it always ended up with the bloody Party!

"How could I tell the Party anything?" Paco asked. "I don't speak the language. So it's up to you, isn't it? If you're prepared to keep this big secret of his, then it's safe. If not, that's your choice."

"I shall tell no one," Dolores said somberly. "I shall keep it to myself because I'm prepared to believe that any man, especially a man who is being guided by the Party, can change."

"And what, exactly, has Señor Donaldson changed from?"

Dolores pursed her brow.

"I want to tell it as much in his words as possible, so you can get the same flavor as I did."

"Understood."

"Ted's first job, back in Moultrie, Georgia, was as a handyman. Then one day his boss fired him, and replaced him with a colored man."

"Why?"

"Because the colored man was prepared to work for less money, of course."

"Couldn't he have offered to take less himself?"

Dolores gave Paco a pitying look.

"It was bad enough he'd been doing the same work as a 'nigger', without being paid the same wages as one," she said. "Anyway, a couple of weeks after he'd lost his job, the Klan held a meeting – a konklave, they called it – just outside his town. Whole families went to it. They took picnic lunches with them. Even the kids were wearing Klan robes and hoods. There were speeches and games in the afternoon. Then, as night fell, the Klan marched down the main street of the town. He says there were thousands of them, from all over the state. There were five or six bands in the parade, but the only musicians who were playing their instruments were the drummers – and all they did was pound out a relentless marching rhythm which sent shivers down his spine. Some of the Klansmen carried burning torches. They looked like they were afraid of nothing and nobody. They acted as if they owned the world."

"So he signed up?"

"Yes, he signed up. Hell, Paco, when you're dirt poor it's nice to find something – anything – which makes you feel important."

"Like the Communist Party?"

Dolores shook her head, almost despairingly.

"Do you want to hear the story or not?"

"I want to hear it."

"The Klan got Ted a new job – in a grocery store. One day the storeowner accused a colored girl of stealing a bag of sugar. She denied it, but, of course, nobody believed her. That night the local Klan went to her shack, dragged her from her bed, and strung her up from the nearest tree. Ted didn't take part in the actual lynching, but he was there to watch, and to give it his support. The next day, when he was clearing up in the store, he found the bag of sugar. It had fallen behind the flour sacks. He says he still dreams about it."

"Dreams about what?" Paco asked, unremittingly. "About hanging a Negro? Or about hanging one who, on that *particular* occasion, wasn't guilty?"

"Are you really such a hard-hearted man?" Dolores asked him. "Aren't you ever prepared to forgive anyone for their mistakes?"

The rebuke was well deserved, Paco thought. Everybody *did* make mistakes. He had certainly made enough of his own.

"I'm sorry," he said. "Tell me the rest."

"Ted couldn't bear to stay in his hometown any longer. He jumped on the next freight train through, and ended up in New York. You can pretty much fill in the rest yourself. He joined the union, then the Party, and when he saw the chance to do some good – coming here – he signed up without a second thought."

"Tell me why he hates Jews," Paco said.

"He doesn't hate them."

"Tell me why other people – people like Mannie Lowenstein – might *think* he's prejudiced against them."

"He was influenced by those around him. Some stevedores are anti-Semitic. Not all – but enough. Now he realizes that that prejudice is just as irrational – and just as unfair – as the one he used to have against the coloreds."

"He's sure he's got over his feelings about the Negroes, is he?" Paco asked skeptically.

"You know that Sam Johnson led a party into Albacete to get some ammunition, don't you?" Dolores asked.

"Yes, I've heard that story."

"And you know that the French clerk there didn't want to give the ammunition to them? That the two French *brigadistas* on guard raised their rifles, and the clerk told Sam that if he didn't leave, he'd be shot?"

"Yes."

"And that it seemed like he really meant it? Which was when one

185

of the other *brigadistas* stood between Sam and the guards, and said that if they wanted to shoot Sam, they'd have to shoot him first."

"Where is all this leading?" Paco asked impatiently.

"Can't you see already? The *brigadista* who put his own life at risk to protect Sam's was Ted Donaldson."

Chapter Twenty-three

The cobbled street outside the cafeteria still glistened with a sheen of early morning frost, though small icicles which had formed on the guttering and window frames were slowly dripping away their frozen lives onto the ground below.

It was that time of the morning when the men had gone off to work, the women were cleaning their homes, and only the aged, after a lifetime of toil, found themselves with time on their hands. Old women, dressed entirely in black, ventured cautiously out of their houses, walking with exaggerated care to avoid slipping. Old men in flat caps prodded the ground in front of them experimentally with the gnarled walking sticks they held in their gnarled hands. All of them, men and women alike, sniffed the air and gave small shudders. Though the weak winter sun had made the air a little kinder than it had been earlier, spring seemed a long, long time away.

Paco and Fat Felipe, ignoring the hazards which older, more brittle bones dared not, strode down the Calle Mayor towards the city walls.

"Imagine hanging somebody just for stealing a bag of sugar," Felipe said. "A bag of *sugar* – for God's sake!"

Paco nodded in agreement, but his mind was elsewhere. He was about to make his second visit to Cindy's sickbed that morning.

The first time, she had seemed much the same as she had been the night before. Was that a good thing, or a bad thing? he agonized.

If she had groaned or cried out, might not that have shown that her poor damaged brain was doing *something* – that it was at least *trying* to claw its way back to the surface? Or could such a groan not equally have been her final protest against the injustices of life before her soul sank into final oblivion?

The two policemen turned onto Calle Pez. Cindy was only a few doors away now – hovering between life and death. They reached Asunción Muñoz's front door. Someone – probably Asuncion herself – had made an attempt to wash away the bloodstains, but there was still enough of a trace to see where Cindy had fallen, and looking at the stain, Paco felt a fresh onslaught of guilt rush through his body.

"You can't blame yourself, *jefe*," Felipe said softly.

"Can't I?" Paco demanded. "Then who can I blame?"

"The man who attacked her."

"He wouldn't have been able to attack her if I hadn't first brought her to San Antonio! He wouldn't have been able to attack her if I'd been by her side, protecting her, as I should have been. She's my woman. She's my responsibility. She's my *failure*."

"*Jefe* …"

"I don't want to talk about it anymore," Paco said firmly. "Do you hear me? The subject is closed."

"Yes, *jefe*," Fat Felipe said meekly.

Paco knocked on the front door, but no one came to answer his call. He forced himself to wait patiently for at least half a minute, then knocked again. When there was still no muted noise of footsteps crossing a stone floor, he turned the handle – and discovered that the door was locked!

Despite the cold air which enveloped him, sweat began to drip from his forehead. People in small Spanish towns did not lock their doors in the daytime. Most of them did not even bother to lock them at night. Yet this door undoubtedly *was* locked.

Why was it locked?

Because the house was empty?

Or as a sign of respect for the dead body which was lying beyond the other side of the door?

While his mind grappled with his growing dread, his hands took independent action, forming fists and hammering desperately on the door.

"Take it easy, *jefe*," Felipe said worriedly.

"Go to hell!" Paco screamed, knowing he must be bruising his hands – and not giving a damn.

The window blind was rolled up, and a frightened white face peered out. Felipe glanced at Paco, and seeing that his boss had not even noticed, he bent his bulky body down to the level of the woman's face.

"It's only us," he mouthed.

Asunción Muñoz moved away from the window, and Felipe heard the sound of a key turning in the lock. He placed his heavy hand on his boss's shoulders, and pulled him away.

"The door's being opened at this very moment," the constable shouted. "Don't go charging straight in, or you'll knock Señora Munoz right across the *salon*."

The door swung open, and Paco looked through the gap at the bed. Concha Prieto was standing over Cindy and mopping the sick woman's brow with a damp cloth.

She wasn't dead! he thought, gasping with relief. She *couldn't* be dead – because Concha would not have wasted her time soothing the brow of a corpse.

He rushed across the room, then flung himself onto one knee by the side of the bed.

"I'm here, Cindy," he said, taking one of her hands between his two. "I'm right here beside you!"

"What the devil's been happening here?" Fat Felipe demanded, angry that his boss had been put through so much for no apparent reason. "Why was the bloody door locked?"

"It was locked because … because we were afraid," Asunción Muñoz stuttered.

"Afraid of what?"

"I … I was upstairs, looking after Concha …"

"I wasn't feeling well," Concha Prieto explained. "I needed to lie down."

"I heard a noise like that of the door catch being lifted, but I thought I was imagining it," Asunción Muñoz continued. "Then I heard footsteps. Very soft footsteps. I went out onto the landing, and called out, 'Who's down there?' Nobody answered, but then I heard the footsteps again. Louder this time – as if whoever it was had given up the idea of being quiet."

"We both came downstairs as quickly as we could," Concha Prieto said. "The front door was wide open, but when I went out and looked down the street, it was deserted."

"So somebody came into the house," Felipe said impatiently. "What of it? Why build it up into a drama? There are always people around who take a morbid curiosity in looking at the sick. And of course whoever it was walked quietly – that's what you do instinctively when you're approaching an invalid. Then your call from the top of the stairs must have startled the visitor – who'd imagined up until that point that he was alone – and made him feel suddenly ashamed of himself for being so nosy. So he left the house as quickly as he could. Who wouldn't have done the same in his place? That's no reason to turn this place into a fortress, is it?"

"The pillow!" Asunción Muñoz said, pointing at the one which Cindy's head rested on.

"What about it?"

"We … we found it lying on the floor by the side of the bed," Concha Prieto said. "It couldn't have just fallen there – not with the weight of that poor girl's head pressing down on it. So whoever was in the room must have pulled it out from under her."

Felipe had not even been sure that his boss had been listening, but now Paco stood up again, and from the black look on his face, it was obvious that he had.

"There could have only been one reason for removing the pillow, couldn't there?" Paco said. "It was going to be a murder weapon. He intended to smother her with it!"

"Yes," Concha Prieto admitted. "That's what we think. That's why we locked the door."

Paco paced the floor, and Felipe watched in awed fascination as his boss transformed himself from the hysterical wreck he had been only moments earlier into the cold calculating professional who, against all odds, had arrested the killer of the headless corpse in the Atocha railway station.

Paco came to a halt. For perhaps thirty seconds he stood perfectly still, as if tuning his mind into the pulse of the room. Then he sniffed deeply. And with that sniff came an image of the *individualista* bar he had visited the previous afternoon.

"Are you on to something, *jefe*?" Felipe asked.

"You're supposed to be the one with the good nose," Paco said. "What can you smell?"

Felipe sniffed, just as his boss had done.

"Garlic," the fat constable said.

"What else?"

"Let me see. Cooking oil. Burnt olivewood. Soap."

"Those are the smells you'd expect to find here," Paco said. "But isn't there something else as well? Something which has no place at all in the house of a widow who lives alone?"

Felipe sniffed again.

"Cow shit!" he said decisively.

"Yes," Paco agreed grimly. "Cow shit!"

Chapter Twenty-four

Paco was striding down the street so rapidly that Felipe was finding it almost impossible to keep up with him. What was even worse, from the fat constable's viewpoint, was that he still had no idea where they were going – or why they were going there.

"Don't go jumping to any hasty conclusions, *jefe*." Felipe pleaded as he puffed. "You know you're usually terribly wrong when you start jumping to hasty conclusions."

"There are so many conspiracy theories floating around in this bloody case that I've been assuming that everything that's happened has had to be part of one of them," Paco said – furious with himself, and furious with the world in general. "So when Cindy was attacked, I automatically accepted that it had to have something to do with Samuel Johnson's murder."

"And didn't it?"

"I thought she must have discovered some clue which would lead me to the killer, and that's why he'd tried to silence her," Paco continued, talking more to himself than to his assistant. "But I was way off the mark. The real motive for the attack – which I would have seen a long time ago if the conspiracy theories hadn't been blinding me – is much simpler than that."

"And what is it?"

"If a coward wants to get his revenge on a man who's humiliated him, he doesn't take it out on that man himself – because he doesn't dare," Paco said. "So instead, he picks on someone weaker – someone he knows his enemy cares about. He hurts the enemy through hurting her."

"You're talking about Iñigo Torres!" Felipe exclaimed.

"Of course I'm talking about Iñigo Torres! He's the one who sabotaged Juan Prieto's tractor. Sneaking behind a woman and hitting her over the head is just his style."

"But why should he have tried to kill Cindy again this morning? Hadn't he already got his revenge on you with his first attack on her?"

"And what if she saw him before he hit her?" Paco asked. "If she regains – *when* she regains – consciousness, he knows she'll tell me who her attacker was, and then he's as good as dead."

They drew level with the *individualista* bar, and Paco pulled his pistol out of its holster.

"Don't do this now, *jefe*," Felipe pleaded. "Wait for half an hour and see if you still …"

"If you don't want to have any part of this, you can go now," Paco told him harshly.

"I wouldn't desert you. You know that."

"Then if you want to stay, don't get in my way."

Paco flung the bar door open, and stepped inside. The few customers who were sitting at the tables, drinking their mid-morning *cafés y copas*, looked up with startled expressions on their faces.

Paco's eyes swept the bar, and once he had made certain that Torres was not there, he leveled his pistol at the barman's chest.

"Where's Iñigo Torres!" he demanded.

The barman's eyes were wide with fright.

"I … I …think that he's … he's at his house."

"And no doubt he's got a solid alibi for the whole morning," Paco said. "Well, that won't do him any good!"

"I … I don't understand, señor."

"I'm going to see justice carried out," Paco told him. "Not government justice! Not even revolutionary justice. Ruiz's justice!"

"You're going to hurt him again?"

"I'm going to kill him!"

"But … but you can't do that. It … it wouldn't be fair to a sick man like him," the barman protested.

Paco lowered his weapon.

"A sick man?" he repeated.

"Yes, señor."

"And how long has he been sick?"

"Only a couple of hours. He was out working in the fields early this morning when his tractor suddenly turned over and rolled on top of him. Five of his ribs were crushed."

Luis Prieto sat alone in one of the *colectivista* bars, an untouched glass of *sol y sombra* in front of him. He seemed completely enveloped in his own thoughts, and did not even look up when the policeman from Madrid walked into the bar and sat down opposite him.

"Iñigo Torres has had an 'accident' out on his land," Paco said. "His tractor turned over."

"So I have heard," Luis replied.

"Exactly the same thing happened to your father, not so long ago," Paco pointed out.

"Are you saying that I was responsible for Torres' accident?" the young peasant demanded.

Paco laughed.

"Without proof? Of course not! But let us just say, for the sake of argument, that it *wasn't* an accident – and that you *were* responsible."

"Go on," the young peasant said cautiously.

"If that were the case, who could blame you? No one can prove that Torres sabotaged the collective's tractor in order to hurt your father, either, but everybody knows that he did. So if you'd decided to pay him back in the same coin, then most people – including me – would see it as no more than justice being served."

"A man should always protect his own family in any way he can," Luis Prieto said.

"And you're very close to your family, aren't you?" Paco asked. "Both your father *and* your sister mean a lot to you."

"What of it?"

"You didn't tell Concha what you were planning to do, did you?" Luis Prieto smiled.

"If, in fact, I was planning to do anything."

"If, in fact, you were planning to do anything," Paco agreed. "And the reason you didn't tell her was that you were afraid she'd try to talk you out of it. But once the deed was actually done, well, that was a different matter entirely. You felt the need to explain to her – perhaps even to justify your actions."

Luis Prieto's smile widened.

"She was the one who brought me up, and so she has always seen me as no more than her *little* brother," he said. "I wanted to tell her that I am not so little any more – that I have grown up enough to be able to defend the family honor."

"But she wasn't at home when you got back to boast of your triumph, was she? She'd already gone to your Aunt Asunción's house."

"You seem to know everything," Luis Prieto mumbled.

"No, far from it," Paco told him. "But a few things are finally starting to make sense to me." He lit up a Celtas. "You went to your Aunt Asunción's house yourself, didn't you?"

"Yes."

"Did you expect to find Concha alone?"

"Again, yes. I thought Aunt Asunción would have gone down to the market to do her shopping by then."

"When did you realize she hadn't?"

"Her coat was still hanging on the rack. And I thought I heard voices from upstairs."

"In order to see the coat and hear the voices, you must already have been inside the house."

"Yes, I was."

"And so you will have seen my *novia*."

"The *yanqui rubia*? Yes, of course I did."

"Tell me about her."

195

"What is there to tell? She was lying on the bed. She wasn't moving, but I could see that she was breathing."

"Think carefully before you answer the next question," Paco said. "Where was the pillow?"

"The pillow? It was under her head, of course. Where else would you expect it to be?"

So there had been two visitors to the house while Concha Prieto and Asunción Munoz had been upstairs, Paco thought. The first had been Concha's brother, Luis, bringing with him the typical peasant smell of cow dung. And then there had been the second, the one Asuncion had disturbed, who had tried to kill Cindy – and might well try again.

"You tell me that family is very important to you," Paco said. "Well, family is very important to me, too – and Cindy is my family."

The young peasant nodded gravely.

"You wish to find the man who hurt her, and punish him. That is only right."

"Yes. But my problem is that I can't look for him and guard her at the same time."

And she would *need* guarding – because if Iñigo Torres was not responsible for the attack on Cindy, then revenge was not the motive behind it.

And if not vengeance, then what?

The only theory which would still fit the facts was his original one – that someone wanted her dead not for who she *was*, but because of what she *knew*.

"I need someone to watch over Cindy for me," Paco said. "Someone I can trust."

"Perhaps one of the *brigadistas* might be willing to ..." Luis suggested.

Paco shook his head.

"Some of them are, no doubt, trustworthy. My problem is that I don't know *which* ones."

"So if you don't want them to guard her, then who?" Luis Prieto

196

began. Then his eyes widened with astonishment as he realized where Paco was heading. "Me! You want me to watch her!"

"Yes," Paco agreed.

"But how do you know you can trust *me*?"

"You have already shown me that you know the value of family, and that you are not afraid to take action when it is called for," Paco said. "I would feel safe if you – and any of your friends you can vouch for – were looking after her."

Luis Prieto shook his head.

"It's all very confusing," he said. "Today you put your trust in me. Yet only yesterday you seemed to think I might have been the one who had killed Sam."

"You certainly spoke about him as if you were glad he was dead," Paco pointed out.

"And I was wrong to ever have had such thoughts," Luis Prieto confessed. "I see that now."

"Did you get your ideas about stringing him up from a tree from Ted Donaldson?" Paco asked.

"What Donaldson said to me, he said in confidence," Luis replied, a sudden hard edge evident in his voice. "If I can't honor his trust, then why should you believe that I will honor yours? But you have still not answered my question – why has your attitude towards me changed since yesterday?"

"A great many things have become clearer since yesterday."

"For example?"

"Yesterday, I wondered what could have happened to make you change *your* attitude to Sam Johnson. He had been your friend, and now, even though he was dead, you saw him as your bitterest enemy. Why was that?"

"You tell me."

"I wondered about your sister, too. Unlike some women from this town, she has not lost a loved one at the front – yet her face bears the same signs of suffering as those who have. And why should such a healthy-looking girl keep feeling so ill? Then there was your father ..."

"What about him?"

"Why hadn't his attitude to Sam Johnson changed as yours had? It could only be because you knew something that he didn't. Put all those questions together, and there can be only one answer, can't there?"

"I suppose so," Luis Prieto agreed reluctantly.

"Your sister must have spoken to Sam, and explained her 'problem'. If he had run away after he had heard the news, you would have tracked him down and killed him like a dog."

"You are right. That is just what I would have done – or have died trying."

"But he didn't run away, did he? He stayed. And if he'd lived longer, I have no doubt he would have gone to see your father, and had a long and serious talk with him."

"Yes. I think you're right about that, too," Luis Prieto admitted.

"And so you were faced with a dilemma," Paco continued. "As a loving brother, you hated Sam Johnson for what he'd done. Yet you have gradually come to see that he cared as much about honor and responsibility as you do yourself, and that he was entitled to your respect."

"Are you saying I couldn't have killed him because I respected him?" Luis asked.

"Not exactly," Paco said. "In battle you could probably kill men you had come to respect, because that is what honorable men do to other honorable men in that situation. But the situation which you found yourself in was much more complicated, wasn't it?"

"*Much* more complicated," Luis Prieto agreed, almost mournfully.

"In a battle you stand face to face with your enemy and, for that moment, you are the only two people in the whole world who matter. In this case, there is also Concha and her wishes to consider. I do not think you could ever have brought yourself to kill the man your sister loved – and I'm absolutely certain you'd never have done it once you'd learned he was the father of her unborn child."

Chapter Twenty-five

The waiter placed the large bowl of steaming *garbanzos* in front of Felipe, and even before his hands were clear of it, the fat constable was attacking the chickpeas with his spoon.

"It is all right if I have something to eat, isn't it, *jefe?*" he asked Paco between mouthfuls.

"Why shouldn't it be?"

"It's just that you're not eating yourself."

"I'm not hungry," Paco said.

He had not been hungry since the moment Felipe had burst into Dolores McBride's house and told him Cindy had been hurt, and he did not feel as if he would ever re-discover his appetite again.

Felipe was different. He, too, was distressed by what had happened to the American woman, but he had never been one to let tragedy – even his own – get in the way of his love for food. Faced with the imminent prospect of facing a firing squad, the fat man would probably have polished off his last meal with gusto.

"We seem to be getting nowhere with this case," Paco said despairingly. "We have no more idea now who killed Samuel Johnson than we did when we stepped off the train in Albacete."

Felipe tore a chunk of bread from the large loaf which accompanied the chickpeas.

"Oh, it's not as bad as that." he said with the optimism that good food always brought him. "We may not be able to point to the murderer yet, but we certainly understand a lot more about the *yanquis.*"

"But all that understanding really amounts to is a realization that we don't understand them at all," Paco said.

"And we have suspects!" Felipe said, refusing to let his enthusiasm be dampened.

"By suspects, do you mean the *brigadistas* who don't have an alibi for the time when Johnson was shot?"

"That's right. You have to admit that's better than nothing."

But not much, Paco thought.

"Let's examine them one by one," he suggested. "Take Clay, the political commissar, first. Why would he want to become a killer?"

Felipe mopped some of the juice with his bread.

"Johnson made Clay very angry when he took some of the other *brigadistas* into Albacete without permission, and practically *stole* the ammunition from the brigade warehouse."

"It's true that Clay is very much the kind of man who always likes to go through the proper channels," Paco agreed.

"There's more to it than that," Felipe continued. "You know what the French are like – Commander Marty may have felt his honor had been slighted. So perhaps he made a deal with Señor Clay."

"What kind of deal?"

"Clay agreed to kill Johnson to avenge Marty. And in return, Marty promised him regular supplies, so there'd never be any need for him to look like such an idiot again."

"I don't think so," Paco said.

"Why not? How often have we heard all these people say that the fate of the individual is of no importance? Ammunition is of more value to the battalion than the life of one man, so perhaps Commissar Clay decided to sacrifice Johnson for the general good."

"I still don't see what Commander Marty would have got out of Johnson's death."

"As I said, his honor had been slighted, and…"

"If you felt *your* honor had been slighted, would you be content to let another man regain it for you?"

"Honor's never been much of a worry to me," Felipe said, reaching for a fresh chunk of bread. "But I take your point, *jefe*. If Marty had felt humiliated enough by what had happened, he would have challenged Johnson to a duel or something."

"Maybe not a duel," Paco said. "But at least he would have followed some course of action he could tell his *compañeros* about. No man could hope to regain his standing by bragging that he had got someone else to do his dirty work for him. And if the battalion falls apart – as it might – then both Marty and Clay will be the losers, because it's their responsibility to hold it together."

"All right, forget about Clay," Felipe said. "What about Emmanuel Lowenstein?"

"We might be on to something there," Paco said. "If I knew that I would be staring death in the face in a few days' time, I'd seize the opportunity to have a little fun at the *fiestas* with both hands. And all the other *brigadistas* did. But not Lowenstein. He claims to have stayed in the barracks – though he's not prepared to say why. That, in itself, is suspicious."

"In a way, isn't the fact that he *hasn't* got an alibi the best alibi of all," Felipe asked.

"What do you mean?"

"If he'd planned to kill Johnson, wouldn't he first have tried to establish at least an alibi of sorts?"

"Perhaps he thought he wouldn't need one," Paco suggested. "There's a war going on in which thousands of people are being killed, and he may have calculated that nobody would pay much attention to one more death. And even if he did think there was a chance there might be an investigation, he could have gambled on the fact that the battalion would be sent up to the front line long before that investigation would produce any results." He lit up a Celtas. "And that gamble, if indeed he did take it, may have been a good one – we *have* got nowhere, and they *could* be sent to the front line any day now."

"But why would he …" Felipe began. Then a look of realization came to his face. "You've thought of a motive, haven't you?"

"A possible motive," Paco agreed, cautiously.

"And what is it?"

"If one of the *brigadistas* can fall in love with a local girl, then why can't another?"

"We know Samuel Johnson fell in love with Concha Prieto, and you're saying it's also possible that …"

"That Lowenstein could have fallen in love with her too. Why not? He visited the Prieto house, just as Johnson did. There is no reason to believe he was any less susceptible to the charms of an attractive young woman than the *Negro* was. But it was Johnson that Concha chose. And suddenly Lowenstein found his principles had turned to dust. For all his talk about equality, he could not stand the thought of being beaten in love by a *black* man."

"I've never understood that kind of love," Felipe confessed. "A man marries a woman because that's what a man does. I can accept that easily enough. But all the high drama and agonizing that some men go through over one particular female seems pointless. Women are like buses – if you miss one, you can be pretty sure there will be another one along in a few minutes. And possibly the next one will be a better cook." A look of horror came to his face as he saw the expression which was forming on his boss's face. "I'm sorry, *jefe*, I wasn't getting personal. I know that you and Cindy are different."

Paco shook his head as if the remark had not bothered him, though it felt like a needle had been driven through his heart.

"Put personal considerations aside," he said. "Whatever Cindy and I are to each other has no part in this discussion. We're two policemen talking through a case, and it's important for me to know *whatever's* on your mind. So if you don't think that jealousy could be a motive …"

"I didn't say that," Felipe interrupted. "But if we're only looking for one suspect, I'd put my money on that big stevedore, Ted Donaldson. After all, Samuel Johnson was a black man and Donaldson did admit to us that he was once a member of the Ku Klux Klan."

"And shouldn't the fact that he's chosen not to keep it secret mean that we can rule him out?"

"That's one possibility," Felipe admitted.

"And what's the other?"

"That it could be a double bluff."

·Go on," Paco said encouragingly.

"How often, in the old days back in Madrid, did a suspect under questioning admit to a part of his criminal history that we didn't know anything about?" Felipe asked.

"Often enough," Paco admitted.

"Now sometimes they'd admit it either because they were so panicked they didn't know what they were saying, or because they thought we already knew all about them. But there were a few instances where I think it was nothing more than a bluff. And what these bluffers were gambling on was that we'd think that anyone who was that honest about his past had to be honest about his present as well. Couldn't that be the case with Donaldson? He confesses that he used to be a racist, and the message that we're meant to receive from him is, 'And because I've confessed, I couldn't possibly be a racist now'."

Paco shook his head in admiration.

"Even after all the years we've been working together, you can still surprise me once in a while," he told his partner.

Felipe positively simpered.

"Oh, I'm not just a pretty face, you know," he said, running his index finger over his double chins.

"So you think that Donaldson is our man?"

"Not necessarily. But if we were in Madrid, our suspicions would be enough to get a magistrate to sign a warrant."

"But will they be enough to get James Clay to do the same thing?" Paco wondered.

Chapter Twenty-six

The two Madrid policemen and their American translator stood in front of the mansion which had once belonged to a rich landowner, and was now the barracks of a group of foreign *brigadistas*, most of whom would never have dreamed of entering such a house in their own country – except through the servants' door.

Dolores McBride took a large key out of the pocket of her combat jacket.

"It wasn't easy getting Jim Clay to agree to go along with this, you know," she said.

"I'm sure it wasn't," Paco agreed.

"Nope, it wasn't easy *at all*. And it didn't exactly help that I couldn't tell him *why* you were suspicious of Ted Donaldson."

"You didn't mention the Ku Klux Klan to Clay?"

"I most certainly did not!"

"Why? I would have thought …" Paco began.

"Then you'd have been wrong," Dolores interrupted. "Aside from the fact that I'd promised Ted I'd never tell anyone in the Party that he'd once been involved with the KKK, if I had brought up your theory about him being some kind of Klan undercover agent, Clay would have laughed in my face. And I can't say that I'd have blamed him – because the whole idea's nothing more than a dime novel fantasy."

Not according to Greg Cummings, Paco thought. But then Cummings was not weighed down by all the ideological baggage that most of the other *brigadistas* were compelled – by their devotion to Comrade Stalin – to carry around with them.

"The only reason I'm going along with this farce is because I want you to see for yourself just how wrong you are," Dolores said.

"Perhaps I am wrong," Paco agreed. "We'll soon find out."

Dolores inserted the key in the lock, and pushed the big door open. She stepped through the gap and into the hallway, with the detectives close on her heels.

"The guys all sleep on the second floor," she said. "The room Ted shares is the third on the left at the top of the stairs."

The spiral staircase curved gracefully round, and as they climbed it Paco felt his mind being catapulted back to his early days in Madrid …

Young Paco Ruiz, only recently discharged from the army and now a probationary police officer, sits in a cramped seat in a dark cinema, and gazes with awe at the flickering images on the screen. A fifteen foot high Douglas Fairbanks is standing half-way up a wide staircase, his sword flashing first to the left and then to the right, as he fights off the attacks from half a dozen enemies.

Paco is thrilled, yet even as he cheers along with the rest of the audience, he is aware that there is at least a part of him which is holding back. He cannot immerse himself as completely in the fantasy as he would have been able to a few years earlier, because he has served in Morocco and knows that naked steel kills, and that even a master swordsman would eventually succumb to any two other men who were even half-way competent.

"What's on your mind, Paco?" Dolores asked, noticing the far-away expression on his face.

"I was thinking it might have been nice to remain a child forever," he confessed.

Dolores shook her head, and her jet-black hair cascaded over her shoulder.

"Weird," she said.

What was weird about wanting to remain innocent? Paco wondered. And what was so good about seeing the world as it really was – especially through the eyes of a homicide detective.

They reached the top of the staircase and turned left.

Dolores counted off the doors.

"This one," she announced.

There was no sign of the four-poster bed which had probably once occupied the room. Instead, a dozen metal cots lined the walls.

"The beds came from an abandoned convent," Dolores explained. "I wonder how the guys like lying in the dips in their mattresses which were dug by the butts of genuine virgins?"

There was no air of expectation about the journalist, Paco thought – none of the tingle which he felt as he was approaching the climax of an investigation. But that was easy enough to explain. Dolores felt no anticipation because she did not expect to find anything of any importance during this search.

And perhaps she was right.

He glanced at the row of cheap cardboard suitcases which had been lined up, military-fashion, exactly parallel to the edge of the beds.

"I don't know which of these cots is Ted's," Dolores said. "I guess you'll just have to keep opening the suitcases until you find the right one."

Paco and Felipe had opened three or four cases each when the fat constable said, "This is it."

They spread the contents of Donaldson's suitcase out on his bed. There was not much there to sum up a life: one cheap suit which had gone shiny at the elbows and knees; a couple of changes of underwear; a few crudely printed handbills announcing union meetings at which Donaldson was one of the principal speakers; a copy of *Das Kapital* in English, a basic Spanish grammar and a third book with the name 'Lincoln Steffens' on the spine.

Paco handed the book by Steffens over to Dolores.

"What's this about?" he asked.

The journalist glanced at the title.

"It's the first volume of his autobiography," she said.

"And does this Steffens man have any known connection with the Ku Klux Klan?"

Dolores laughed loudly.

"You really do have the Klan on the brain, don't you, Paco?"

"Well, *does* he have a connection?" Paco persisted.

"No, not even close. Lincoln Steffens was a journalist from what we call the 'Muckraking' school, back in the States. He wrote about corruption. Big city corruption, mainly. He was a bit too liberal for my personal taste, but you gotta say, the man was a gutsy investigator."

"So he wasn't a communist?"

"No," Dolores admitted, "but he certainly wasn't the kind of writer who a member of the Party would get censured for reading, either."

She was holding the book loosely between her thumb and fore-finger, and a single sheet of paper, which had been stored inside the autobiography, fell from it and floated gently to the floor.

Paco bent down and picked it up. It was an ordinary piece of cheap writing paper, the sort which could be purchased from any *papelería*. From its layout, it was obviously a letter, and – not surprisingly – it was written in English.

But it was what was at the top of the letter which caught Paco's attention.

"2.28.71," he read.

"What is that? Some kind of date?" Dolores asked.

"Seems to be," Paco said. "Are you *yanquis* so far advanced of us Europeans that you need to have twenty-eight months in your calendar?"

Dolores giggled.

"No, we don't. We just write the month and day the other way round to you backward folk."

"So that would be the twenty-eighth of February?"

"Yeah. What did you say the year was again?"

"Seventy-One."

"Eighteen Seventy-One?"

"No, just seventy-one. And unlike the rest of the date, it's written in Roman numerals – LXXI."

Dolores suddenly turned very pale.

"Give me that," she said, almost snatching the letter from his hand.

"Is it …?" Paco began.

"Shut up! I need to think," Dolores said curtly, cutting him off. "I'm pretty sure that 1923 was Year Fifty-Seven, so this year would have to be …" She frowned as she did the mental arithmetic, "… yes, 1937 is Year Seventy-One. There's no doubt about it."

"But Year Seventy-One of what?" Paco asked.

Dolores shook her head from side to side, as if she were having difficulty accepting what was before her eyes.

"Year Seventy-One of the Klan," she said heavily. "Do you want me to translate the letter for you?"

"Yes," Paco agreed. "I think you better had."

"It's addressed to the Exalted Cyclops."

"The what?"

"The head of the local chapter of the KKK. It reads, 'Greetings to the leaders of the Invisible Empire. As was ordered by the Klonvocation, I have begun the work of destroying this rabble of niggers, Commies and yids. And I have already had some success – there is one nigger now who is no longer able to cast his lascivious eyes over our pure white womanhood …'"

"Go on," Paco said.

"That's all there is." Dolores' hand suddenly went limp, and the letter floated back down to the floor. "I don't believe it," she gasped. "I simply *won't* believe it."

"Do you have any logical reason for saying that?" Paco asked.

"No, but …"

"Look at this, *jefe*," Felipe said.

He was holding up a gray woolen sock with a hole where the big toe had forced its way through the fabric.

"What about it?" Paco asked.

Felipe pointed to the part of the sock where the anklebone would project when it was on a foot. There was a stain there – a reddish brown one.

Paco had no doubt that it was blood.

Chapter Twenty-seven

There were four of them in the town hall committee room – Felipe standing by the door, Paco and Dolores sitting at one end of the table, and Ted Donaldson facing them from the other end.

Paco studied the big stevedore. In his time as a police officer, he had interrogated hundreds of suspects. Some of them had exuded a powerful air of defiance, and it had been obvious right from the start that they would still deny their guilt even in the face of incontrovertible evidence. Others merely *thought* they were tough, and after half an hour or so would break down and confess. There were those who would immediately try to make a deal, and those who would willingly admit to scores of crimes they could not possibly have committed. There were the weepers, and there were the screamers, the comedians and the would-be orators. Ted Donaldson, he decided, fitted into none of these categories. The stevedore merely looked bewildered.

"Ask him about the gray sock," Paco told Dolores. "Does he deny that it's his?"

When the journalist had finished relaying the question, Ted Donaldson shook his head.

"No, he doesn't deny it," Dolores confirmed.

"Where did the bloodstain on it come from?" Paco said.

And he was thinking to himself, 'Did it come from my Cindy's wound, you bastard? Did you make the mistake of accidentally brushing against her when you'd knocked her to the ground? Did your ankle touch her poor bleeding head?'

"He says that he cut himself when he was out on maneuvers, but he didn't even realize he'd been bleeding until he returned to the barracks and took the sock off," Dolores translated.

"When was this?"

"A while ago. Three or four days. He's vague about the exact date."

"Can he show us the scar?"

Donaldson shook his head again.

"He says that it wasn't really a very deep cut to begin with, and anyway, he's always been a quick healer."

In the old days, back in Madrid, he probably wouldn't even have started interrogating Donaldson until he'd been armed with a report on the blood, Paco thought. But this wasn't the old days. Even if there were still technicians in Albacete who could do the work, there simply wasn't time to consult them.

He lit up a Celtas and sucked the smoke greedily into his lungs.

"Ask him about the unfinished letter," he said.

"He says he knows nothing about that."

"But it's in his handwriting, isn't it?"

"He says it's *similar* to his handwriting – very similar – but it's not exactly the same."

"So it's a forgery?"

"That's what he claims."

A handwriting expert would have been able to rule on the question within a matter of minutes, Paco thought – but as in the case of the blood technicians, there wasn't one available.

"Does he know what's meant by the term 'Exalted Cyclops'?"

Donaldson nodded emphatically, then spoke passionately for perhaps a minute and a half.

"He says that of course he knows what it means," Dolores translated. "He was once an active member of the KKK – he hasn't denied that – so he's familiar with all the terms and modes of address. But he claims that you don't have to be a Klansman to know how to use the terminology. It's been in the newspapers – there have even been books about it."

"Is that true?"

"About the books and the newspaper articles?"

"Yes."

"I guess so."

Donaldson spoke again, this time looking Paco unflinchingly in the eye.

"He swears he didn't kill Samuel Johnson, and nor did he attack Cindy," Dolores translated.

"Did I mention Cindy, you *hijo de puta*?" Paco demanded, speaking directly to Donaldson, even though he knew the other man would not understand. "Did I even *suggest* that the two cases were connected?"

"No, you didn't," Dolores replied. "But he says he's not a fool, and it's obvious to him that the two are not only connected, but are just one part of a much larger conspiracy."

"What kind of conspiracy?"

Dolores posed the question, and as Donaldson answered it Paco saw a look of pure horror start to spread across the journalist's face.

"I had no idea – no idea at all – that anything like that was going on in his mind," Dolores said, when Donaldson fell silent.

"Anything like what?"

"He says … he says it's a Zionist conspiracy. He knows all about it because he's seen a copy of the Protocols of the Elders of Zion, in which the Jews have laid out their aims for world domination. He claims that the Jews want Republican Spain to lose this war."

"Why?"

"Because that will make European fascism stronger – so strong that the other European powers will have no choice but to go to war with it themselves. It will be a long and bloody war, and when it's finally finished, the whole of western civilization will have been destroyed. Then the Jews will step in and take over."

"But that's totally insane!" Paco said.

"I know it is. *The Times* of London exposed the Protocols as a complete forgery as long ago as 1921. But it hasn't stopped Adolf

Hitler from using them for his own ends – and it hasn't stopped people like Ted Donaldson from still believing that they're true."

Donaldson had been listening intently, as if he'd been trying his best to understand what was being said. Now he pointed his thick index finger at Dolores, and started to shout.

"What's he saying?" Paco asked.

"That he knows I'm not translating his words properly. That I'm probably a dirty Jew myself."

Donaldson could not have understood these words any better than he'd understood the previous ones, yet they seemed to infuriate him more. With a roar he rose to his feet, and flung himself across the table at Dolores.

His big hands formed claws as he reached for her slender throat. His eyes blazed with a killing rage. Then, suddenly, he grunted and fell face down on the table.

"That should keep him quiet for a little while," Felipe said, matter-of-factly, as he examined the butt of his pistol to see if its collision with Donaldson's head had done it any damage.

"Are you all right?" Paco asked Dolores.

Though Donaldson's powerful fingers had not had time to so much as brush against her skin – though he was now lying harmless and unconscious – the journalist still had her hand protectively over her throat.

"I'm … I'm fine," she said, unconvincingly.

Paco looked down at Donaldson.

"How long will he be out for?" he asked Felipe.

"A man as tough as him? Half an hour. Maybe a little longer."

"He needs to be tied to a chair before he comes round," Paco said. "Can you manage that by yourself, Felipe, or will you need help?"

"I can manage it well enough," the fat constable said. "Why don't you take a break, *jefe* – you certainly look like you could use one."

Chapter Twenty-eight

Standing with his back to the town hall, Paco watched the two old men cross the Plaza Mayor. They walked as most old men did – slowly and carefully – well-aware that their own bodies were making the world an increasingly hostile place for them to inhabit – but though they were heading for the far corner of the square, they kept turning their heads towards the *ayuntamiento*.

The word had spread already. Paco thought. The old men had somehow heard that an arrest had been made, and though they knew they would see nothing but the solid walls behind which Donaldson was being held, they still could not stop themselves from looking.

That kind of curiosity was not confined to obscure villages in the *quinto coño*. In Madrid, in the old days, it had been quite common for a small crowd to gather outside a police station when it had become known that a suspect in a particularly sensational murder was being held there.

Paco remembered people in these crowds shouting questions at him as he left the building – not because they knew he was one of the officers involved in the case, but merely because he was one of the privileged who had been *inside*, and might possibly have heard something.

Have they charged him yet?

Has he confessed?

And behind those hoarse pleas for information there had always been one basic assumption – that because the suspect had been taken into custody, he must be guilty of the crime.

Why was it, Paco wondered, that people who came into contact with policemen in their daily lives – and were well aware that those officers had their flaws like anybody else – still endowed the force with an infallibility when it came to a murder investigation?

"Do you mind if I join you for a few minutes?" asked a woman's voice immediately to Paco's left.

He turned. Dolores McBride was standing a few tentative feet away from him, still looking shaken after Donaldson's attack.

"I asked if you'd mind if I joined you," Dolores repeated.

"Of course not," he replied.

But he'd wanted to say, "Yes, I do mind!"

Wanted to tell her that he'd rather be alone with his thoughts – with his doubts!

But after all she'd been through to help him, it would have been churlish to dismiss her like that.

Paco offered her a Celtas, but Dolores shook her head and took a packet of American cigarettes from her breast pocket.

As Paco was lighting it for her, her free hand went instinctively up to her neck.

"He didn't actually touch me, did he?" she asked.

"No, he didn't," Paco assured her.

"But it feels as if he did." She ran the hand softly over her throat. "You didn't try to defend me, did you?" she asked accusingly. "When Donaldson was trying to attack me, you just sat there."

"You're right," Paco agreed.

"Why?"

"Because I *was* sitting, and Felipe was on his feet. He was in a much better position to handle the situation, and I didn't want to get in his way."

"So you *knew* that Felipe would handle it?"

"Of course. We're a team. We both know what the other's thinking. I know how he'll react almost before he does himself."

"It must be wonderful to be in that situation," Dolores said wistfully. "I thought I was in it myself until a few minutes ago."

"Did you?"

"Oh yes. I thought every member of the Party was as much a comrade as every other member of the Party, and I could trust them all absolutely. I guess that now you see me as some kind of fool."

"Not at all," Paco assured her.

Dolores grinned ruefully.

"You're being very kind, Inspector – but you're not being very honest. I *am* some kind of fool. A prime example of one, in fact. If there was a blue ribbon for idiots at the county fair, I'd walk away with it every time."

"You're being too hard on yourself," Paco told her.

"Here I was going on about how the Party changes people," Dolores continued, as if she hadn't heard him. "Here I was saying that you were out of your mind to talk about the KKK being able to infiltrate the brigade – and it turns out that you were right all along."

"Donaldson still hasn't admitted to being a member of the Klan," Paco cautioned her. "He hasn't even admitted that he was the one who killed Samuel Johnson."

"No, he hasn't, has he? I guess he wouldn't give the Jewish-Negro conspiracy – which he seems to see all around him – the satisfaction of getting his confession," the journalist said.

They heard the door of the town hall swing open behind them, and suddenly James Clay was standing next to them.

"Since you're both out here, I assume the interrogation is over," the political commissar said.

"Tell him that it's a long way from being over," Paco replied, when Dolores had translated Clay's comment.

The commissar frowned with displeasure.

"But you must have all the evidence you need to convict Donaldson, surely?"

Paco took another drag on his cigarette.

"To convict him?" he repeated. "You seem to have confused my role in this investigation, Señor Clay. I'm a policeman, not a judge."

"In point of fact, you're actually neither of those things," Clay reminded him. "But you are still the most competent person in San Antonio to rule on Ted Donaldson's guilt or innocence."

"And suppose I pronounce him guilty?" Paco asked. "What happens to him then?"

"I've been in touch with our headquarters in Albacete," Clay told him. "If Donaldson's found guilty of killing Sam Johnson, I have been granted the authority to execute him."

Paco shook his head in amazement.

"Yesterday, you were absolutely convinced that it was impossible for any of your *brigadistas* to have committed the murder. Now you're apparently prepared to execute the first *brigadista* who falls under suspicion. What's changed?"

"*Nothing* has changed – including my position on the matter," Clay said haughtily. "Yesterday, I said the killer could not be a *brigadista*, and events have proved me right. Donaldson never *was* a member of the brigade, he was only *pretending* to be one in order to serve the ends of the despicable organization to which he has dedicated his life. Now we know the truth, thanks – to some extent – to your efforts. And the sooner the execution is carried out, the better it will be for the morale of the battalion."

"And what if Donaldson were to turn out to be innocent, after all?" Paco asked.

"Do you have any evidence that he is?"

"Nothing concrete."

"Are you likely to be able to produce any evidence before we are sent up to the front line, in two or three days' time?"

"Not likely, no," Paco admitted.

"Then let me explain the situation to you once more. The brigade needs someone to blame for Sam Johnson's death, and Donaldson is the obvious candidate. Even if he *were* innocent, the sacrifice of his life would still be justified in terms of the general good."

"You can't build a general good on a foundation that's rotten," Paco protested.

"Perhaps we must agree to disagree on that," Clay said. "But such

216

considerations are irrelevant anyway. And why? Because we both really know that Ted Donaldson callously murdered Samuel Johnson simply for being black, just as we know that he tried to kill Cindy Walker because she had started to become suspicious of him." The commissar checked his watch. "I intend to have Donaldson shot by a firing squad at dawn in this very square. You have until an hour before then to come to me and say that you endorse my decision."

"And if I don't?"

"With, or without, your approval, the execution will go ahead."

Clay turned his back on them, and strode away across the square. He walked like a man who was convinced of his own importance, Paco thought, watching him go – a man determined always to convey the impression that everything he did was significant.

And perhaps I'd act in that way, too, if I'd been born with a silver spoon in my mouth, he told himself. Perhaps I, too, would want to prove to myself and others that I could make my own mark on the world without the help of my family connections.

In his mind's eye, Paco saw the scene which would be enacted the following dawn.

The firing squad would gather together in the main room of the barracks, some time before the sun came up.

Who would be in charge of them?

Probably Sergeant Greg Cummings, who, despite being a liberal, seemed to command the respect of his men.

Most of the squad would never have killed another human being before, and perhaps to give them the courage they would need to pull the trigger, Cummings would pass the brandy bottle around.

As the hour approached, they would march in their own clumsy way from their barracks to the town hall, where the prisoner would have been kept under guard. If those watching over him had an ounce of compassion in them, Donaldson would have been drinking too, though they would have been careful not to let him have so much that he needed to be carried to his place of execution.

How would Donaldson act as he was marched under escort into

217

the square? Would he still be protesting his innocence? Or would he, by that stage, have reached a dull acceptance of the fact that he was about to die? Perhaps he would be thinking of the black girl he saw lynched, the girl whose death – he now claimed – had made him turn his back on the Klan.

He would be positioned against a wall, and feel the brickwork pressing against his back. He would watch – still unable to entirely comprehend it – as the rifles were raised to shoulder height. Perhaps, for a brief moment, he might experience a flash of hope – suddenly find himself believing that he was never meant to die in this way. Then he would hear Greg Cummings shout the order to fire, see the flames shoot from the barrels, and maybe even hear the crack of the bullets before he felt a brief searing pain – and then felt nothing at all.

"Is everything all right?" Dolores McBride asked worriedly.

"Nothing's all right," Paco replied. "It hasn't been since the day General Franco landed his army in Morocco."

Dolores was silent for a few seconds, then she said, "Donaldson might have come round again by now. Want to go be back inside and see if he's willing to talk some more?"

"No," Paco said. "Before I see him again, I need a drink."

"I've got a bottle of top-class hooch back at my place," Dolores told him. "We could slip back there, if you like."

Paco shook his head.

"I wouldn't appreciate company," he said. "I need to be alone to do some serious thinking."

Chapter Twenty-nine

Fundador would have been his drink of choice, but Paco knew that once he started on the brandy he would not stop until the bottle was at least half empty. So instead, he ordered a glass of red wine from the barman in the *individualista* bar and when it arrived, he drank it slowly, thinking, as he sipped, of cold winter mornings and of men standing with their backs to walls and facing a row of rifles.

He was just about to order a second wine when he felt a soft tap on his shoulder, and turning round saw the stocky figure of Mannie Lowenstein standing there.

"What do you want with me?" Paco demanded irritably. Then he added, "I'm sorry, you don't understand, do you? I forgot for a moment that you don't speak Spanish."

"I do speak it – at least, enough of it to get by," the *yanqui* replied.

"But how could you, when you've only been here for a few…?"

"I have several comrades from Latin American countries back in New York. I learned it from them."

"So why, when I was questioning you, did you pretend that you didn't understand a word of what I was saying?" Paco asked suspiciously.

"Because I was afraid that if you learned I could speak Spanish, others would soon find out, too."

"Why should that bother you?"

"If my superiors in the brigade discovered I could speak the language, they would probably decide I could be best used in some administrative job, coordinating with the Republican authorities."

"And you didn't want that to happen?"

"It is a Party member's first duty to serve unquestioningly wherever it is decided that he can be most useful," Lowenstein said earnestly. "If I am ordered to work as an administrator, I won't complain about it. But that is not the same as saying that I would deliberately put myself into a situation in which that outcome became inevitable. I came to Spain to fight for what I believe in – not to push paper around."

"Aren't you putting yourself in that situation now?"

"Perhaps I am, but there was no choice in the matter. I had to let you know I speak Spanish, because we need to talk."

"Talk about what?"

"The rumor which is going around the barracks is that Ted Donaldson has been arrested for Samuel Johnson's murder," Lowenstein said, avoiding a direct answer. "Is that true?"

"I have been asking Donaldson some questions about the murder, yes," Paco admitted.

"It's also rumored that the case against him rests in part on a letter he is supposed to have written, and in part on a bloodstained sock which was found in his kit."

Only three people knew that. Paco thought – himself, Felipe and Dolores. No, there was a fourth! To detain Donaldson, he had needed to get James Clay's permission, and in order for that to be granted, Dolores had had to tell him what they had discovered in the barracks. And the political commissar, instead of keeping the information to himself – as a leader of men should – had quickly turned it into barrack room gossip.

"Let us say, for the sake of argument, that the rumors you've heard are true," Paco said. "What has it got to do with you?"

"If Ted Donaldson is proven to be guilty of the murder, then there is no doubt that he should be executed for his crime," Mannie Lowenstein said. "But I don't think he *is* guilty."

"He's certainly guilty enough of hating the Jews," Paco said. "If you'd heard what he had to say about them just half an hour ago, you'd have absolutely no doubt about that."

Mannie Lowenstein gave him a melancholy smile.

"If we decided to shoot all the men who had something against the Jews, the world would be a much emptier place," he said. "Our role is not to eliminate them – though that is something we have seen others try against *us* – but to educate them to understand that we all share the same basic humanity."

"It's a fine thing to have a noble aim in life," Paco said dryly. "But I think even you would see some difficulty educating a man who believes that the... what was the phrase? ... the Protocols of something or other..."

"The Protocols of the Elders of Zion?" Lowenstein asked.

"That's right," Paco agreed. "Even you would see some difficulty in trying to educate a man who believes that those protocols are genuine."

Lowenstein looked shocked.

"Donaldson actually said that? He said he believed the Protocols were genuine?"

"Yes."

"He said it to *you*?"

"Yes."

"But how could he do that? You don't speak English, and he doesn't speak Spanish."

Paco sighed at the other man's pedantry.

"All right," he agreed. "He said it to me *through* Dolores McBride."

For perhaps fifteen seconds, Lowenstein seemed to worry over the idea, then he said, "Even if Ted Donaldson does hold those extreme views, it doesn't necessarily mean he was the one who killed Sam Johnson. If we could just consider the evidence together ..."

"That can't happen," Paco said firmly.

"Why not?"

"Because, whatever the rumors going around the barracks might say, you're still a suspect yourself, at least as far as I'm concerned."

"If I'd killed Sam myself, why would I want to try and persuade you that Donaldson hadn't?" Lowenstein countered. "Surely it would suit me perfectly to have another man blamed for a crime I'd committed."

"I don't pretend to even begin to understand the way in which you *yanquis* think about so *many* things," Paco said, "but I do know that since you refused to explain to me why you didn't go to the *fiestas* along with everyone else, you must remain one of my suspects."

Mannie Lowenstein hesitated for a second, then said, "And if I were to explain it now?"

"Then I would ask myself why, if it was a true explanation, you had held it back before."

"I held it back because I was ashamed."

"Ashamed? Ashamed of what?"

"Of my failure to put the past behind me, and to embrace the Party as fully as I should have."

"Go on," Paco said encouragingly.

"I abandoned my belief in the God of the Jews a long time ago. But it's not always so easy to abandon the external trappings of the religion I was brought up in. The truth is that I did not go to the *fiestas* simply because they were held on a Friday."

"Is that supposed to make any sense to me?"

"It will, if you think about it. Friday night is the start of the Jewish Sabbath, and however much I told myself I was being irrational, I could not defile the Sabbath simply for my own selfish pleasure. Do you believe me?"

A policeman learns to recognize statements which have an undoubted ring of truth about them – as this one did.

Paco nodded.

"Yes, I do believe you."

"So I am now no longer a suspect?"

"You are no longer a suspect."

"And does that mean that you are now prepared to discuss the evidence against Donaldson with me?"

"It means that I'm willing to listen to what you have to say," Paco replied cautiously.

"Then that will have to do," Lowenstein said. "Let us take the letter first. If I needed to send someone a letter, which I knew would incriminate me if it were discovered, I wouldn't leave it half-completed in a book. I'd write it at a single sitting, and as soon as I'd finished it, I would post it."

"There are censors who might examine the letter here in Spain, and probably in the United States, too," Paco said. "Knowing that, I would not have written anything so incriminating at all."

Lowenstein gave him a long, assessing look.

"So you have doubts about it, too, do you?"

It would have been pointless to lie to a man as intelligent as Lowenstein.

"Yes, I have my doubts, too," Paco admitted.

"And then there's the question of the sock to consider," the *brigadista* continued. "If I'd attacked your young woman myself, I would have inspected all the clothing I'd been wearing for bloodstains, the moment it was safe to do so. And if I'd found some blood on one of my socks, I would either have tried to wash it out or have thrown the sock away. What I would not have done, *under any circumstances*, is leave it around for a policeman to find."

"Neither would I," Paco agreed. "There can be only two reasons why the sock could have been there in his suitcase. The first is that Donaldson is an incredibly stupid man ..."

"He isn't that," Lowenstein interrupted. "Whatever else his failings, he is easily capable of recognizing incriminating evidence."

"... and the second is that Donaldson's explanation for how the bloodstain came to be there is the true one. In which case, the fact that the sock was still there tells us more about *someone else* than it does about Donaldson himself."

"I don't understand," Lowenstein confessed.

"If I had been trying to frame Donaldson for Samuel Johnson's murder, I would have planted the letter exactly where it was," Paco explained. "But I would have removed the bloodstained sock."

"Why?"

"Because its presence raises just the sort of questions you and I have been asking each other. Why didn't he check his clothing after his attack on Cindy? Can he really be *that* stupid? But *because* the sock really has *nothing* to do with the case at all, the man who planted the letter didn't even know of its existence."

"You're saying that, as far as you're concerned, Donaldson was definitely framed?"

"Nothing is ever certain in this world," Paco said, "but I'm convinced enough of his innocence to do whatever I can to prevent his execution."

"So you'll talk to Clay. You'll express the same doubts to him that you've been expressing to me?"

Paco shook his head.

"That would just be a waste of time. Clay has decided that Donaldson must die, and it will take more than a few nagging, unanswered questions to persuade him otherwise."

"What *will* make him change his mind?"

"Fresh evidence which clearly points the finger at someone else."

"And where do you hope to find that?"

Paco shrugged his shoulders.

"I have absolutely no idea of even where to begin to look," he confessed.

Chapter Thirty

Dusk was falling by the time Paco returned to the town hall. A small crowd of people had gathered outside the building, but instead of bombarding him with questions, as their counterparts from the city would have done, they contented themselves with staring at him.

He found Dolores McBride just inside the *ayuntamiento* lobby. An American cigarette was drooping lethargically from the corner of her sensuous mouth, and the evidence of the numerous butts which had collected around her feet suggested that she had been chain-smoking.

"You've been away a hell of a long time!" she said.

"I told you, I had some serious thinking do," Paco replied. "Has Donaldson regained consciousness?"

"Yeah. Nearly an hour ago now. I've been in to see him two or three times already."

"And has he said anything interesting?"

"He hasn't said anything at all! Didn't even react to the fact that I was in the room. Looked right through me – like I wasn't really there."

"Which is an improvement on trying to kill you," Paco pointed out. "Why do *you* think he attacked you?"

"I should have thought that was obvious from what he said *before* he went bananas. He'd decided I was part of the international Negro-Jewish conspiracy, and wasn't translating what he said accurately."

"And were you?"

The journalist laughed.

"Was I what? Part of the international Negro-Jewish conspiracy?"

"No," Paco said, straight-faced. "Were you translating what he said accurately?"

Dolores shrugged.

"I guess so. I may have missed the odd nuance here and there, but I got across the main points he made accurately enough." She glanced down the corridor at the room which had become the interrogation center. "You want to give it another shot?"

"Why not?" Paco replied, without much enthusiasm. "I suppose there's always the chance he'll be able to give us a useful piece of information."

"You mean, like a confession or something?"

"Or something," Paco agreed.

Felipe had tied Donaldson to a chair in the council chamber. The fat constable made a thorough job of it, and however much the big stevedore had twisted and strained, he would not have been able to break free. Not that the prisoner was making any attempt to escape. He hardly moved when Paco and Dolores entered the room. Only his eyes, burning with a blazing hatred as they fixed on the journalist, gave any hint of how he would behave if he were not restrained.

"Ask him who he thinks killed Sam Johnson," Paco said to Dolores.

"Ask him *what?*"

"Who he thinks killed Johnson."

"But we already know that he did it himself."

"So give him a chance to lie."

Dolores translated the question, but Donaldson made no response.

"Ask him again," Paco said. "Tell him we'll never find the real killer unless he decides to help us."

Dolores repeated the question, and this time Donaldson answered.

"He says that this is all a waste of time," Dolores said. "I probably won't give you a fair translation of what he said, and even if I do, it won't make any difference, because you're just as bad as the rest of them. You want him dead, he knows that, so why don't you stop playing games, and just get on with it?"

There was a sudden sound of pounding feet in the corridor outside, then the door handle rattled violently. Paco had locked the door when he entered the room, and whoever was outside must have realized it, and now began banging frantically with his fists.

Felipe looked at Paco for guidance. Paco drew his pistol, then gestured to his partner to open the door. Felipe stood well clear of the possible line of fire, and stretched over to pull back the bolt.

"You can come in now," Paco called out. "But do it slowly."

The door swung open, and he saw Luis Prieto standing in the corridor. The young peasant was red in the face, as if he'd been running as fast as he could.

"You must … you must come quickly!" he gasped.

Paco felt his stomach churn. He could taste the bile in his mouth, and he wondered if he was about to throw up.

"Is it … is it Cindy?" he forced himself to ask, though he was dreading the answer.

"Yes."

"Is she… is she dead?"

The boy shook his head.

"No! Not dead! Far from it, señor. She's just regained consciousness."

Chapter Thirty-one

Paco sprinted down the cobbled streets. He was hardly aware of where he was – only of where he was going. Twice, he slipped on the ice and fell sprawling onto the ground. Twice, he was up again in an instant, oblivious to any damage he might have done himself.

Cindy's going to live! Cindy's going to *live*!

The words echoed round his head as the sound of his footfalls bounced off the cobbles and hit the walls.

He came to a panting halt at Asunción Muñoz's front door, and Luis Prieto drew level with him a second later.

"You move quickly for an old man," the young peasant said.

Then he knocked on the door and called out, "Open up! It's us."

The bolt was drawn, the door swung open. Paco barged his way past Luis's *compañeros*, and dashed across the room to the old iron bed.

To Cindy!

She looked very pale – almost as pale as death itself – but there was life enough in her beautiful eyes.

"You took your time getting here, Ruiz," she said, her lips forming into an exhausted smile. "Tied up in an important card game, were you?"

"You've guessed it," Paco replied, returning her smile. "But even so, I'd have come right away if I hadn't had such a good hand."

He wanted to touch her – to hold her to him – but he didn't dare without the doctor's permission.

"How are you feeling?" he asked.

"How do you expect me to feel?" Cindy asked. "There's a herd of horses running wild in my head, and I feel like shit." She paused for a second, as if gathering her strength. "We need to talk. Now!"

"So let's talk."

"I mean we need to talk *in private*." Cindy said, gesturing with her eyes towards the corner of the room.

Paco turned to the three young men who had been guarding his *novia* since early that morning.

"I owe you more than I can tell you," he said. "Tomorrow I'll buy you as much drink as you can hold – and then some more – but I can handle things from now on."

"Are you planning to stay here all night yourself, or do you want us to come back later?" Luis Prieto asked.

Was he planning to stay there all night? Paco asked himself, as his other world – the one which was not centered on Cindy – came flooding back to him.

How *could* he stay all night when another man's life was hanging in the balance, and only he could save it?

"I have to go out again later," he said. "Come back in half an hour. No, better make it closer to an hour."

Luis Prieto nodded, and he and his friends headed for the door. As they closed it behind them Paco knelt down and – very carefully – took Cindy's hand in his.

"Do you know what happened to you?" he asked.

"Sure, I know what happened to me. I was walking down the street, minding my own business, and some son-of-a-bitch hit me over the back of the head with what felt like the Statue of Liberty."

Paco grinned.

"And do you happen to know exactly which son-of-a-bitch that might have been?"

Cindy shook her head as much as was prudent.

"I didn't even hear him sneaking up on me. One second I was walking along, the next I had a whole galaxy of stars exploding before my eyes."

"The reason you were out there on the street was because you were looking for me, wasn't it?"

"That's right."

"Because you had something to tell me?"

"Right again."

"Was it about the brigade? Had you thought of something which might point us towards Samuel Johnson's killer?"

Cindy looked puzzled.

"No, it wasn't about that at all."

Paco felt a stab of disappointment, but it was instantly washed away by a sea of anger and self-loathing.

How could he let the murder intrude on this moment, when all that really mattered was that Cindy was going to recover? he wondered.

"So what *were* you coming to see me about?" he asked.

"I wanted to tell you all about me and Greg. I should have told you the night before, but I was so damn mad at you that I decided I'd just make you suffer a little bit longer."

Like you're making me suffer now, Paco thought.

And suddenly, he saw how wrong he'd been. How pig-headed. How selfish. If he really loved this woman as much as he told himself he did, then his main concern should not be his own feelings, but her happiness.

"If you want to leave me and go back to him, I won't stand in your way," he promised. "But be very careful. Make sure he stays faithful to you."

"*Faithful* to me!" Cindy repeated incredulously.

"I don't know if you've slept with Cummings since we arrived in San Antonio – and I don't *want* to know – but if you have, you're not the only one. He's been sleeping with Dolores McBride, too. He was in bed with her at the very moment you were attacked."

Cindy made a gurgling sound, and for a moment he was terrified that what he had just told her had caused a relapse.

And then he realized that she was laughing – uncontrollably.

"What's the matter, Cindy?" he asked worriedly. "Have I said something funny?"

"Oh Paco," Cindy spluttered between her giggles. "Oh Paco, Paco, Paco – how could you possibly have got everything so completely wrong?"

Chapter Thirty-two

Time could play strange tricks on the mind, Paco told himself. A night's passionate love-making could appear to be over in a moment. An hour's surveillance on a cold, deserted street could drag out for so long that it felt like a whole day. And so much had been going on inside his head since Cindy had made her astonishing revelation that though not more than ten minutes of real time could have ticked away, he seemed to have been absorbed in the problem for an eternity.

"You've gone very quiet, Ruiz," Cindy said, as she watched her lover pace the room, not even stopping as he lit a new Celtas from the stub of his old one.

Paco flicked the remains of the old cigarette into the fireplace, and drew heavily on the fresh one. If he'd heard her words, he gave no sign of it.

"I said you've gone very quiet," Cindy repeated, much louder this time.

Paco stopped pacing, and turned towards her. "I'm sorry? What was that?"

"I've given you an idea, haven't I?"

"No," Paco corrected her. "You've given me a solution."

"Are you saying that you know who killed Sam Johnson?"

"Yes, that's exactly what I'm saying."

"And who attacked me?"

"Yes. That as well."

"Was it the same person?"

"That doesn't matter."

"Well, thanks a lot! It's good to know I don't count for much round here," Cindy said, only half-joking.

"That's not what I meant," Paco said hastily. "What I should have said was that it doesn't matter who actually *struck* the blow, because it was part of a team effort – only one piece of a much bigger scheme."

"So there's more than one person involved?"

"At least two. Possibly more."

"Do you know *why* they killed Johnson?"

"Not exactly, but from the picture I've built up of the poor bastard, I've got a pretty good idea."

"My, but you have been a busy boy while I've been unconscious, haven't you?" Cindy said admiringly.

No, he hadn't, Paco thought, angry with himself. Or if he *had* been busy, then so much of that 'busyness' had been a complete waste of effort.

Cindy had found it amusing that he had been so wrong about her present desires – and her hopes for the future. But it wasn't entirely his fault. He'd been manipulated. He had been presented with a set piece – a theatrical staging performed entirely for his benefit – and he had fallen for it completely.

Should he have seen through it? he asked himself.

Perhaps.

But in his own defense, it had to be said that his background had worked against him – as the players had probably known that it would. He was not a *yanqui* or a Northern European. He did not come from one of those countries which had thrown off its traditional restraints. He was a Spaniard, for God's sake, and had been brought up in a society where young women were chaperoned even when they were only out for an innocent walk with their *novios* – a society in which the sexual act outside marriage was so taboo that no one would ever even dream of using it as a way of misleading the police.

He heard the front door softly click open behind him, and he turned

233

around. It came as no surprise to him to see that Greg Cummings and Dolores McBride were standing in the doorway.

Cummings had a broad, relieved, smile spread across his craggily handsome face.

"Thank God you've regained consciousness," he said to Cindy. "Don't you ever dare go scaring us like that again, young lady."

Cindy smiled back at him. "I'll try not to," she promised.

"Things have been real boring round here without you," Dolores told her. "It's kind of hard to go on being gorgeous when you've no one to compete against."

Paco forced a smile to his own face, just as if he, too, were joining in the general good humor and the relief. But his mind was engaged in a cold – desperate – calculation.

As long as Cummings was still in the doorway, Cindy was safe. But Cummings would not *stay* in the doorway forever. Part of his plan had to be to walk across the room to the bed. And once he had accomplished that maneuver – once he was kneeling down beside Cindy, shielding her from the rest of the room, he would be in complete control of the situation.

He had to be prevented from ever reaching the bed, Paco told himself.

But how?

It wasn't possible to deal with Cummings *and* Dolores at the same time – and of the two, the woman was probably the more dangerous.

"Yeah, you sure enough scared the hell out of us for a while back there, Cindy," Greg Cummings said, moving a step closer to the bed, as a concerned friend would.

Paco's right hand reached up for his shoulder holster. "Don't even think of it!" Dolores warned him.

Her pistol was pointing straight at his heart, and the hand which held it was as steady as a rock.

Paco let his arms fall down to his sides.

Cummings saw the pistol, too.

"What are you doing, Dolores?" he asked. "You don't pull a gun out when you're amongst friends."

"But we're *not* amongst friends," the journalist countered. "And there's no point in pretending any longer that we are, because our clever policeman from Madrid has worked it all out. You have worked it out, haven't you, Paco?"

There seemed no point in denying it.

"Yes," Paco agreed. "It took me long enough, but I've finally worked it out."

"Would someone mind telling me what the hell is going on here?" Cindy demanded.

"You wanted to know who killed Sam Johnson. Well, they did," Paco told her. He turned to Cummings. "Did James Clay play any part in this nasty little plot of yours?"

"Clay!" Cummings repeated contemptuously. "Our esteemed political commissar! Of course he didn't! Even if he could be trusted, the man would have no stomach for such an undertaking. Appointing him was one of the biggest mistakes the Party Committee in New York ever made. He has no idea of the realities of power. He would just have sat there in his cozy little office and let everything around him fall apart."

"But *you* weren't prepared to let that happen, were you?" Paco asked.

"Far *wiser* heads than mine were not prepared to let it happen," Cummings said. "I have been acting on the instructions of men who know what sacrifices need to be made to build a workers' paradise. My orders come not from spineless jellyfish of the ilk of James Clay, but from Moscow."

"From Joe Stalin himself?"

Cummings laughed.

"Do you seriously think that the General Secretary, burdened as he is with so many other responsibilities, has time to deal with a minor local matter like this? No, I work for the men whose job is to relieve Comrade Stalin of some of his burden, just as I relieve them of some of theirs."

"Wait a minute!" Cindy protested. "You're not a communist, Greg. You're a liberal."

"If you wish to conceal a tall, strong oak tree, do you put it on a treeless plain?" Cummings asked. "No! You plant it in a forest of lesser trees. I have been hiding my true self in a forest of weak, puny liberals for a long time. And it worked. You knew me well, but you never suspected that under my pink trappings beat a heart which was pure red."

"But why…?" Cindy asked.

"I've been a secret weapon – a sleeper – held back until I could be used with maximum effectiveness. Until now!"

His little speech sounded as if it had been rehearsed, Paco thought – and it probably had! For long years, Greg Cummings must have yearned to tell the people he knew that he was playing a role which he secretly despised. He must have imagined this moment many times, and have polished and practiced the words he would use until he was as proficient as any actor.

It was a very bad sign that he felt free to deliver his long-anticipated speech now. It could only mean that it didn't matter to him that this particular audience learned the truth – because this particular audience would not live long enough to pass it on to anyone else.

The only chance that he and Cindy had of surviving was to stall their would-be assassins until Luis Prieto and his friends returned, Paco told himself.

And when would that be?

Three-quarters of an hour! And then only if the young men were on time!

But he still had to try – had to hope that Cummings and Dolores liked having an audience so much that they would put off the executions until help had time to arrive.

"Why did you murder Samuel Johnson?" he asked, beginning the process. "Was it because he was black?"

The fact that such a question could even be posed seemed to take Greg Cummings completely by surprise.

236

"No, of course it wasn't because he was a Negro," he said, sounding genuinely offended. "I'm no racist! He had to die because he was a bad communist."

"He took ammunition from the depot in Albacete without waiting for the proper authorization from the Party," Dolores McBride said. "He gave his support to the collectivists in San Antonio, when Comrade Stalin had already clearly stated that they were not ready for collectivization, and that what we should be doing was to encourage a bourgeois revolution in Spain by throwing our weight behind the *individualistas*."

Attack their precious Joe Stalin! Paco's brain told him. Make them want to make *you* believe in him as *they* do, even though they're intending to kill you in a few minutes.

"It's not that Spain isn't ready for collectivization – it's that Stalin isn't ready *for it* to be ready," he said. "Do you really think he believes in world revolution? Of course he doesn't! He's against collectivization here simply because he doesn't want to offend Britain and France by seeming to support it. And *why* doesn't he want to offend Britain and France? Because he knows he'll need their help if there's a war with Germany – their help to defend *Russia*. He doesn't give a damn about what happens in Spain. And he doesn't give a damn about you! You're nothing but his puppets – and when he's finished pulling your strings so hard that they snap, he'll throw you away with no more thought than a child would throw away a broken toy."

"Sam Johnson was a danger to the Party," Cummings said woodenly.

It was almost as if Cummings hadn't heard a single word he'd said, Paco thought. Or perhaps he had heard, but had chosen not to understand. The man had dedicated his life to the Party. Could anything ever persuade him to accept the fact that he had never been anything more than a dupe of Russian nationalism?

"So Sam Johnson was a danger," he said aloud.

"Yes," Cummings agreed. "If he hadn't been a natural leader, his attitude would not have been a problem. But he *was* a natural leader – and the men would have followed him anywhere."

"And he would have *protected* them," Paco said. "If some ignorant time-serving bureaucrat in Moscow had issued an order which had put his men at risk, Sam would have ignored it. He would have saved lives!"

"Discipline must be maintained at all costs," Cummings said. "It is not our place to question our orders."

"Even if those orders are stupid? Even if they're verging on being criminally insane?"

"The Party can *never* be stupid," Cummings told him heatedly. "At all times, in all circumstances, the Party is always right."

Paco did not dare to glance down at his watch for fear of alerting Dolores and Cummings to what he was doing, but his best estimate was that another five minutes had passed.

Not long enough! Nowhere near long enough! The time which he had managed to use up so far was like a hairline crack compared to the vast canyon he still had to fill.

"Who actually killed Samuel Johnson?" he asked.

"Why should that matter?" Dolores replied, almost pityingly. "It was the Party which eliminated him. The finger which actually pulled the trigger is of no relevance at all."

"And no doubt it was the Party that decided that Cindy had to die," Paco said. "But who acted as the instrument of the Party? Who tried to batter her to death in the street, and, when that didn't work, attempted to smother her in this very room. It was Cummings, wasn't it?"

The sandy-haired man looked at Dolores, then, when she nodded, turned to Cindy. His earlier arrogance had disappeared, and instead there was a pleading look on his face, almost as if he were begging the woman in the bed for her forgiveness.

"I had no choice," he said. "You knew far too much about my past for us to let you live. If we hadn't tried to silence you, you would have led Ruiz to us eventually. But please believe me, Cindy, it hurt me to do it."

"But nowhere near as much as it hurt me, you son-of-a-bitch!" Cindy said spiritedly.

And despite the perilous situation they were in, Paco found himself smiling.

"Who forged the letter from Ted Donaldson to the Exalted Cyclops?" he asked.

"That was me," Cummings admitted. "When it became obvious that you weren't going to give up on the investigation, we thought at first of killing you. But then we decided that wouldn't work – because we knew that the authorities in Madrid would only send another investigator in your place. So we had to give you what you wanted – a murderer."

"Why Donaldson?"

"He was expendable. He would never have amounted to much more than cannon fodder, and the fact that he had once been a member of the Klan gave him a believable motive for the killing."

"You knew he'd been in the Klan because you'd heard him talk about it to Luis Prieto when you both visited the Prieto house."

"That's right," Cummings agreed. The imploring look had drained from his face when he had turned away from Cindy, and now he was once more the arrogant intellectual. "In his own fumbling, cloddish manner, Donaldson was trying to explain to the Spanish boy that the Klan was evil – and that he should know just *how* evil because he had once been a member of it himself. I said nothing at the time, preferring to store up that particular piece of information in case it became useful later, as indeed it did."

The man was scum, Paco thought. And Ted Donaldson, for all the stevedore's failings, was worth ten of him.

He could bear to look at Cummings no longer, and turned instead to Dolores.

"You pretended you thought it was a waste of time to go through Donaldson's kit, but all the time you knew what we'd find – because you'd planted it there," he said.

"Spot on!" Dolores agreed. "And I must be a pretty good actress to have had you so completely fooled."

She was, Paco agreed. She had played the role of the skeptic to perfection when they had been searching the barracks.

Nor had that been her only triumph. She had played the role of loyal Party member to perfection, too, though, strictly speaking, that had not been a role at all. She *was* loyal – but her loyalty belonged to quite another branch of the Party than the one she openly professed to belong to.

"Did Donaldson really say all that stuff about an international Zionist conspiracy?" he asked.

"Hell, no," Dolores replied. "I'm sure there's a streak of anti-Semitism still running through Donaldson's veins, but most of the garbage I spouted was my words, not his."

"And he sensed that, didn't he? Even though he couldn't understand the words, he guessed you weren't translating what he was saying. That's why he tried to attack you."

"And got cold-cocked by your fat friend for his trouble," Dolores said. She looked Paco straight in the eye. "What's with all these questions, anyway? Why should you be so interested now?"

"I'm a detective by nature, as well as by profession," Paco said. "I just like to slot all the pieces of the puzzle together."

"So you just like to slot all the pieces of the puzzle together, do you?" she asked. She shook her head. Her jet-black hair swirled sensually around her shoulders, but the hand which held the pistol remained as steady as ever. "No, I don't buy that. There's got to be another reason you're so happy to stand here chewing the fat. You're waiting for something, aren't you?"

"What could I be waiting for?" Paco asked.

"Perhaps for the cavalry to come to the rescue? Well, let me tell you, that isn't going to happen."

No, Paco thought sadly, it *wasn't* going to happen. Dolores and Cummings had the upper hand, and they were not about to give it away now.

"Here's the way it's going to play." Dolores said. "You and me, Inspector, are going to go for a little walk."

"And Cummings?"

"He'll stay here to look after his long-lost love."

240

His long lost love. Now there was real irony

"Let her live," Paco pleaded. "She'll keep quiet about all this."

"Will you, Cindy?" Dolores asked. "If we spare you, will you just walk away and forget everything?"

"You know goddamn well that I won't!" Cindy spat. "If you hurt Paco, you're as good as dead yourselves. It doesn't matter where you go. You can run back to Moscow with your tails between your legs, and I'll *still* find you."

Dolores turned back to Paco, and shrugged helplessly.

"You heard her," she said. "We don't have any choice, so let's try and make this as quick and dignified as we possibly can, shall we?"

She was going to kill him – but not yet. Whatever story she and Cummings had concocted to explain away two more killings, it involved him dying somewhere else, and from that knowledge he drew a sliver of hope.

If he could find some way to overpower Dolores on the way to wherever it was they were going …

If he could then get back to Asunción Muñoz's house before Cummings had had time to dispose of Cindy…

If… if… if…

It *was* a sliver of hope – but no more!

"Do we at least get to say goodbye to each other?" he asked Dolores.

"Sure – as long as you can do it from where you're standing now."

He and Cindy had faced death together before, but never with the certainty with which they were facing it this time.

Paco looked across at his woman and marveled that, even at such a moment, her face could express more love than fear.

"We were good together," he said.

"Wrong as usual, Ruiz," Cindy replied. "We weren't good – we were the best."

Chapter Thirty-three

The air on the street seemed colder than it had earlier. But perhaps it wasn't. Perhaps the chill he felt biting into his bones was no more than a manifestation of the huge sense of failure which had begun to sweep over him.

The moment that Cindy had told him what all Cummings' students had known about their teacher for a long time, warning bells should have started ringing in his head. He should have been on his guard, expecting Dolores and Cummings to arrive even before they did. Instead of applying his mind to slotting the last few pieces of the puzzle into place, he should have been making plans to take Cindy somewhere safer. But he hadn't done any of that – and now it was too late.

"Are you still watching that building right across the street to make sure it doesn't move?" asked a voice behind him.

"Yes, I'm still watching it."

Dolores was just in the doorway of the house, he calculated, which put her at least two meters from him. If he swung round now and tried to grab her gun, he would be dead before he even got close.

"Now here's how it works," Dolores said, briskly and businesslike. "When I give the word, you turn left. You do it in a single smooth movement. No hesitation, no jerkiness. One second you're looking *across* the street, the next you're looking *down* it. And you don't check over your shoulder to see where I am, because that would be a *big* mistake. Once you're facing in the right direction, you wait for the order and then you start walking – real slow and real steady. You keep to the dead center of the street. If you deviate by as much as an inch from the path I'm expecting you to take, I'll shoot you where you stand. Understood?"

She was good, Paco thought – far too good to ever make any of the mistakes he'd been hoping she would.

"I asked you if you understood," Dolores said.

"I understand."

"Good. Turn now."

He turned, listening for sound from within the house. But there was only silence.

He imagined the scene.

Cummings standing a few feet from Cindy, watching – even though she was as weak as a lamb – for any false moves.

Cindy herself, lying there, perhaps preparing for death, perhaps still hoping that her Spanish knight in shining armor would find some way to rescue her at the last minute.

But that wasn't going to happen – because Dolores was being far too careful.

He wondered how Cummings would decide to kill the woman he loved. He probably wouldn't shoot her, because that would make too much unnecessary noise. Maybe he would strangle her. Or perhaps he would use a pillow to smother her. He had already tried that method once, and failed. But this time he would succeed, because there would be no one to disturb him.

Stop it! he ordered himself angrily – stop thinking about Cindy, and start thinking about how to overpower Dolores.

"OK, move off," Dolores said.

Her voice told him that she was now in the street behind him. But not close enough!

Not nearly close enough!

He took one step forward, then a second.

Cummings would be moving into position for the kill now, because he wouldn't want to stay in the house any longer than he absolutely …

Stop it! Stop it!

"You're doing just fine, Paco," Dolores said soothingly. "Just fine. A few more minutes, and it will all be over."

He heard a noise – a slight shuffling sound – coming from the shadows just ahead of them.

Dolores had heard it too.

"Is somebody there?" she called. "Step out where I can see you!"

She was distracted. He would never get a better chance than this. Paco swung round, going into a crouch to make himself a smaller target.

If he could spring at her...

If he could manage to knock her to the ground...

He was still fine-tuning his plan of attack when he heard an explosion and felt something heavy – something burning – slam into his shoulder with the force of an express train. He toppled over backwards, and as he did so, his brain began screaming out its protest at the pain which was quickly spreading through his whole body.

If he were to survive this – if he were to have the slightest chance of saving Cindy – he had to get back to his feet before Dolores had a chance to fire again. But even as he struggled against the pain, he knew that he would never make it.

His confused, agonized mind registered a number of disparate sounds.

A slight plop.

The sound of a body falling hitting the street.

A man – Cummings – screaming the word 'bitch' in English.

Running footsteps.

He forced himself to his knees, and crawled painfully back towards the door of the house he had just left. A body blocked his passage, and because he did not have the strength left to clamber over it, he had to waste precious seconds on a detour.

He reached the door on his hands and knees – like a dog instead of a man, he thought – and looked through pain-filled eyes into the room.

He saw Cindy, propped up in the bed on one shaky elbow.

He saw Cummings, staggering around the room with his hand over his right eye and moaning,

"You've blinded me! You've blinded me!"

And he saw Mannie Lowenstein, standing between the two of them, holding a pistol.

"What do you want me to do?" Lowenstein asked softly.

"Shoot him!" Cindy screamed. "Kill the fucking fairy!"

The *brigadista* nodded gravely, then raised his weapon.

The explosion from the silenced pistol was no more than a loud plop. Cummings stopped moaning, and his legs collapsed from under him. As he hit the floor, a patch of red began to appear – like magic – around his heart. Lowenstein walked over to the fallen man, and put two bullets in his head.

Perhaps minutes had passed – or perhaps it was only the pain which made it seem like minutes. Lowenstein had manhandled Paco into a chair and was now leaning over him.

"Can you hear me?" the *brigadista* asked.

"Yes," Paco gasped. "I can hear you."

"We need a story to explain away this mess – and we don't have long to produce it."

"Cummings!" Paco croaked. "It was Cummings. He killed Johnson. He … he was working for some rogue branch of the Party in Moscow."

Lowenstein shook his head.

"It *can't* have happened like that – even if it did," he said. "If the brigade does not believe in the unity of the Party, it believes in nothing. If a popular *brigadista* like Greg Cummings could not be trusted, then who can be? Cummings died a hero's death. All we need to decide now is who killed him."

He was right, Paco thought. Whoever took the blame, it couldn't be Cummings.

The idea which came into his head was not in the least funny, but – perhaps because his judgment was distorted by the pain – he seemed to think it was.

He started to laugh, even though it hurt to do so.

"Why … why don't we learn from Hitler?" he asked. "Why don't we blame it on the Jews?"

"The Jews!" Lowenstein exploded, as if he could hardly believe what he'd just heard.

"Perhaps I should have said *a* Jew."

"Me? You want me to take the blame?"

"No, not you," Paco said, trying to sound more serious. "The Jew I have in mind is thousands of miles from here. And nothing we can do or say will hurt him."

"As long as he lives, a man can hurt. Is the Jew that you have in mind already dead?"

"No, not yet," Paco admitted. "But with the shadow which is hanging over him, he might as well be."

Chapter Thirty-four

There were four of them waiting for the midnight train to Madrid, though only three of them were planning to take it. The blonde woman still found it tiring to walk for more than a few yards, and was sitting in a wheelchair. Her *novio*, his shoulder in plaster and his arm in a sling, stood next to her. Beyond him were his fat assistant and the political commissar of the Lincolns based in San Antonio.

James Clay had insisted on seeing them off, though Paco suspected his motive had more to do with making sure they were really leaving than it did with courtesy. Clay had not gloated for a full fifteen minutes, but now, as he bent over Cindy's wheelchair, it looked as if he were about to start again.

"Commissar Clay says that he knew right from the start the murderer couldn't have been one of the *brigadistas*," Cindy translated.

"Tell him he was quite right about that, and I was quite wrong," Paco said cheerfully.

Clay frowned.

"Of course, there *was* one moment when I wavered in my belief," he admitted.

"When was that?"

"When I was going to have Ted Donaldson shot."

Paco chuckled.

"You might fool others, Commissar, but you don't fool me," he said.

"I beg your pardon!" Clay replied, as always more than willing to take offence when he thought his dignity was being challenged.

"You never thought Donaldson was guilty," Paco said. "You only *pretended* to, in order to flush the real murderer out."

Clay smiled.

"I might have known you'd spot that," he said. He became serious again. "How long had Dolores McBride been working for Leon Trotsky, do you think?"

"We'll probably never know the answer to that," Paco admitted. "She was very clever at hiding her true allegiance. If Trotsky hadn't become desperate – if he hadn't seen for himself what a great success the International Brigade was going to be, she might have stayed hidden for years. But Trotsky *did* see it, and realized he had to do something soon. That's why he took the risk of having Dolores exposed. He just couldn't stand the thought of Comrade Stalin having yet another triumph."

"But why Johnson?" Clay asked. "If she really wanted to destroy the brigade, why not kill someone important?"

"I think Johnson's death was no more than a rehearsal," Paco said confidentially. "I believe – though I can't prove it – that her next target was the one intended to strike the really devastating blow. I'm almost certain that what Greg Cummings had found out was that she was planning to kill *you!*"

"And that's why she shot him?"

"Yes. If only I'd arrived a few minutes earlier, I might have been able to save his life. As it was, all I could do was avenge his murder."

"It's a pity you had to kill her," Clay said. "If she'd lived, we could have put her on trial. That would have shown the world what a villain Trotsky really is."

"The world already knows it," Paco said. "At least, the part of the world which has stopped believing the capitalists' lies does. Still, I would have taken her alive if I could have. But you know what Trotsky's fanatical followers are like. They've come to accept their own lies – and she chose to die rather than admit the truth."

The train, hissing steam, rumbled heavily onto the platform.

"There's one more thing I should say before we go, Commissar Clay," Paco said.

"And what's that?"

"I hope you'll do all that's within your power to keep away from the front line."

"Keep away from the front line!"

"Yes. And I'll tell you why. Any man can be a front line soldier, but it takes a *real* man – a man with balls – to force himself to stay back at headquarters and make sure that everything is running smoothly there."

"Perhaps you're right," Clay agreed. "I'll certainly give the matter some thought."

The train pulled slowly out of the station. Cindy took one last look at the few lights still twinkling in Albacete, then turned to face Paco.

"I've seen some snow jobs in my time," she said, grinning, "but the one you did on Clay takes the prize. Weren't you afraid that you were going a bit too far with all that guff about the wonderful Comrade Stalin and diabolic Trotsky?"

If his shoulder had permitted it, Paco would have shrugged.

"Men believe what they want to believe," he said. "It suits Commissar Clay to see things in those terms, and if I talk back to him in the same meaningless jargon, that only proves to him that I'm at last starting to show a modicum of intelligence. And as to what I said about him staying away from the front line ..."

"Yes?"

"If he chooses to believe he'll serve the cause better in Albacete than he could on the battlefield, that can only be to the advantage of the combat troops who would otherwise have to follow his orders."

Cindy grinned again.

"You just can't help interfering in other people's lives, can you?"

"No," Paco agreed. "That's probably why I'm a detective."

"Do you want to tell me why Greg Cummings tried to kill me now?" Cindy asked.

"Certainly," Paco agreed, "but first we have to go into a little of the essential background."

Cindy gave a loud stage groan.

"Oh, not that," she pleaded. "I'm not sure I could stand another session of hearing just how clever you've been."

"And you won't," Paco promised. "The person who held the vital piece of information which cracked this case was you."

"OK, I'll buy it," Cindy said, resignedly. "Give me all the 'essential background' I'll need."

"Dolores and Cummings had absolutely no idea what a hornets' nest they'd be stirring up when they killed Samuel Johnson," Paco explained. "They thought that in all the confusion of war, nobody would have the time to pay much attention to it. What they hadn't foreseen was the effect it would have on the morale of the battalion itself, so it came as a complete surprise to them when the government sent me in to investigate."

"*Us* in to investigate," Cindy said.

"Us in to investigate," Paco agreed. "And that caught them on the hop. Up until that point, they hadn't seen the need to provide themselves with alibis, and suddenly they *did* need one."

"So they decided to give *each other* alibis?"

"Exactly. But they needed a reason to explain *why* they were together."

"Do people need reasons?"

"*They* did. They'd been working together, on behalf of their boss in Moscow, for some time. But in order to keep that fact hidden, they had been feigning complete indifference to each other. So it would have been highly suspicious if they'd suddenly become close friends – close enough to prefer each other's company to the *fiestas* on the night that Samuel Johnson was killed. Unless …"

"Unless they could explain it all away by pretending they'd been having a secret affair," Cindy interrupted.

"Yes. No man's going to want to watch fireworks when he can have sex instead. Why should anybody even think to question that they were screwing when Johnson was killed? Not only that, but as a bonus they could use the same alibi to cover them for the attack on you."

"And this time, they'd have a witness to the dirty deed?"

"That's right. Dolores always intended me to catch them at it – she deliberately invited me to visit her at six o'clock because she thought that if I found them deep in an 'act of passion', it would never occur to me that they'd only been together for a few minutes. And she was quite correct – it didn't. Of course, I should really have spotted the clues, and not been fooled for a moment."

"What clues?"

"Dolores put on a show for me – parading around naked. Cummings, on the other hand, quickly covered himself up. Now why was that?"

"The answer to the first part of that question could simply be that the vain bitch wanted you to see what a beautiful body she had," Cindy said, only a *little* bitterly.

"She did – but not because she was vain. She wanted me to be looking at her, rather than at Cummings, in case I noticed that, despite the fact that they were supposed to have been rutting like goats, he didn't have an erection."

"Well, of course he didn't have an erection!" Cindy said. "Greg was a homosexual through and through. All his students knew that, and the only reason we kept quiet about it was that he was such a nice guy that we didn't want to get him into trouble."

"And that was why you had to be eliminated – *because* you knew. The alibi only held together as long as I thought of Cummings as being heterosexual. Once you'd told me the truth, as you did just after you regained consciousness, I started looking in the right direction at last."

"So they tried to kill me to protect Greg's little secret."

"That was the main reason – but it wasn't the only one. I needed a translator, and if I couldn't use you, I'd have to use Dolores. That put them right inside our camp. They could find out exactly how the investigation was going and – if necessary – throw in a few red herrings to put me off the scent."

"How did Mannie Lowenstein manage to pick up the scent?" Cindy asked.

251

"He didn't – not completely. And if Dolores hadn't overplayed her hand, he probably wouldn't have got it even half-right. But she *did* overplay her hand."

"You mean when she put all those words about the Protocols of the Elders of Zion into Ted Donaldson's mouth?"

"I mean *just* that. Lowenstein knew there was a streak of anti-Semitism running through Donaldson. He'd pointed it out himself during the meeting in the council chamber. But he'd seen enough of the man to realize Donaldson wasn't extreme *enough* to believe that there was an internationalist Zionist community bent on dominating the world. So if Donaldson hadn't made those outrageous statements, then Dolores was lying. And if she was lying, it had to be because she had something to hide. That's why he followed her – and that's why we're still alive."

"I could have worked all that out for myself, you know, given time," Cindy said, yawning.

"I'm sure you could," Paco replied, covering his mouth with his hand to hide his smile.

"I'm suddenly very tired," Cindy told him. "I think I'll try to grab a couple of hours sleep."

"After all you've been through, that's probably a very good idea," Paco agreed.

Cindy closed her eyes and was soon asleep. Paco turned his head to look out of the window. He couldn't see the rolling Castilian countryside in the darkness – but he knew it was there.

They would be back in Madrid in the morning, he thought. And after that, there would be a few weeks of recuperation before he was sent out to the front again. He wondered if he would survive the war, and if – with the strong chance that the other side would win – he even really wanted to.